THE FORGER OF FACES

Also by Catherine Butzen

Shades of Immortality, Book #1: Painter of the Dead

Thinklings Books
1400 Lloyd Rd. #552
Wickliffe, OH 44092
thinklingsbooks.com

Shades of Immortality, Book #2

THE FORGER OF FACES

Catherine Butzen

Thinklings
Thinklings Books, LLC
Wickliffe, OH

PROLOGUE

2010 BCE

"Brother!"

The slim, bald-headed Meren came hurrying through the pillared hall. His amulet of Amon and leopard-skin cloak showed him to be a powerful man in a strong and influential priesthood. He ignored all attempts to stop him as he entered the innermost rooms.

The man lying on the bed of leather strips was built like Meren: short and slim, with a sharp chin and high cheekbones. He was Meren's brother, but he looked more like the priest's sickly father. He had lost a shocking amount of weight since they last met, and his right shoulder was twisted. Corded muscles stood out under sunken skin. One leg flexed with misshapen bone, unable to straighten.

"Anhurmose," Meren said. He thumped down next to the low bed, heedless of his dignity or who might be watching. "Brother! Amon protect us."

The man on the bed wheezed. "Please," he said. "Pray for me."

Meren bowed his head and placed his hands on Anhurmose's damp brow. "Hear us, O Amon," he said softly. His voice fell into the rolling cadence of the priests' chant, a rhythm as familiar as the rising of the sun.

"Hear us, O Hidden One, who knows the secrets of the living heart. Hear us, O Sekhmet, into whose jaws disease and ailments shall leap and never return again. Behold, that which is bound is unbound. Behold, he who is afflicted is granted release. Behold, he is made master of himself again, and life, health, and strength abound in him."

The prayer seemed to have some effect. Anhurmose let out a breath and closed his eyes. The twisted limbs eased. "Thank you," he rasped.

"What happened? It's never been this bad before."

Anhurmose huffed a short, dry laugh. "I fell," he said. "Like an idiot.

1

We'd almost cleared the rebels, and I climbed onto the village's bakehouse to get a better look at the land. They had archers in the reeds—took a shot at me. I ducked and fell off the damn roof."

"Only my brother," Meren said with a weak smile. "Win his battle but lose his footing."

"Only me," Anhurmose agreed. "Nothing's broken—I don't think. I had the healer in earlier. He's sworn to silence. But now everything..."

A spasm of coughing cut him off. His face contorted, one clawlike hand clutching his chest. Meren took his brother's hand, and Anhurmose squeezed, teeth bared as he pushed through the spasm.

"Anhurmose. This is past healing now."

Anhurmose squeezed his brother's hand harder. "I can feel it," he said. "Tight—in my chest, all the time now. Can't sleep. Meren, *please*."

Meren closed his eyes. His brother's voice was only a thready whisper.

"Meren. *Save me.*"

Tears beaded in the priest's eyes. The amulet of Amon lay heavy against his chest, the gold and stones warm. For this moment, the amulet might have been alive, but it would be cold and dead again as soon as he put it down.

Everything he had ever been taught, as a boy and as a man and as a priest of the greatest god of Kemet, warned him that there would be no turning back. Death was one half of the whole, a natural part of the order of the world. Meddling with its workings risked damaging things that must not be damaged. The healers knew it: when they spoke to their patients, they offered to battle with sickness, not cure it.

But...as much as this looked like a known disease, perhaps it wasn't. Perhaps his brother, his closest friend, was actually cursed. To cut down a soldier and general in the prime of his life with such an ugly and disfig-uring ailment certainly seemed like a curse, and Meren could imagine the dangerous powers called upon to make such things happen.

And if Anhurmose was cursed, then a priest of Amon must exert every possible effort to defeat it. "There may be a way," Meren said at last. "I didn't think it was worth trying. Some knowledge is better left to the gods."

Anhurmose's breath was coming fast. His withered hand squeezed Meren's with all its little might.

"Please, brother. Help me live."

Meren squeezed back. "You will live. I promise."

CHAPTER 1

"I don't wanna live forever. I mean, it sounds good, but
what am I gonna do? What if I get bored? And what if I get
lonely? Who am I gonna hang around with...?"

—*Dr. Ernest Menville*, Death Becomes Her

Asleep in bed, Theodora Speer dreamed about fire.

Fire turned the snowy graveyard orange in the middle of a winter
night. Burning hands planted red burns on her body. A smiling priest,
wrapped in a leopard skin, calmly explained his rights and duties while
he cradled his brother's mummified corpse.

Weirdest Christmas ever.

The alarm shrilled. Theo opened her eyes, blinking away the memories of fire and ash. She turned over and looked at the clock.

Three forty-five a.m.

"Blech." She wiped her eyes and stretched, shivering in the pre-
dawn chill. Nobody should be awake this early unless they hadn't gone
to bed yet.

Theo rolled out of bed. The dark room was silent except for the
gentle whoosh of the air conditioning system. On the other side of the
bed, blankets were rumpled but cold.

She'd gone to bed with her boyfriend. She remembered drifting off,
her head resting on his chest, soothed by the too-slow beats of his heart.
That had been after ten p.m., but Seth might have been up for hours
already. His internal clock had broken a long time ago.

A quick check of her phone confirmed the horrible, no good, very
bad hour. It also showed four missed calls. All from her mother.

No, thank you. She reminded herself to clean out her voicemail
inbox and headed for the kitchen.

3

The whole suite was clean and sterile: the kitchen chrome and granite, barely used. The man who owned the place sat at the kitchen table with a cup of tea in one hand and a crumbling parchment spread out in front of him. A mug of coffee steamed on the counter.

"Good morning," Seth said as Theo shuffled past him, yawning. "Did you sleep well?"

"Ugh, mornings are the worst," Theo mumbled. She grabbed the coffee and drank herself into something resembling wakefulness. "I mean yes. For as much sleep as I got." She smiled at him over the rim of the mug. "Thanks again for letting me stay over."

He rolled up the parchment and turned in his chair. "It was my pleasure," he said.

Theo set down the mug and touched his cheek. Seth looked tired: dark circles under his eyes and a furrow in his brow. He was fifty-three, according to his ID. He appeared younger. But he was older—much, much older.

At this time of morning, he wore gray sweatpants and a white t-shirt. His black hair, brushed carelessly out of the way, reached the nape of his neck, showing off strong features, broad shoulders, and whiskey-colored eyes with a hint of an almond shape. A square of medical gauze covered his right eye.

People looking at Seth Adler occasionally had the feeling that something wasn't right about him. Something put together wrong, features that didn't add up. One of Theo's friends in the museum's art loft had taken her aside. "So," he'd said. "Plastic surgery, right?"

No, Seth never got work done. But there was a reason others didn't trust his looks. In the time Theo had known him, he'd gone through three bodies.

This one, at least, was holding up pretty well. It was her work.

Theo slid into his lap. Seth kissed her, quick and gentle. The hands that held hers were covered in thin, branching scars.

"Good morning to you too," she said, smiling against his lips. "Did *you* sleep well?"

"Mm. Well enough."

She smoothed a lock of black hair out of his face. "You don't need to lie. I could feel you tossing and turning."

"It was nothing," he said. "Just dreams."

"I thought you didn't dream much."

Seth's good eye flicked to his work on the tabletop. The parchment looked old: hundreds of years, and probably a copy of the original. Something from very far back. "It's happening more now," he said, looking back at her. His lip curled at the admission. "With the new body."

"Do you want to talk about it?"

He shook his head. "Not this early in the morning."

Theo knew a deflection technique when she heard it, but he wasn't wrong. Too early, and she was barely awake yet. It was going to be a long day.

"Ugh, you're right." She pushed herself to her feet. "I'd better get dressed. I can't believe they scheduled such an early flight!"

Seth's hands settled on her hips. He looked up at her, the single eye glinting. "Stay," he said. "The museum can send you somewhere else."

Theo laughed. "Sure! I'll flake out of my first big assignment since Christmas. That'll really convince them that I'm trustworthy."

"I can have them change their minds."

"Seth. No." She touched his chin. The lines around his eyes were deeper now. "You know that'll make it worse. Half the museum thinks I kept my job because of you."

Seth frowned, but he let her go. Theo turned away and headed for the bedroom.

Six months ago, in a graveyard, she'd faced down one dead man for the sake of another. Seth's long-lost brother, Meren, had captured them both. He'd demanded that Theo recreate the ancient magic that had once made Seth into something more and less than human.

Shabtis were the key. Ancient Egyptian grave statuettes, each made of clay and holding the heart of a sacrificial animal. Four thousand years ago, when the man called Anhurmose of Waset had been dying, his brother Meren had crafted hundreds of those shabtis with a special incantation on them. Every time Anhurmose had died after that, his soul had been reborn in a powerful new body formed from one of those shabtis.

Meren had tried a different path to immortality. His method should have been better, but it had left him a maddened spirit, endlessly possessing others' bodies. He'd spent centuries hunting down his brother's new identity, wanting shabtis that would give him a form of his own.

To save Anhurmose, now called Seth, Theo had made Meren a

shabti. And then she'd painted the sacred symbols of life on her hands and burned Meren to death with their touch. As the sun had been about to rise, she'd used blood and clay to make the dying Seth one more shabti, and placed his own ancient heart into it.

It almost hadn't worked. Seth's clay bodies had been weakened by the night, and if the sun had risen on him before she finished, he would have died forever. His new body had been born injured: the right side battered, the right eye half-blind. But he'd been alive. And when the police had turned up, they'd found two injured people rather than a lunatic and a living mummy.

Which had still looked pretty suspicious.

At the end of it, Theo Speer the underpaid artist was in a sort-of relationship with Seth Adler the CEO, and that was all anyone at work needed to know. How did she keep her job, if not because of her sort-of boyfriend?

This week's assignment was a chance to prove that she pulled her weight. Theo knew she could do it.

In the bedroom, Theo stripped out of her sleeping clothes and pulled on jeans and a Columbian Exposition Museum of History t-shirt. She pulled her pale blonde hair into a ponytail: low, over her ears, to conceal the burn marks Meren had left on her scalp. Other scars formed a sacred marking over her heart. No one was going to see those unless she picked a *really* sexy dress.

Seth came into the bedroom. Cloth rustled as he pulled the day's suit from its hanger. It was going to be ninety degrees outside, but the world would end before Seth turned up to work wearing something other than a suit.

"A thought occurs," he said with a sideways glance. "Most exhibits don't need an advance guard to help prepare them for new museums. Is *Treasures of the Middle Kingdom* that much of a challenge?"

"It's mostly *your* tomb goods. Are you surprised it's causing trouble?" Theo joked.

Seth chuckled dryly and closed the closet door. "Enough trouble to need a dozen people?"

"Well, only a few artists." Theo put in her earrings, tilting her head to examine herself in the mirror. The reflection showed Seth's broad back, the flex of his shoulders as he slipped on the white linen shirt. *Focus! You've got places to be.*

"It's mostly the marketing guys and internal management," she said as she flicked open her suitcase. Everything was already packed, but that wouldn't stop her from double-checking. Better safe than sorry. "They're having a mini-conference with the other museum. You know, get together, congratulate each other, share special ways to bore their employees to death."

"Sounds like a waste of time."

Theo rolled her eyes. "Come on, don't they have time-wasting BS in corporate finance too? I bet you have guys taking three-hour 'business meetings' around lunchtime."

"Of course I do." Seth pulled a tie from the rack. "But they damn well stop when I catch them."

"Well, not all of us are scary CEOs. They don't listen to me." And this would be a new museum with different rules. In the Columbian, Theo knew the turf: which security guard could be bribed with marshmallows, which directors would be hungover on Monday morning and unlikely to drag out a meeting, and which exterior security cameras were angled just right to let her nicotine-deprived fellow artists sneak a smoke on public property. In New York, she would need to tread carefully.

She looked up to see Seth knotting his tie, not bothering with the mirror. "Wait! Oh, damn."

"What's wrong?"

Theo wrinkled her nose. "You tied your tie. I wanted to do that."

He cocked an eyebrow, bemused. "Feeling domestic, *djed?*"

She tucked a strand of hair behind her ear, nodding. Warmth bloomed in her chest at the nickname. It was an ancient Egyptian word meaning strength or stability. *Di djed nebet,* he'd once said. *The lady gives me strength.*

He stripped off the tie and held it out to her. Silently, Theo draped it around his neck. The slow heartbeat pulsed against her fingertips as she tucked the tie under his collar and wrapped it just like her mother had taught her. The silk slid easily through her hands.

"There." She adjusted the knot and stepped back. The icy-blue silk picked up the cool undertones of his skin, and the slight sheen of the weave added a speck of light against the slate-colored suit. He was a portrait: Theo Speer's *Man of Wealth and Taste.*

"Thank you," he said, as if she hadn't just acted weirdly sentimental over a tie of all freaking things. "I didn't know you could do that."

"Yeah, well, Mom wanted me to have the skills for 'appropriate company.'" Theo shrugged. "I think she figured that I was gonna be a disappointment. I had to teach Aki how to do it."

He touched the blue silk knot. "Nicely done. Nothing the board of directors will be able to complain about."

"Oh, come on," she teased. "Like you care what the board thinks."

"Mm. But I do care about maintaining the image that gets things done. The board expects me to be a heartless professional, and so I must appear." He tapped long, callused fingers against his chest, over his slow heartbeat. His voice was too solemn to be serious. "Restoring my original heart may have ruined their business model."

Theo put her hand over his. "In that case," she said, just as solemn, "I promise I'll consult them next time we do creepy magic in a graveyard."

He snorted. "Please don't. The PR department would resign en masse."

Seth had lived for thousands of years. But he went through each day like everyone else, and he dealt with the same headaches that Theo did. She was secretly glad for that. The struggle kept him human.

* * *

Even in the middle of a crowded airport, it was easy to spot the rest of her group from the Columbian Exposition Museum of History. Or rather, to hear them. Zack McMann, second-in-command of Fabrication, was sharing his opinions with the rest of the gate.

"Ronnie James Dio was the *best*. Get outta here with that Hetfield crap!"

"Come on!" scoffed Frank Fischer, Publicity. "Sure, Dio had a good voice, but Hetfield's got power. You need power if you're going to sell metal."

Theo sat at the edge of the group and unslung her shoulder bag. The rest of the group—six all told—nodded or ignored her. Two of them were sleeping. Another one was trying to. Dave Garcia, also Fabrication, tapped avidly at his phone and occasionally shot glances at Fischer and McMann. Probably live-tweeting their arguments again. @museumfights had about sixty thousand followers the last time Theo had checked.

(Nobody was supposed to know who ran that account. Whenever a group manager asked, everyone shrugged. Unofficially, Dave got away with it as long as he was funny.)

"Hey, Theo!" McMann turned to her. "Help me out here. Dio or Hetfield?"

"Which one was in NSYNC?"

McMann and Fischer shot her disgusted looks and went back to their argument. Theo winked at Garcia, who nodded to her and tapped out another tweet.

Working backstage at a museum meant you met a wide variety of different people. Publicity and Marketing folks were talkative, social, and annoying. Fabrication tended toward the quiet and harmlessly creepy, with McMann being a glaring exception. Higher up the ladder, you got the department heads and the curators, all extroverts whether they liked it or not. They had to glad-hand donors and deal with the press, which sometimes left them with fixed grins like strychnine victims.

"Ah, fuck. Who let you in here?"

And then there was Aki Lee.

Theo turned in her seat. Her best friend and fellow artist wore the same clothes he always wore: skinny jeans, Converses, and one of a rotating selection of tasteless t-shirts. (Today, it was "Alferd Packer Restaurant & Grill: Have a Friend for Dinner!") With wild black hair and battered Ray-Bans, Akeela "Aki" Lee may have always looked like he was nursing a hangover, but he was still ready to commit wanton acts of abstract impressionism.

They'd first met at the exclusive Greenfield School in Oak Park, Illinois, when they were ten years old. Aki had been the scholarship student, son of a single mother who built chicken-wire sculpture dresses for the Chicago arts scene. Theo, on the other hand, had had mediocre grades...but her family knew the right people.

They'd both spent a lot of time disappointing their parents. That was a solid start for a friendship.

"Look at you," Theo said fondly. "Whose gutter did you crawl out of?"

"I refuse to answer on the grounds that you might recriminate me." Aki flopped into the seat next to her. "Too bad I can't go back there, though. Jesus, New York."

"What's your problem? I'm looking forward to this."

"I will too, in a couple of hours. Right now, I feel like roadkill. So I'm gonna be angry for a while."

"And I thought I was kidding about the gutter. You want some

Advil?"

"Oh fuck me yes."

Theo snorted and fished out her makeup bag. In the wild art-school days, their friendship had often revolved around who could do more shots. In their late 20s, it was around who carried the hangover supplies.

* * *

The flight was short: barely more than two hours. Theo's luggage came back to her with no trouble, though there was a sticker on it that said that for her convenience and safety, it had been searched. And then they were released into the wilds of New York.

New York.

Their destination was the Heritage Museum of History, just off Central Park. Theo and the others boarded the train, trying not to look like tourists. Their luggage gave them away, but surrounded by twenty or thirty other tourists on the train out of Kennedy, they blended into the herd. Theo held her laptop bag close and watched the people passing by.

Scene: a husband and wife poring over a map together. Both had the tanned, healthy look of hiking enthusiasts, and their wedding rings were new. Designer clothes, the latest sneakers, shiny smartphones. A honeymoon trip to the Big Apple, exploring the urban jungle.

Scene: an older woman staring blankly at the floor. She, too, was well-dressed, but she wore it carelessly, rumpling her Louis Vuitton like it was a $10 t-shirt. So accustomed to nice things that she no longer saw them? Or depressed and down on her luck, wearing out luxuries she'd bought when life had been better? One image, two pictures.

Theo turned away, focusing on the flickering lights lining the subway tunnel. No more images, no more magic. In the dark glass, she could see a reflection of a teenager glaring at her turned back. Probably caught her looking and thought she was judging them.

Theo shrugged it off. Their stop was coming up.

Hauling their luggage, the small group of museum personnel clambered up out of the subway and into the wide square. It was only a hop, skip, and a jump to their destination, but Theo looked up—and up—and up.

The plaza in front of the museum thronged with people. Back home, the Columbian Museum was set apart from the rest of Chicago, on top of a windy hill traversed by chilly white steps and raked by the wind off the lake. But the Heritage Museum might have been in the middle of a street fair. The plaza was lined with dozens of vendors offering tacos, curry, noodles, hot dogs, fried beef on a stick, and innumerable artisan sandwiches and desserts.

People manned kiosks and little tables, handing out pamphlets or giving speeches to any curious passerby. Walking past with the others, Theo caught snatches of pleas on behalf of women in the Sudan, women in America, gay men in the South, reptile breeders in the South, and people afraid of the aliens currently occupying the White House. The full spectrum of American democracy was available for sampling. Artisan politics, sprinkled with your choice of cause and delivered hot and freshly outraged.

"Freaks and geeks," Aki said, surveying the buffet of opinions. "We'll fit right in."

"Do I want to know who's which?"

"Your boyfriend is 150 times your age. Kind of a foregone conclusion."

"Which makes you the geek."

He gave her a sharp look. "Yeeeees," he drawled. "Problem?"

"Nah. I just think it fits you perfectly." She shot a sideways glance at him. "Especially the part where 'geek' used to mean 'circus act.'"

"You're lucky I'm hard up for friends, or I'd kick your ass for that."

"You and what army?" Theo teased. She dodged a completely unserious punch to the shoulder and jogged ahead into the plaza. The museum was waiting!

Beyond the modern day stood the huge, solid cliff of the Heritage Museum of History. Old patiently waiting behind the new, history and the future blending together.

The building was a neoclassical box: huge and square, but festooned and fringed and draped with porticoes, goddesses, Corinthian *and* Doric columns, and a vast Parthenon wedge of mythological figures parading across its crowning arch. Huge slabs of marble and travertine limestone caught the morning light, their cream-and-tan dapples blazing yellow-white in the sun.

But something about its shape stood out to Theo's eye: something awkward, almost crooked. She wondered if the slab the building rested on was starting to crack. She blinked hard, trying to get a sense of it. Was it the shadows?

No, the shadows were fine. Weirdly reddish in the morning sun… Huh. She glanced up, but the sky was clear. On travertine like that, the shadows should be sharp and dark. Instead, they were low-lying and fuzzy at the edges, tinting the columns rust-colored.

"Not bad," Aki said beside her. Theo blinked again, and the optical illusion vanished. "C'mon, let's go set up before Publicity grabs all the good workstations."

Theo grinned and hitched her bag, settling it against her hip. This was what she lived for! Bright lights, big city, beautiful project waiting for her. She was going to help make something amazing happen and bask in art and culture and history—the kind of history that was safely removed and clean under glass.

Yeah. This was going to be good.

CHAPTER 2

The staff and management of La Belle Epoque Antique Dealers has been deeply saddened to hear of the passing of your father, Faruq. I find myself surprised at his passing; that irascible old Egyptian gave the impression of being ancient even when we were young men, and many of us in the antiques trade believed that he would haunt us and our descendants until the end of the world. I suggest that you bury him with a stake through his heart.

Please accept the enclosed donation for his charitable foundation. Our most sincere sympathies for your loss.

—Excerpt from a letter to Seth Adler
from Pyotr Bestuzhev of La Belle Epoque, Inc.,
on the occasion of the "death" of Seth Adler's "father"

Adler Financial had occupied the same offices for nearly forty years. Senior managers, men who had been interns when the move was made, still referred to the building as the new office. Men and women hired last week also called it the new office. If something worked, there was no point in changing it.

The tone was set by the man at the top.

Seth, then called Rachid al-Adhur, had founded the company in the 1890s. He'd never had the gift of prophecy, but Rachid could see that there was money to be made in handling other people's money. And he'd needed money, then, more than ever. His tomb had been plundered a bare few years before, and his possessions—his shabtis—scattered across the world.

He'd reclaimed many of the lost shabtis. But there was more work to do, and the resources of the Adler identities opened doors. Since then, he had been several generations of Adler fathers and sons in turn.

Seth arrived at work just after six o'clock in the morning. Old habit: if you haven't slept well, then the enemy probably hasn't either, so now's the perfect time to charge.

Even at this hour of the morning, the furious Chicago summer already had its grip on the city. The sun struck in through the floor-to-ceiling glass windows, warming the deep chestnut and walnut furniture in the bright office.

By noon, it would be almost a hundred degrees, with full humidity. Thick, wet air boiled people alive but made each breeze a magnificent relief. The sun blazed, throwing lights from building to building and making the mirrored glass façades wink at him. And behind it all, the smell of the lake, almost like the rankness of the riverbanks of home.

Seth checked his email and got to work. The early morning hours were the best time of day to actually get things done. Out of ten or twelve hours at the office a day, at least six were booked solid with meetings: meetings about corporate culture, about regulatory compliance, about ongoing negotiations. Meetings about lawsuits, too, which were always interesting.

(Theo and her friends feared lawyers. Lawyers were the modern lector-priests, keepers of strange arcane knowledge that mortal man could not decipher. They were capable of bringing great darkness—a curse upon your wallet.)

He worked steadily until nine, reviewing reports and figures. The stock market, international affairs, the weather, even planned sporting events: all of them could make or break a business deal. Adler Financial handled corporate funding and investments, which meant keeping clients happy while walking on eggshells.

After centuries of war, corporate finance was easy. Assume everyone is lying and proceed accordingly.

The first meeting started at nine o'clock. The board of directors, of course. Then came another meeting with department VPs and group managers. Most didn't require his input. He listened, mentally sorting and filing the information streaming past him. New regulatory requirements in the EU (they were ahead on cybersecurity compliance), technology requirements (cutting-edge not welcome unless thoroughly tested), new problems with a long-term client...

Hmm.

At the head of the conference table, Seth shifted in his chair and uncapped his fountain pen. The VP of Customer Relations stopped in the middle of his sentence. Joseph Baedler, 43. He'd been in the job two months. Solid promotion from the managerial ranks.

"Continue," Seth said.

"Right. Yes. Uh. Like I said, Flyte BC wants their contact protocols changed. They've limited their available hours and want everything copied to third-party data storage. Fourth-party, actually, since they've already got their cloud service provider looped in."

"Keeping extra records of transactions. They're collecting information." That was Roger Woodes, their lead legal counsel. He considered, glanced at the recording device on the table that was keeping the minutes, and quoted from memory. "'The aforementioned is a personal opinion with no bearing on the position of Adler Financial, its officers, or any of its adherents.'"

"Uh, we don't... We haven't received any information requests."

"They know we're not in the mood for this right now. They're trying to rattle us. When it's time to re-up our agreement, they think we'll be nicer to them." Woodes leaned back in his chair. "'The aforementioned,' 'personal opinion,' etcetera."

The VP of Marketing disagreed. The VP of Client Success agreed, but wavered. The VP of Implementation insisted that this was a distraction from issues with their current platforms.

Seth interrupted. "When did they start saying this?"

That, Baedler knew. "First complaint was May 17th."

Five weeks ago. Hmm.

Flyte's layers of management were thicker than armor plate. Seth would figure on eight workdays for news about a problem to reach the upper echelons. And they met with the Adler Financial representatives around the first of each month, so the problem should have been known and raised by May 1st. Unless it hadn't been a problem *until* May 1st.

"Who's the contact rep for Flyte?"

Baedler flipped through his notes. "Uh, that's Hank Langley."

"The kid with all the NASA gear in his office?"

"Yes. He replaced India Jackson when she went on maternity leave."

"Find someone else," Seth said. "Move Langley to one of the new-tech accounts. Reassign Eli Ramirez to Flyte."

Woodes chuckled. "You have inside information? As your lawyer, I'm supposed to warn you about that."

"Not really. Langley is a young go-getter who thinks a mile a minute.

Flyte lost a lot of value when they tried a risky portfolio last year. They don't want someone impulsive and aggressive handling their account."

"I don't know about that." Carl Twyler, VP of Compliance. "After all, they know that it isn't Langley actually picking the investments."

"Certainly," Seth said. "But they're still seeing a kid who's always racing ahead. They're anticipating a mistake and want the records to show it."

"Are you sure?" said Twyler. "Sir."

"Yes. Switch the rep and tell Flyte we're sending them someone who used to work with Jackson."

The VPs nodded and murmured acknowledgment.

As the meeting wrapped up and people streamed out of the conference room, Woodes drew level with Seth.

"C'mon," Woodes said. "What was that about, really?"

"Instinct," Seth replied. The two men walked down the hall together. As the last of the VPs peeled away toward their own offices, he slowed, letting them get well ahead of him.

Woodes slowed too and waited. "Instinct and...?" he said, low-voiced.

"Instinct and Marcus Thompson."

"Flyte's CFO?"

"He's sick," Seth told him. "Liver cancer. He found out last autumn, just after their aggressive portfolio crashed. The last thing he wants to see is a fresh-faced reckless kid working on Flyte's account..."

"...and risking Thompson's legacy," Woodes said. Seth nodded. "That's good. Thompson's a crusty jackass, and cancer would send him into overdrive. How'd you know?"

He'd overheard two men whispering on the far side of a crowded hall. Difficult to explain, though. "Rumors on the golf course."

"No shit. Hey, you finally started playing?" Woodes's voice rose slightly as they began walking again. "I keep telling you, it's great. Your dad used to play, you know."

Seth winced. His previous identity, Faruq Adler, had indeed played golf—strictly to blend in. Hated every second of it. Every round of golf felt like a failed hunting expedition, trudging through the grass and the trees. Never catching anything but boredom.

"I tried," he said. "Probably never again."

"Well, if you're anything like your dad on the course, you should keep trying it. His short game stank, but he could drive it like Nicklaus." Woodes clapped Seth on the back. "And if you go golfing again, maybe you'll pick up some more useful info for us, huh?"

Woodes was the only lawyer remaining from Seth's previous life. While Seth appreciated the chance to see an asset pay off in the long term, Woodes persisted in thinking of him as Faruq Adler's son. And as "Seth" was a supposed fifty-three to Woodes's sixty-eight, that meant Woodes occasionally treated him like a son or a younger brother.

Seth excused himself and headed for the nearest kitchen. Like every company in this era, Adler Financial ran on coffee. Caffeine had little effect on Seth; his magically animated body was highly resistant to all forms of poison. But coffee was a social event and useful for keeping people alert. A lot of long late-night watches could have gone very differently, back in the day, if his men had been drinking coffee instead of beer.

He was halfway around the corner from the kitchen when he heard his name spoken inside it. A voice. No, two voices: youngish, one male and one female.

He sorted through his mental files until he found them. Caleb Johansson and Ming Zhou. Two of the latest crop of interns.

His bodies were built for combat, but he'd never failed when stealth was needed. He moved slowly, soft-footed, and cocked an ear to the conversation.

"So he was at one of those white-tie things," Johansson was saying to Zhou. "The pricey dinners the old people have every year. And a security guard, who's actually an art thief, recognizes him and thinks 'I can pin some crimes on this guy.'"

"That's crazy," Zhou said. "So what happened next?"

"Well, the boss is backstage at this big museum with this artist he likes, and the artist sees the criminal steal something. But the criminal security guard drugged her, so she thought it was Mr. Adler. Mr. Adler can prove he wasn't there, but I guess he really likes this woman, because he meets her again. Meanwhile, the security guard tells the cops that both Mr. Adler and the artist are involved in this, and the cops try to arrest them!"

"Wait, I heard about this!" Zhou said. "They turned up in a mortuary. Or a graveyard."

"Someplace weird, I don't remember, but there's dead guys." Johansson didn't have the vocabulary expected of a corporate intern.

"The security-guard criminal caught both of them. Mr. Adler gets beaten up and ends up going blind in one eye. But anyway—the important thing—when word gets out, we lose four clients in one afternoon. Big ones."

"That was right after I was hired. Everyone was freaking out. I thought it was a new Great Depression!"

"No kidding. The way I hear it, the board was this close to kicking out Mr. Adler entirely. But Mr. Adler walks right out of the hospital—one arm and leg busted up, wearing that eye patch—and stares down the whole board. He gets on the phone with every top client personally and puts out the word that the company isn't going down. Two of the ones who dropped us sign right back on.

"And then you know what he does? He pays the legal fees *and* the medical bills for the guard who blinded him!"

Zhou frowned. "He knows that's super suspicious, right? Like a pay-out. And I heard Mr. Klinger got fired when he asked about it."

"No, Mr. Klinger got fired because he was dumping stock in the firms that dropped us. If they wanted to fire everyone who ever mentioned it, this place would be empty."

"I'm surprised the board didn't remove him," Zhou said. "When I was at Brown, our business ethics class spent weeks on cases like this. Even if he didn't do anything illegal, it doesn't make people confident about the firm."

"On the contrary," Seth said.

Johansson jumped and Zhou almost dropped her coffee cup. Seth stood in the kitchen doorway. He could hear their pulses racing from across the room. One had gone pale and the other red at the sight of the boss they'd just been gossiping about.

"Holy—" Johansson swallowed. "Mr. Adler."

"Mr. Johansson. Ms. Zhou." Seth crossed the kitchen and took a coffee cup from the rack with his good hand. "Regarding your class on business ethics, Ms. Zhou, the issue was one of personal morality. Mr. Zimmer, the culprit, is an unhappy and unhealthy man who deserves a chance at rehabilitation."

He poured himself a cup of black coffee. "And while it did some damage to the firm initially," he added, taking a sip, "those clients who took their business elsewhere now have to explain why they're against helping the sick. A small outlay of capital ensures our reputation as an ethical firm, which is worth more than a pair of fly-by-night startups who can't balance their own books."

Johansson and Zhou watched him silently. He took another sip of coffee and looked at them.

"Carry on," he said.

He stepped aside. Taking it as a hint, they hurried out, shooting each other alarmed glances.

* * *

Seth discarded the half-full coffee cup as soon as he was back in his office. Like any drug or poison, he required a titanic amount of caffeine to actually gain any benefits from it, so he usually didn't bother with the stuff. Drinking it was just another part of blending into the American workplace.

American culture was a strange blend of the hard and soft. On the one hand, the system was utterly cutthroat and used every possible tool to gain an inch of advantage over competitors. On the other hand, each company presented itself as "The Company That Cares" and "A Family Firm," embracing customers while knifing each other in the back. It was as if gladiators had gone into the arena with happy smiles painted on their helmets.

Tell Americans you're hard and unyielding and they will trust you, because they think those are negatives. And any man who confesses his negative qualities must be honest.

The injuries from the graveyard lingered. The night, the time when the sun was in the underworld and death held sway, was always the weakest time for his shabti bodies. Theo had had only moments to revive him from his imprisonment in his own withered mummy: if the sun had risen while his soul had been trapped there, he would have died again. As it was, his right side—the one that had faced the east—was weak and scarred. A limp in the right leg, wounds on the right hand, a film on his right eye that he covered with a square of gauze.

The gauze was necessary. Contrary to Johansson's version of events, an eye patch would send the wrong message to the company. However, most people found it uncomfortable to stare at a visible injury. The corporate world did not have the same opinion of scars as the pharaoh's generals.

In due time, he would find a solution. As of now, he did not know whether this body would cure these afflictions over time. And what was six months of inconvenience in the span of his life? At the very least, the gauze served to further differentiate his appearance from his former selves.

Such considerations were more important than ever now. Gods help him if this body was examined with modern medicine. His old bodies had bled clay; this new one actually had blood, but who knew what a blood test would show? Hearing that the board intended to move against him merely gave him a good excuse to leave the hospital, and leaving had won him an additional reputation for perseverance in the face of personal hardship.

Now the board was friendly again, and everyone acted like it hadn't happened. Unless you were a pair of interns who hadn't learned to survive in the corporate world.

Seth moved to the window. Down below, the street was deadlocked with morning traffic. Humanity moving in waves, surging as the lights changed.

Theo would make a picture out of it all, but he couldn't see the art. Overlaid on the street below was the street as it had been fifty years ago, a hundred years ago. He saw streets in Cairo, Paris, Moscow, Istanbul, Hong Kong, Calcutta, Reykjavik, Toulouse, Manaus, Rome…Jerusalem…

Why was he thinking about Jerusalem? Had he really dreamed about it last night?

Sir Peter the Gallant. Thinning red hair and a pockmarked face. Lived up to his name until things got difficult. The walls of Antioch above them. Dead horses in the traces, their bodies already half eaten—

He shook off the thought. Those days were long, long gone. His business was in the here and now.

Of course Zhou and Johansson would gossip about their boss. It was a constant throughout history: if you want to know what's going on, ask the underlings.

The security guard, Mark Zimmer, had been possessed by the ghost of Meren. Zimmer's own soul reclaimed his body when Meren took the new shabti form Theo made for him, but the soul had not aged since Meren took it. Now he was a child's mind in a grown body.

In times gone by, people called men like that spirit-touched. Men afflicted, whose minds were not right. Sometimes they were holy fools or monsters. Today, of course, there were names and syndromes and certain diagnoses. Zimmer was under professional care. Things had changed.

Everything changed. The world moved on, constantly rewriting its own history, and each time it declared that *this time* everything had been gotten right. *This time,* all the old illusions of the past had been swept away, and the ultimate truth had been finally discovered.

And in a hundred years it would have shifted once more, and the ultimate truth would turn out to be something else entirely, and the previous ultimate truth would have joined the rest of the old illusions of the past. And everyone down there in the street, thinking about work or school or family or the future, would be dead, and the future they'd envisioned for their world—the brave new existence driven by radium or gland transplantation or cold fusion—would be dead with them.

History was littered with the corpses of unborn futures.

A voice rose in the back of his mind. Memories surged.

"Imagine it, Maximilian. The Holy Land will be free again!"

The smell of sweat, the reek of the dead. Water running through his fingers, dyed red by the dust and dirt—

He hadn't slept well. That was all. If he focused on work, things would be better.

CHAPTER 3

Who is more beautiful to look upon? Behold, they receive her before the throne of the immortals, and no word of reproach is spoken there nor hymn of praise made lesser by her presence. She goes forth into the daylight and is garbed in gold, as is her right.

—Prayer for the soul of an unknown woman,
c. 1250 BCE

The Columbian party shoved their luggage into a corner of their new workspace. Check-in at the Super Saver motel didn't start until three p.m., and there was work to do now. Frank Fischer went off for mysterious Publicity things, and Aki was immediately grabbed by the Heritage Museum's graphic design department. The others dived into the process of unpacking and setting up an entire exhibition.

Some of what they called the "furniture" had already been moved into the exhibit hall. Free-standing columns with printed text, the bases for figure replicas that would come later, the (currently glassless) cases: furniture that defined the floor plan of the exhibit and how visitors moved through the space.

The genuine artifacts were already in climate-controlled storage. They would be installed at the last minute, with extreme care.

But in between lay the custom work, and that was why the Columbian team was there. This was the exhibit's first stop on a multi-national tour, and now they were in the shakedown phase of the operation. Theo and company would be fixing and reworking the installations and custom pieces that turned out not to work in their new setting.

Seth liked to say that "no plan ever survives contact with the enemy." A quote from some old general. Theo could've told him something similar—except for "plan" read "floor plan," and for "enemy" read "those jerks in the layout department."

Something was seriously wrong with the exhibit hall. The Columbian Museum was inspired by an ancient temple, all high ceilings and fluted columns, but the Heritage Museum was older and built to use every available inch. Instead of the pillared halls of academe, *Treasures of the Middle Kingdom* was going to be spread out across small, oblong rooms and low corridors.

"Oh. Great," Theo said. This was not the space that had been advertised. "What happened to getting that space in the south wing? This looks like a closet."

"I think it is," said Dr. Calvin Harper (Columbian Museum, Assistant Coordinator of Mobile Exhibitions). "But it's a closet in the Heritage Museum, so we have to take it."

"Well," she said, looking up at the ceiling. "We're going to have to trim those mural pieces for a start, or fold them back." She frowned. "Wait. Would that be damaging museum property?"

Dr. Harper laughed. "'If you have to ask...'"

"'...then you already know.' I'll start folding."

Theo quickly made notes. When an exhibition had too many artifacts and not enough space, you had to choose carefully. The tone of the institution putting on the show would determine what stayed and what got packed up again.

Originally, *Treasures of the Middle Kingdom* had been slated for the museum's famous Laramie Hall. Wide rooms, columns, high ceilings—exactly the sort of temple atmosphere that the whole thing was designed for. But apparently, someone had lost some paperwork or decided that they didn't actually like successful exhibits that much. Now *Treasures* was trying to fit into an awkward collection of side galleries.

The last-minute shift to a different set of rooms had upset their whole plan. Harper desperately wanted a group of shabtis to have appropriate placement in the Tomb Room, while Stiegler wanted them in the prime position of the second-to-last chamber to capitalize on the publicity of the thefts. Markov, of Preservation, wanted to scrap everything that wasn't genuinely four thousand years old and kept bitching about "stupid toys and pretty pictures. How the hell are we supposed to establish safe boundaries for the artifacts if we've got all this shit all over the place?"

Half a dozen docents and miscellaneous Heritage Museum personnel were on-site with clipboards, crowbars, and the other tools of the traveling exhibition. One or two of them even seemed excited, despite the long hours of hard work that lay ahead. One group removed wrappings from the placed furniture. Others swept the floor for the third time, fighting a continual battle against sawdust.

After forty minutes of inter-departmental arguing, Theo managed to nail down where four of the big murals would go. She didn't even have to kill Stiegler or Markov, though she thought about it really hard.

The murals were printed on massive rolls of canvas. Each was bundled with a collection of spars that, if you followed the instructions exactly, would allegedly turn into an appropriate bracing frame. Theo had assembled several of them over the years, and as far as she could tell, the manufacturers went out of their way to ensure at least one screw-up per frame.

This time, they had been given three side pieces and one end piece. With a sigh, Theo sent an intern to the carpentry department to beg for help.

"What's the problem?" said a voice. Theo turned, adjusting her bandanna.

A tall man stood a few feet away, watching the activity with a boyish grin. He was about fifty-five years old and had the strong frame and thickening middle of an athlete now comfortable in middle age. Dark hair going gray, Massachusetts accent. She didn't recognize him, but the nice-ish suit and museum ID on a lanyard said that she should probably answer him.

"The frame pieces are wrong," she said, wiping sawdust off her hands. Fresh frames always had raw edges. "We need one of the carpentry guys to come down and cut about two feet off the B spar."

"Oh, I see." The man looked down at the bundle of frame pieces lying across the makeshift trestles. "Is it a Cott-Tite frame?"

"Yep."

"I'm not surprised. They're always *this* close to going out of business. Sure as hell hate to work there, huh?" He held out a hand. "I'm Alan Armstrong. Assistant curator of Egyptology. Friends call me Al."

"Theodora Speer. Art and Environment, Columbian Museum." They shook hands. Dr. Armstrong's brow furrowed.

"Oh, right—Theodora! Are you the one who was...?"

"I designed most of the murals, yes."

Dr. Armstrong chuckled. "That's not what I was wondering, but I bet you know that," he said, making Theo's stomach twist. "We heard the security-guard story. Did he really think he was an Egyptian priest?"

"I don't know what he thought he was," Theo said flatly.

"I'm sorry, I don't mean to upset you!" Dr. Armstrong stepped back and held up his hands. "No weapons! I just hope it didn't scare you off Egyptology. We don't bite, I promise."

"Of course not," Theo said. "Is there something I can help you with, Doctor?"

"Nah. Just came down to see how things were going. It's been a long time since we've had something new on the Middle Kingdom." He chuckled. "Everyone wants the pyramids or Tutankhamun! No love for ol' Montuhotep and his boys. Guilty as charged here, too—I was an Old Kingdom guy at Oxford. Ask me anything about Abydos! Or wait, don't. I'm sorry, I just talk and talk and talk when I get the chance. I'm not annoying you, am I?"

"Of course not," Theo repeated. Nothing a curator did could be annoying, not when you were employed by a museum. It was an unwritten rule of the career. "Things are going well with the exhibit prep, so I don't think you have anything to worry about. If the frame actually worked, then we might have something to report."

Dr. Armstrong grinned again. He had a boy's teeth, bright and even and too small for his big, broad face. "Now that's what I wanted to hear! Academics supposedly love wit and all that crap, but give me old-fashioned *sarkasmos* any day. Wait, hang on. Do you speak Greek, Theodora?"

"I'm not interested in languages, to be honest," she said. When was he going to go away? He seemed nice enough, but she didn't want to waste time being chattered at.

Then, belatedly, she felt ashamed. Her own boss, Dr. Van Allen, had given her a chance to explain in the wake of the graveyard incident. His decision to send her on this job only six months later was a sign of trust. The least she could do was act professional.

Not that Dr. Armstrong noticed anything. "No surprises there," he said cheerfully. "Everybody has their own thing, right? And I can't draw a straight line with a ruler. *Sarkasmos* means 'to tear the flesh,' which I think is very appropriate, don't you? It's where we get the word 'sarcasm.' But we're not supposed to have fun here—it's all very serious. Someone gets offended. The only time they don't get offended is if we're talking about fakes and forgeries. Do you like fakes? We have a real collection here."

Theo blinked. Armstrong clearly didn't skip the triple mocha espresso. "I don't know," she said. "I don't really work with them. Every collection has forgeries, of course."

"Oh, don't they just," Dr. Armstrong said. "More than anyone ever admits."

"Come on!" she replied with a smile of her own. "You can't tell me that the world-famous Heritage Museum ever bought a fake!"

"Of course not!" Dr. Armstrong said. "Never, ever, ever. We certainly don't have a collection on the other side of the museum campus." He winked. "I'm sure the Columbian doesn't have a collection either."

"We have a few examples on display—mostly Egyptian and Greek. But big fakes get thrown out."

"What a waste," Dr. Armstrong said. "Fakes are an art all their own. You should visit our fakes while you're here. The archive's closed to the public, but I could give you a tour."

"Really?"

"Really."

All right, then. Dr. Armstrong was a little strange, but he was about as frightening as a baked potato. And...well, she was curious. What kind of fakes could a big old museum like this have collected over the years? "I'd like that. Thank you."

"Excellent. When do you wrap up for the day?"

"Probably around eight. There's going to be a lot to do."

"Ha! No kidding. Let's say eight o'clock, OK? Building H, on the south side of campus. Good luck with your frame!"

And he was off, waving and shouting to one of the Heritage Museum's representatives on the other side of the hall. His voice echoed and re-echoed off the marble.

Theo shrugged and went back to work. Curators lived in their own worlds.

* * *

They wrapped up at 7:40. Most of the furniture was in place, and Theo's team set up five frames and hung two of the canvases in the room closest to completion. The Cott-Tite frames were still broken, of course. Grass grows, birds fly, Cott-Tite frames take forever to fix.

There would be nine rooms total, labeled in hasty Post-Its stuck to the floor plan: the Entryway, the Hall of Egypt, the Hall of Kings, the Hall of Medicine, the Tomb Room, the Afterlife Room, the Scene of Judgment, the Egress, and most important of all, the Gift Shop. The Scene of Judgment and the Afterlife Room, which relied on central set pieces and only supplemented with smaller genuine artifacts, were the closest to complete. With her mural of the Opening-of-the-Mouth ritual hoisted into place in the Afterlife Room, Theo was free to go.

Like every museum, the Heritage Museum was one-tenth display and nine-tenths backstage. Only a small part of its collection was on show. The rest lurked in basements and attics, being stored or archived or analyzed or preserved.

In Theo's own Columbian Museum, which topped eighteen stories on the aboveground side, it was easy to get lost in the warren of tunnels below. Oversized Storage, with its one-ton clay jars and stone statues, seemed to attract the lost and bewildered. You could usually find a misplaced tourist there, eyeballing a colossal Olmec head like it was about to jump out and bite them.

The Heritage Museum built out, not up. New departments and labs were parceled across three city blocks of museum campus in the heart of the city. Building H turned out to be a four-story, vaguely Neoclassical building from the end of the nineteenth century, nestled between a small public library and an offshoot of parkland.

Theo knocked on the glass-fronted door and was admitted by a lone security guard. He glanced quickly at her temporary badge and didn't bother to look through her bag before pointing her down a dingy fluorescent-lit corridor. Theo followed it into a vast open space and stopped.

Inside, the old building had been cored like an apple. Only the rooms at the outer walls remained intact, linked by metal catwalks and fire escapes. In the middle of the vast space sat the tower of crates.

Crates upon crates upon crates. Stacks of them, shrouded in plastic or canvas drop cloths, marked with yellowing labels from thirty or forty or ninety years ago. Building H was pulling double duty as a second-rate Oversized Storage.

Someone had made an exhibition area on one side of the main floor. Old wooden cases, lined with yellowing glass, contained a jumble of unfamiliar specimens. They ringed an open space backed by the stacks of crates. In the center of the space lay the mummies.

It might have been a small-scale exhibition, except that artifacts from every possible culture were on display together, and many of them were glaringly obvious fakes.

Dr. Armstrong stood by the nearest case. He had a pleased, proprietary air: the king surveying his kingdom.

"Come on in!" he said. "What do you think?"

"I think it's a *lot* of fakes," Theo said. Armstrong laughed. "Why are they set up for display?"

"It's my pet project." Armstrong swept out his arms, gesturing to the vast space. "We have so much great stuff in storage! Weird little old things like this. I've been trying to get an exhibit put together for next year. Anyway, their furniture has value."

Theo peered at the nearest case and saw what he meant. It contained a pair of Aztec chocolate pots, brightly painted and in suspiciously good condition. The case itself was old, stained wood, with fluted edges and carved flowers around the rim. The etched label on the case was deeply tarnished brass.

"Fakes through the ages," she said. "I suppose if no one else is using the old cases, anyway…"

"Precisely. Here, let me introduce you to my favorites."

But it wasn't the chocolate pots or the painted wooden panels or even the golden skull jewelry that he pointed to. Instead, Dr. Armstrong led her over to the mummies.

There were half a dozen of them, all in shockingly good condition. An Old Kingdom priest: *Hai-Ti, Lesser Priest of Osiris, Speaker for the Dead.* A battered torso, its legs replaced with crude wooden spars: *"The Other Woman," name unknown.* A Ptolemaic court official, Egyptian in death and Greek in life: *"The Minister," name unknown.* A pair of mummified heads, side by side in the same case: *Tilamentu and Khnumwaset, sons of Amoneferu, Overseer of the Fisheries That Lie Upon the Eastern Bank.* Laid out beside each was a small handful's worth of grave goods. Green faience shabtis watched her from the Minister's case.

"These are all fake?" she said.

"Every single one. The X-rays don't lie." Armstrong nodded. "They're just junk and butcher bones. Hai-Ti is an old Woolworths mannequin. But…didn't the forger do great work?"

He looked down at Hai-Ti's case, gently resting his hands on the surface of the glass. His gaze looked past the dust and smeared fingerprints, his expression familiar. Theo saw it in the mirror sometimes.

She moved from case to case, peering in at the faces underneath. Uneven here—bad symmetry there. Hard to mistake for human if you actually knew what a mummy looked like. But if you were a buyer who couldn't see past the gold and the thick mask of tar and natron...well, they'd be breathtaking.

"Oh! Look at this one!" she said. "The head. Look at the brush marks! Who made these?"

Armstrong groaned. "We don't know! And that's the problem. We have these great pieces, but they were dug out of old collections and stuffed in a closet! I've been trying to rescue them."

"Are they all from the same time?" Theo peered closer at the fake head. "Look at that paint...1930? 1928?"

"Who knows? We lost a lot of records in a fire a while back. And nobody keeps the provenance on fakes."

Now it was Theo groaning. The word "provenance" gave her flashbacks. Provenance documentation proved not just what an item was, but where it had come from and who'd handled it. Without provenance, you couldn't do anything with a piece, no matter how beautiful it was.

And in their weird, misshapen way, these were beautiful.

"This is my favorite," Armstrong said, pointing. A case rested on a small dais, partially covered by a dusty sheet. Gold glinted as he pulled back the sheet.

The mummy shone with wealth. It was a woman: swaddled in intricate lozenge-patterned bandages, a gold plate resting on her chest, golden sandals peeking out of the frayed fabric over her withered toes. An elaborate thick-braided wig had been set on top of the bandaging, making the whole thing look like an old rag doll with yarn hair. The wig was bobbed with a sharp angle at the jawline, its ends waxed and dressed with gold beads.

"There," Dr. Armstrong said, laying his hand lightly on the case. "Princess Penedjmet. They called her Seventeenth Dynasty when she was taken in. But the design is all Late Period. Someone passed an old-style fake off as even older!" He patted the case with an almost fatherly concern. "Isn't it great? And it's just junk underneath."

Theo peered at the case.

"Pig parts," she guessed. "Those bones look real. Fill it out with rags and papier-mâché..." She frowned, thinking about it. "The skin is...onionskin paper? And lacquer?"

Armstrong slapped a hand on the case. "Exactly! Exactly! I knew we should have gotten an artist in here earlier."

Theo let out a breath. The huge building echoed, replaying the doctor's whoops of excitement. He didn't seem to care about disturbing the library-like stillness of a museum: he was having fun talking about his favorite subject. Why couldn't the Columbian have more people like him?

"It's beautiful," Theo said softly. "It's a special form of art. You know what an 'exquisite corpse' is, right?"

"It's an art term, isn't it? Something French?"

"French surrealists. They had a name for everything. An exquisite corpse was a collaborative art project—something where everyone adds a piece without knowing what the whole thing is going to look like."

"I think I see where you're going with this," Armstrong sing-songed.

Theo traced a fingertip over the glass, outlining the shape of Penedjmet's short, beaded wig. "That's what these are. They're art, but not the kind of art that anyone planned to make. Homemade. They're too delicate for photography, right? Too bad. But I'd love to sketch them."

"Well…" Armstrong turned, looking guilty. "I might've been hoping you'd say that. I have a secret plan."

"Oh. Your exhibit?"

"Yes! I have most of the funding I need, and I have the authority to make it happen. But the senior curators wanted an independent opinion. Do you think these are worth exhibiting? As the work of an unrecognized master artist?"

He was asking her professional opinion? Theo had to admit she was flattered.

"Well," she said, "any known fake is a *failed* fake. You can't really call a failure a masterwork. But some fakers…well, they were masters, right? Han van Meegeren, John Myatt, Elmyr de Hory…"

"Van Meegeren! What an artist. It takes guts to defraud the Nazis."

"Exactly!" Theo said. "Exactly! But it's not just technique, right? Van Meegeren's stuff is really obvious to us, because he painted his era's idea of what an old painting should look like. Maybe forgeries aren't really masterpieces, but they're part of history. They're…they're a history of how people saw history."

Armstrong lit up. "That's it! That is *it!* Not just forgeries or failures. These are treasures. These can inspire people and teach them!"

He grasped her hand. His face was bright with the sheer, innocent glow of pure intellectual pleasure. Theo disentangled herself as gently as she could.

"As assistant curator of Egyptology," Armstrong said, "I'd like to commission you to create some exhibition artwork. I know you've worked on Egyptian reconstructions—your work in the *Treasures* gallery is fantastic. We really need your touch on this! I'll be officially launching this project kick-off next month, but until then, I'll pay you professional rate out of my own funds. We have to get on top of this right away!"

Excitement rose in Theo's chest. Armstrong was enthusiastic about her work—and, more to the point, he was willing to *pay*. It would mean longer hours (no way she'd be able to do this during her normal day, not with *Treasures* taking all her time), but it was an independent commission from a major New York museum. Talk about a career boost!

But...

"I signed a non-compete agreement," she said. "You'll need to talk to the Columbian, Dr. Armstrong. Or get an artist from your own department."

"My department is slammed with prepping for the fall shows. I want you for these preliminaries!" he insisted. "I'll call your guys at the Columbian and make it happen."

"I hope you do," she said. "It's been a while since I got to work on something like this. Do you think I could have access to this room for a while? Just to sketch?"

"Absolutely. Absolutely. I'm going up to the office right now—I'll arrange for your key card! You hang out here and get to know them, OK? I think Princess Penedjmet will look great on a mural."

Armstrong bounded out, and Theo felt a twinge of affection for the strange curator. He was weird, but he loved his work.

Now she was alone. Theo began to walk the perimeter of the room.

The low light wasn't just for atmosphere. Whether or not they were real mummies, these things were still a hundred years old and not made to last. Varnish discoloring, surfaces flaking. There would have to be restoration work done at some point, that was for sure. Flash photos would damage the surface. Definitely better to draw them.

She squatted down, putting herself eye-to-eye with the Minister's twisted head. The forger had relied on texture and artfully applied damage to hide his anatomy mistakes. One eye socket was larger than the other, but a casual viewer wouldn't spot it, because extra ridges of onion-skin-and-lacquer had been layered into and around the smaller socket. Theo's sister used eyeliner the same way to hide a droopy lid.

Maybe the forger was a woman. If Theo saw something similar on Princess Penedjmet and the other female fakes, then there might be an argument for the woman's touch.

"What do you think?" she added to the Minister. "Were you made by a woman? Who knows? Unless we find a monogrammed lipstick in your body cavity or something." She giggled.

The Minister's set, hard-lined face seemed unimpressed with her line of thought.

"There you go again," Theo said to herself. "The last time you talked to the artworks..."

The last time: those strange, stiff rows of broken shabtis, things made with more care than skill, waiting on their Plexiglas shelf for a public to finally appreciate them. She remembered talking to them as she'd sketched them, touching the glass and once even kissing it. Why not? They were beautiful pieces and criminally under-loved, in her opinion. *My little guys. You're going to be awesome—I promise. Soon!*

And in doing this, she'd reached out to the spirits hiding within those shabtis. The man for whom they'd been made felt the connection she'd innocently formed, and had reached out back to her.

Two nights ago, she'd told him she was going to New York. They'd been in bed, sweat cooling in the evening air—windows open, a breeze raking in from the lake and taking away the humidity of the Chicago summer.

His arms around her. Strong. Solid. Feet tangling under the sheets like teenagers on their first giddy night together. He kissed her neck, dragging a shivering sensation up her spine that made her squeak like—well, like one of those teenagers. He'd left pink marks on her neck. She called him a vampire, sometimes. His hand caressing the scarred *tyet* symbol on her left breast, his heart thundering against her back as he held her closer like he could keep her there forever.

He didn't want her to go. It would mean at least a week away, and he didn't like New York for some reason. *Bad memories,* he'd said. But he'd been around so long. What place wouldn't have bad memories for him? Theo pointed out that she wasn't moving there, just going for a week or two.

I'll miss you, she'd said, and meant it.

Seth marked the point where her life turned strange. Part of her attachment to him was selfishness: he made her feel special, reminding her that she had done *magic* and that she had him now, that strong, solid man painted in shades of immortality. But his presence also reminded her that she had technically killed someone.

Meren had been human, once. His magic had saved Anhurmose, created the man she knew today. But without his own heart or his own mummy to anchor him, Meren's soul lost its memories and its mind. In the end, it was nothing but a raving ghost. In that graveyard, Theo had painted the sacred symbols on her hands, and her touch burned him to death.

She didn't regret killing Meren. But she couldn't forget it. Sometimes, she dreamed about it.

Like last night.

Ugh. A good project was just what she needed.

Theo sat on the floor next to one of the cases. She crossed her legs and leaned her cheek against the cool wood, breathing the smell of dust and varnish—and, hidden deep beneath it, a tantalizing hint of cedar. The gentle breeze of the air circulation system stirred a few loose strands of hair. In that vast space, every footstep echoed, but now there was nothing but silence. Nothing but her and six fake mummies.

She took out her tablet and began to throw down a few quick, loose sketches. Nothing too detailed: just letting her fingers do the walking and seeing what they came up with. Definitely no charge for this part of the process.

Getting colder in here. The high AC was calibrated for one-off visitors who might spend two or three hours in the building; the number of summer colds among museum staff suggested that eight or twelve hours a day in the AC might not be so good for you. Theo pulled her light jacket over her shoulders and continued to sketch.

Something rustled.

Theo raised her head. "Hello?" she said. She looked over her shoulder and scanned the room. The back of her neck prickled.

There was no one there.

"Great," she said to herself. "It's too late for this."

Footsteps announced the return of Dr. Armstrong. "Done!" he said. "You'll be getting your key in a couple of days, once the paperwork has cleared. There's too much paperwork around here, honestly... But can we get this started soon? I'll have the lawyers send you a copy of the standard commission contract, and we can talk about that…say, tomorrow at three o'clock? Can the Chicagoans let you go for a while?"

"I think they'll survive without me," Theo said, smiling. "I'm looking forward to this, Dr. Armstrong."

"Me too! I can't wait to see what you come up with. These old things…I mean, a modern fake is just a fake, but an old fake is really a curiosity. It's a window into what people used to think."

She walked Dr. Armstrong to the door. He happily chatted about his vision for the project, and Theo let the ideas flow through her mind. Fake artifacts, real art: beautiful objects made for a scam. The words "The Lies of 1910" on a banner ten feet high, demanding people's attention.

After Dr. Armstrong closed the door behind him, the temperature dropped a few degrees. Theo turned back to the main room.

A curl of mist wound around the base of the Greek artifacts—and Theo was no longer alone in the room. Her scalp prickled. The light was changing, blue bleeding into purple and wine-red.

Red mist poured from the cases. It swirled across the floor, clinging to the concrete like dry ice. Tendrils gripped at the edges of the cases and churned against the glass, finding cracks.

In seconds, the redness overwhelmed the last of the room's blue hues. Now the shadows were deep sepia brown. The mist was the color of brick drying in the sun, dull and worn, tired as it crawled toward her. Theo clutched her bag, heart hammering.

From the mist came the hands. Dozens of them. They lunged weakly from the oncoming tide of mist, groping blindly for the floor or the furniture. They tried and failed to hold on to the solid world around them.

A ragged sigh breathed into Theo's ear. A breath, a moan of pain.

Please don't leave us, a voice whispered.

She jolted a step back, her shoulder blades hitting the door. The hands were already withering away. Their shapes shifted and tore, dissipating as the clouds of mist dispersed. In moments, the redness was gone, and the voice fell silent.

CHAPTER 4

I have never discovered what the gods want from me. I
fear the day I find out.

—Excerpt from The Iudex Diary

Dimness blanketed the offices of Adler Financial. It was past eight
o'clock at night, and almost everyone had finished for the evening.
Shadows collected in the corners of the darkened cubicles. Office doors
hung half open, left behind by people eager to escape from the world of
numbers.

"All clear," Seth murmured, stepping back into his office. The clean-
ers wouldn't come through until around midnight, so he had time alone
to focus.

Finance was never entirely alien to him. He learned as the world
did: from army logistics to managing estates to the first tentative
twitches of what would become the behemoth stock market. Losing one
fortune in the South Sea panic had taught him how much modern
finance was like war.

But the tools of modern finance were a pain in the ass. Particularly
Microsoft Excel.

Seth was buried in yet another column of numbers, his mind on
price fluctuations, when he heard footsteps approaching. He looked up
to see a familiar face in the doorway.

"Adler," Woodes said, "hell. When even the lawyers are leaving, it's
time to pack it in for the night."

"If the lawyers are leaving before midnight, then I'm paying them
too much," Seth replied. He saved the document and sat back in his
chair.

"I'm the last one out," Woodes said. "And we both know you're not gonna do shit about me leaving. The Cambert brief is on hold until Tuesday."

"Interview their suppliers. Dig through their garbage. You've got four lawyers and seven clerks on retainer—"

"And they can't do it," Woodes cut in. "I told you, I can only get you the best of the applicants. And this year's bunch can't take a piss without checking precedent. Face it, kid: Cambert can't win, but it'll take time to make 'em lose."

"What about McMichaels?" Seth said. "They were supposed to send their discovery requests today."

"Delayed until the first. They want to interview Zimmer."

That would go well. A piranha pool of corporate lawyers, interviewing a cursed child in a man's body about a night full of ghosts.

"No," Seth said immediately. "His last statement called me an immortal and said Ms. Speer killed a monster with magic fire. What do they expect to get from him?"

"For a start"—Woodes heaved his bulk into the leather armchair in the corner—"they'll get proof that you *aren't* using medical care to bribe the person who conveniently lost his marbles and took the fall for everything."

"Mm. When you put it like that…"

"Well, it'll look more official in the filings." Woodes shook his head. "Look. We're not getting out of this easily. You can talk about reputation and ethics all day, but this guy almost crippled you and you're paying for his care? Giving his sweet ol' parents stipends to look after him? Sure looks like you're hiding something. We're lucky it's only the two civil suits."

This was the less fortunate side of modern business. McMichaels Security was suing in the belief that Zimmer, one of its contractors, had been unfairly scapegoated and its reputation thus damaged. Cambert Tool & Die (a minor but heretofore reliable account, now helmed by a new go-getter CEO) was suing for breach of contract. Cambert specifically alleged that Seth's decision to return to work immediately after the accident had prejudiced his judgment during vital negotiations. The Zimmer mess would haunt Adler Financial for years.

As far as the law was concerned, Mark Zimmer was an insane security guard who'd nearly killed Seth out of some paranoid obsession. There was no way to make these twenty-first-century people understand that Zimmer was only one in centuries of Meren's victims. With Meren gone, the real Zimmer was helpless. Having him cared for was just mercy.

That explanation wouldn't fly with the shareholders, though. Or the lawyers.

"His parents are retired," Seth said. "They live on almost nothing. Zimmer's treatment costs more than they could possibly afford. Should I have let him go to jail or end up on the street?"

"I know, I know," Woodes said. "But there's what's right and then there's what's true. And what's true is whatever people see."

"Truth is truth." Sacred *maat,* both truth and order. The key to the universe.

"Look at it this way. You're looking through a keyhole into a room. You hear a gunshot and see someone fall. A minute later, a guy leaves the room. Everything you've seen is true—but you can make up all kinds of shit about it, and you don't have the full picture. Nobody has the full picture, because we're not mind readers with 360-degree vision." Woodes pointed a finger at Seth. "And what's true, as true as the view through that keyhole, is that you gave a guy a free ride after he took the fall for a shitload of thefts."

Woodes was tired. Seth had made things harder for the whole company.

Still. It was done and would not be changed. Anhurmose was in full agreement with Seth on this point, as were his selves down the centuries. Mark Zimmer deserved what he had gotten. And so had Meren.

If you will lead men, judge men, send men to their deaths—then you must give them what they have earned.

In the old days, that meant leading the prayers and making offerings on their behalf. As the smoke curled up toward the hot cloudless sky, he'd blessed his soldiers in the names of Isis, Osiris, Horus, Amon, Montu, and their special patroness, Neith. Today, it was more about 401Ks and company contribution match plans, but for him, the sentiment was the same.

Bless the fighters. Treat the wounded. Bury the dead. Zimmer was being treated, and Meren was dead.

"We're all going to die someday," Seth said. "Don't you want to be able to look back and say you did the right thing?"

Woodes stood up. "You sound like your father," he said. "He used to talk about that. Shit, we'd talk. Ten-Scotch lunches. He'd knock off impromptus about ancient history and everything old is new again...Jesus."

"Well, we're very alike."

Woodes opened the door. "Nah," he said. "I used to think that, but you're definitely something different. Less robotic." He laughed. "Shit, I'm tired. Gonna pack it in. Don't work too late, kid."

"The market waits for no man," Seth told him. Woodes laughed again and closed the door behind him.

Less robotic?

The power of a real heart at work, then. This body was little different in appearance from his ordinary shabti forms, but it was much closer to true life. Perhaps Woodes was capable of perceiving that.

Seth's fingertips tapped at the desk. Thoughts clicked smoothly into place, familiar as a sunrise.

The lawyer is old. Experienced. Should have retired by now. Unable to retire? Unwilling? Lacking something—money, time, opportunity? Enough perception to see old and new bodies. Highly placed and trusted.

If Woodes became a threat at some point in the future, he'd be a damaging one.

Nobody would believe the truth of Seth's condition, even if someone as solid as Woodes were to reveal it. Yet Seth couldn't provide simple proofs. The façade of the Adler family would not stand up to closer inspection.

Perhaps it was time to offer the old man a generous retirement package. It wouldn't be the first time—or even the fiftieth—that he'd paid off an asset who was becoming inconvenient.

Glancing down, he grabbed his phone. Much as he hated having a constant electronic leash tied to him, the thing was useful for organizing his work. He composed a quick reminder note to himself: *prepare to deactivate RW.*

As he thumbed through the phone, he stopped. Theo's contact picture looked back at him.

It was a photo of an oil painting. A blonde woman stood with a paintbrush in hand, the hood of her orange winter parka draped across her shoulders like a ceremonial stole. She'd thought it was funny when he asked her for it, but she'd painted it anyway. A tomb painting of someone who had never appeared in a tomb.

He dropped the phone onto the table and stared blankly at the screen of his computer.

It had been a long time since his last relationship. There were many, many women over the centuries, but few of them ever knew what he was. Some found things out, thinking he was a sorcerer or alchemist. Some might have guessed at more, but…memories were scattered. Only recently had he begun to recover them.

Now he was in a new body that was also an old body. It held the shape of his shabtis, but there was blood in his veins and a human heart in his chest. Theo had put it there.

Pulled to pieces and put together again, like Isis had done for Osiris.

But she wasn't Isis. Isis was divine, the mother of all, a creature of surpassing beauty and potent magic. Theo was human. Caught up in her work and treasuring some of the strangest things. Fragile. Transient. Here today, gone tomorrow.

What would happen to him when she died? He had once thought he outlived the priest who made him, but Meren's soul had lingered in this world. Would the magic still work with his priestess dead? Would his memories of her be preserved forever, just like his memories of Kemet?

Ha. Trapped with 21st-century English in his head for all eternity. Remembering a woman who had not only loved him, but put him back together.

He remembered his first wife, would remember his wife as long as he lived his unnatural life, but at least *she* had thought her husband properly dead and buried. And she had gotten children by him, which was what really mattered in those days.

Theo had none of that. However their connection ended, Theo would die someday. And she would die knowing that Seth went on.

Gods damn it all, he didn't want to think dark thoughts tonight. Not with last night's dream still lingering in his head.

Think on it, Maximilian—

The smell of burning flesh and wood in his nostrils, a scream—

It was clear he wouldn't get any more work done. He turned off the computer and stood, stretching out the kinks in his muscles. He'd have to find something to settle his nerves.

CHAPTER 5

And so they took up four thousand jars of beer and dyed it red with beetle shells. This they spread upon a field. The goddess Sekhmet, her thirst for blood unquenched, seized upon the jars and drank down every drop.

—Excerpt from "The Deeds of the Gods,"
recorded c. 980 BCE

The Super Saver motel was only five blocks from the museum. At seven a.m., the air was already warm; unlike in Chicago, no high winds whipped at pedestrians or swatted newspapers into people's faces. But pigeons flocked around the statues, as crazy-eyed and gimpy as the ones back home.

Theo stopped in the square in front of the museum and tilted her head back, squinting at the bright morning sky. A cluster of sparrows landed on top of an abstract sculpture and began quarreling fiercely, pecking at each other and flapping their wings. Faint wispy clouds promised another bright, hot summer day.

Another day away from Chicago. Another day away from Seth...

But also another day away from her family, which she didn't mind so much.

Mom and Dad had been asking to meet Seth for weeks now. Wanting to know about this mystery man their girl was spending so much time with.

Dora, honey, why don't you bring him over for dinner?

Yeah, sure. Theo was going to introduce cool, sophisticated Amy Rose Clarendon Speer to a fifty-year-old boyfriend. She could already imagine the lecture: "I know you're *sensitive*, Dora. You don't need to date someone just to prove you can. We'll love you even if you never meet anyone for real."

Magic she could handle. She had burns and scars that said she could. Parents? Nobody had yet invented a charm for that.

At just after seven a.m., Building H was dark. Nobody let her in when she knocked on the glassed-in door. Looking up, she spotted the blink of a security camera and waved at it. Sometimes that worked...but not this time.

No strange mists fogged the glass. No reaching hands or whispering voices, unless she counted the museum docent across the path arguing with his husband on speakerphone.

"What do you mean, I'm acting weird today?" he was hollering. "Suddenly it's on me? I get this job and you start saying I'm crazy!"

Theo sighed. Something was going on in that building, but the mystery would have to wait until later. Time to clock in.

* * *

Aki greeted her with a fresh copy of the exhibition bible, which had sprouted a peacock fan tail of Post-It notes overnight. His bright red t-shirt, featuring a semi-tasteless Colorado intramural basketball logo, had been turned inside-out in preparation for being hidden under a button-down.

"Welcome to hell," he said. "You're framing the C and F murals. I'm in meetings until two, so don't even think about asking for help."

"I'm working on Cott-Tite frames, and you get to sit on your butt in a conference room?" Theo griped.

Aki gave her the dead-eyed stare of a man who's already lived through too many meetings.

"Theo. We're talking about the exhibit presentation deck design. It's seventy-six slides long." Pause. "In Spanish Joy."

Theo winced. Art styles went in and out of fashion just like anything else, and the current favorites among museums were Spanish Joy and the weird, blobby CalStar. Theo, whose motto was "realism forever" *(Viva la Renaissance!)*, filed it all under "ugly corporate design" and went on with her life. But Aki, who had serious opinions about impressionism and the different movements within Pop Art, took Spanish Joy as a personal insult.

"I'll notify your next of kin," she said. "Did the carpenters ever give us the new spars?"

"Nope."

"Their mistake. Now they get to deal with me." Pocketing the Post-It notes, Theo headed for the door.

"I'll help you hide the bodies!" Aki called after her.

The carpentry shop was impossible to miss. It was one of the largest workshops on the lower floor, and the smells of sawdust and varnish were detectable from several rooms away. The huge open space echoed with the buzz of saws and the whine of drills. Long workbenches were set double or triple widths apart, making plenty of room for the huge sheets of plywood and two-by-fours that the carpenters used to frame new temporary walls and build structures for installations. There were no windows: the whole space was illuminated by the harsh white glare of shop lights.

The shop lead, Mr. Martinez, frowned as Theo presented a copy of the request. "We never received this," he said, flicking through his notes from the previous day. "We don't cut Cott-Tite frames, anyway. It breaks our distribution contract to display them altered."

Theo's shoulders slumped. "Do you have any spare pieces?" she said. "We have six murals that need framing—two eight-by-tens, two eighteen-by-twenty-fours, a six-by-four, and a twelve-by-eighteen."

"Check storage. We always have a few Cott-Tite parts in the back. But for the eighteens, we'll need to build new frames. When do you need them?"

"As soon as possible."

From the look on his face, Martinez had been expecting exactly that response. "Not gonna happen," he said bluntly. "We're already building out two galleries for *A Voyage on the Titanic* and setting up pavilions for *Dances of the World.* If you want me to put manpower on this, I need a request from someone higher up."

Theo shrugged. "I'll ask our team lead about getting that request in. Can I take frame pieces from storage, anyway?"

"No problem. Just write down whatever you take. You need someone to carry those down for you?"

"The big pieces, yeah. The eights I can manage, but the tens and twelves will probably snap if I try it by myself."

"Well, have fun with that," Martinez said dryly.

Great.

In the end, Theo shanghaied a couple of interns into helping her carry the spars. Generally speaking, if you talked like you knew what you were doing and moved fast enough, interns could be talked into anything. They were sort of like shabtis that way, except they didn't dissolve into clay dust when they'd fulfilled their duty.

Theo smiled wistfully at the memory as she got to work. She'd made shabtis for herself, once—to help her find Seth. She didn't regret doing it, but she wished she'd found a way to keep them alive when their job was done.

She was starting to learn that when it came to magical creatures, she was a bleeding heart.

* * *

At two fifty-nine, Theo looked up from a tangled mass of wood and metal struts, only to find herself temporarily blinded. The man standing in front of her wore the world's loudest Hawaiian shirt with a professional gray blazer and slacks.

"Hi!" said Dr. Armstrong, from somewhere above the explosion of fuchsia and lime. "Still dealing with the frames, huh? Got a minute?"

Theo blinked, trying to see through the hibiscus flowers imprinted on her eyeballs. "Of course," she managed to say.

She straightened up from her crouch and wiped her hands on a rag, removing a fair amount of the sweat, sawdust, and oil. Dr. Armstrong held a manila folder, which he presented to her with a grin.

"That's the contract I promised you," he said. "There's a copy in your work email, too, but I wanted you to have a paper copy. It's a lot easier to work on things in paper, y'know? Take your time to look at it."

"Thanks." Theo mopped the sweat off her face and wiped her hands again before taking the folder. "I've already started some sketches. They're great subjects."

Armstrong nodded. "Aren't they? Incredibly skilled work! I don't want to rush you, but..." He wavered. "When can I see them?"

Theo hid a smile. Armstrong's hopeful expression took her right back to childhood. Until getting moved to the Greenfield School, she'd been the only artistic kid in class, and the others always wanted her to draw pictures for them. (Usually a superhero, a wizard, or a superhero fighting a wizard.) Her classmates always had that same expression as they hung around at recess, waiting for her to finish the drawing they'd begged for.

But she was a professional now, and this could mean a lot for her career.

"When they're done," she said. "I want these to be the best sketches you've ever seen!"

"Of course. Of course." Armstrong looked disappointed, but he switched topics in a flash. "What do you think of the forger? Do you think we'll get a portrait of him? Her? Them?"

Theo considered. "That would be interesting," she said. "I mean, I'm not a psychologist. But it's interesting to think about. Who was this person? Where were they from? It makes you wonder."

"Doesn't it! I can't wait to see what you come up with." Armstrong checked his watch. "And now I have to run. Damn. My number's on the paperwork in there—call me any time!"

And he hurried off, taking his blinding shirt with him. Theo carefully tucked the paperwork into her tablet bag and went back to work on the spars.

Yeah, she'd be reading it. Carefully. But unless that contract was insanely awful, she bet on signing it. A commission like this? The thought warmed her. *Residuals,* her inner voice sang, imagining financial independence and professional respect.

* * *

The frames and the installations kept Theo late. Just after eight o'clock, she let herself out the side entrance, nodding and smiling at the night guards on duty. They nodded back, clearly not interested in making friends with a random visitor. Considering what had happened the last time she got close to a security guard, that was all right with Theo, but being agreeable still helped when you were the outsider.

Everyone said you could get robbed and murdered in New York, but not on this side of town. Historical buildings blended with clubs and trendy eateries. The nightlife was alive and hopping: sushi places and tapas bars, art galleries lit up with after-hours wine parties, the distant thump of bass from a nearby club, and the much-more-present deep grinding bass from a low-rider trailing some questionably legal but definitely fragrant smoke from its windows.

Her cell phone rang. She grabbed it, wondering if Seth's name would turn up on the display. She had a hell of a lot to tell him!

Instead, her stomach dropped.

Mom.

"Hello?" she said.

Her mother's voice came through, bright and clear, as if she were next to her instead of hundreds of miles away.

"Dora! Finally. Is it so hard for you to turn your phone on?"

"Mom—"

"Oh, never mind. Listen, Dora, we're dropping by tonight. Be home from six to eight, remember—traffic is bad right now. So you'll need to leave work now."

"I'm not home, Mom," Theo said carefully. "I'm in New York."

There was a moment of silence.

"What are you doing in New York? I told you we wanted to see you this week."

"Something came up, Mom. They needed help moving an exhibit."

A sigh. "Dora, sweetheart, we got you that place because we want you to be safe. You know how you get sometimes. Don't you think it's careless to go running off to some other city without even telling us?"

"I forgot. Mom, you always say you don't want to pry—"

"I would never pry, Dora. *Never.* I'm just worried about you. Ever since you were attacked like that, you've been making so many careless choices."

Theo swallowed. The guilt curdling in her stomach, the suppressed pain in her mother's voice, were all too familiar.

"It wasn't careless, Mom, I swear. It's for my career. It means they trust me to handle something delicate."

Her mother huffed. "Of course that's what they say. They're probably afraid you'll sue them."

"Mom—"

"If you can't make time to see us, I understand. We know kids have to live their own lives. But, Dora, don't ignore me when I'm trying to help you. You could be spending your time so much more productively—"

"But, Mom—"

"Don't interrupt me! You already let us support you and pay for the apartment. We're happy to do it, sweetie, because we believe in your future. And it hurts to see you throwing yourself away on a job that doesn't care about you like we do."

Theo took a deep breath. Silence fell on the other end of the line. "Mom," she began. "My job—"

"I can't talk about it any more," her mother cut in. "It hurts too much to see you unhappy. Let's focus on the good, Dora. If you can't make time for us now, we understand. When are you coming back?"

One week. Two, if she was lucky. "I'm not sure," Theo lied. "It's pretty crazy here. They moved the exhibit into—"

"Well, let me know as soon as you do. You're still recovering from trauma, Dora—you shouldn't be straining yourself."

"I'm not straining—"

But that was the last word as far as Theo's part of the conversation went.

Amy Rose Clarendon Speer impressed upon her wayward daughter the importance of safety; pointedly reminded her that they'd be more than happy to get her a gallery showing of *real* art ("Let me make some calls, Dora"); and structured her energetic, doubtless loving remarks in such a way as to imply that she cared deeply, unlike the man who was currently not by Theo's side and whom Theo never actually cared to bring around.

At the cocktail parties and Harvard class reunions, they called it tact. To Theo, it felt more like vivisection.

"Mom, I have to go," she said. "I'm walking back to the hotel."

Before her mother could object, Theo ended the call and shoved the phone back into her purse. Her eyes stung, and she blinked hard, trying to force away the creeping sadness.

She looked up at the sky. It was far from dark: the velvety purple of a city nighttime blotted out all but the strongest stars and planets. To Theo, it was beautiful. A sky like an emperor's cloak.

There was the Big Dipper, looking pale and faded at this time of year, hanging low on the horizon. There was the Little Dipper. There was Cygnus the swan, Cassiopeia, Draco, Scorpius. The red star Antares glowed in the scorpion's heart.

Red, again.

Now that the long day was over and the excitement of the contract had settled a little, she found herself thinking about Building H again. Something was definitely strange there.

She gazed at the distant pulse of Antares and wondered what magic would bring into her life next.

Theo felt herself poised on the edge of something, facing another leap into the unknown: the same leap she'd taken the night she saw Seth die for the first time. But this time, it was all in her hands. She could leave Building H alone and let its red mystery go unsolved if she really wanted to.

But did she want to?

No. Every artist had a streak of crazy in them that came out in different ways, and she was no different. She'd always chased perfection in her work, looking for the fold of cloth or the fall of light that would add an extra dimension to the picture and bring a world to life. Learning about magic had simply given her one more thing to pursue. Hands and voices and red shadows? She had to know more.

Besides… She laughed to herself. If she dragged this visit out as long as possible, she could keep dodging Mom's calls.

CHAPTER 6

"Many wounded. We cannot evacuate."

—Major Charles Whittlesey,
October 1918

They called him Adder, or Uncle, or even Grandpa.

In the beginning, they didn't trust him. He was thirty to the young soldiers' eighteen. He was dark-skinned and they were mostly white men, the sons of Irish and German immigrants. He didn't eat or sleep as much as they did, and he rarely talked. They thought he was some kind of freak.

Then they reached France, and things went to hell. Now Altair al-Adhur was Adder, or Uncle, or even Grandpa to them.

Morning in the forest was a haze of cold fog. They were dug in deep on the hillside, trenches and foxholes on a slant. The ground was churned up into thick mud studded with knots of dying grass roots.

The bodies mostly lay where they'd fallen. A few of the braver souls who crawled to the stream for water would pull a fold of cloth over the faces of the ones they knew. More often, they'd stop to rifle their pockets for supplies. The food had almost run out, and a tin of fish or fruit from a dead man's pack meant a chance.

Adder lay motionless in the shadow of a fallen log. The trench was almost twenty yards away, and dawn hadn't yet reached the thickest parts of the forest. A short knife was strapped to his left forearm, and a pair of dead rabbits was tied to his empty ammunition belt. Three canteens on his back.

Rabbits were easy to catch. They didn't sense him as a living thing. Sometimes the Germans didn't, either, which made Adder a good scout.

A desultory shot buzzed overhead. Adder held his breath, slowing his heartbeat, and waited. Only one shot, no more.

The rainclouds thickened, shading the sky. He crawled. Stopped in the shadow of a moldering stump. Crawled.

It took him almost forty minutes to reach safety. With a muffled groan, he slid over the muddy lip of the trench and landed on Private Red Schwartz, who swore in *sotto voce* Yiddish and kicked him.

There were six of them in the mess, dug into two intersecting shallow trenches on the south side of the hill. Davis, Red Schwartz, MacConaghie, Napolitano, Liebermann, and Sgt. Dorff. Adder made seven. There'd been eleven when they broke through into the pocket, but that was four days ago.

The sergeant crawled over to Adder. He was a strained-looking white man, barely twenty-one, who held the group together with string and fingernails.

"Report," he whispered. Wind shook the trees overhead, sending rain spattering down on their helmets.

"Water and meat," Adder told him. He handed over the catch. Dorff nodded.

"Good work." That was all he said.

The rabbits were passed down the trench to Napolitano, who'd done some cooking for the mess when they were allowed to have fires. His family were butchers. He started skinning the kill—quietly.

Quiet was the order of the day. Someone whistled a lick of "O'Brien is Tryin' to Talk Hawaiian" and others shushed him.

Quiet, and keeping your head down. Others were doing the same in this wet patch of woods. What was left of their battalion hunkered down, filling the hillside with holes and trenches dug with the speed only men not wanting to get shot could manage. All around them, hidden in the dank tangle of woods, were the Germans.

"How's it looking, Grandpa?" said Davis through a mouthful of biscuit.

"Quiet," Adder said. "Spotted a couple of stragglers to the east. The major was back and forth all night, checking maps with Quinn. They sent out a runner just before dawn."

"That's it, then," said Schwartz. "We'll have mortars clearing the Huns in a couple of hours."

Adder didn't know. This whole war was going wrong.

In his long, long life, he'd seen many wars and many breeds of warrior. From his earliest days soldiering on the hot sand of the Red

Land to the ugly battlefields of tangled death that Bonaparte liked so much, he had dipped in and out of wars whenever he wanted. Last year, in late 1917, he'd decided to dip in again. As far as his contemporaries in Chicago knew, the aging Rachid al-Adhur was taking a tuberculosis cure in Colorado while his "son" Altair al-Adhur went off to fight.

He could use a war. Fighting meant promotion and power as the basis for establishing a new identity. His role as Rachid in Chicago was tiresome: now that he'd built a business that would fund his search for lost artifacts, he wanted a new role that better suited his temperament. Altair al-Adhur, newly thirty, was slated for a swift rise through the ranks of the American army. He had lifetimes upon lifetimes of soldiering experience. What did this war have to surprise him with?

But this old dog was having trouble with his new tricks.

"Never mind the mortars," Sgt. Dorff said. "Keep your head on what's happening here. It's another fine day, courtesy of Uncle Sam and the US Army. Button your lip and join us in a morning's light soldiering, eh?"

Davis saluted. "We'd be delighted, Sarge," he said. "Will the ladies be joinin' us for tea and cake?"

"No ladies, unfortunately, but the sons of bitches over the ridge haven't heard," the sergeant said. "Until we get those mortars, we have to assume that the Kaiser's boys will be visiting. Head down, eyes open, don't waste a single bullet. And one more thing."

He opened his mouth, about to give an order that would never be heard. This was the morning the Germans broke into the pocket, and no man would ever know what it was the sergeant meant to say. But instead of the crack of rifle fire or shouts in German, scorpions poured from Dorff's mouth. Yellow-green, tiny, a river of chitin: the deathstalker scorpion of Kemet scuttled in a tide down the front of the frozen sergeant's uniform and flowed across the ground. Schwartz and Napolitano and Liebermann and Davis and the rest remained motionless, statues in a museum, as the tide of scorpions poured over them and crawled in a rasping, clicking wave toward Adder.

* * *

Twisting violently in bed, Seth knocked over the lamp and sent his phone flying. It slammed into the wall before snapping back on its charging cord and cracking against the table.

Seth pressed his hands to his face. Sweat poured off him now. His blind eye watered: in the darkness of night, when the West and death were closer, even this new body was weak. His skin prickled with imaginary claws. The shadows seemed to be populated with scuttling horrors.

"Gods save me," he muttered in Kemetic. "Gods save us all."

His memories of Kemet had always been sharp. Preserved in the clay of the shabtis made for him, they were refreshed every time he died—and he had died many, many times. His language, his old life, his wife and his children and his brother, all kept fresh through the centuries. Everything between then and now faded into a hazy dimness, preserved only in the diaries he painstakingly copied and re-copied. Without his own heart, he could not hold the memories forever.

He finally had his heart again. He'd wondered if, instead of Kemet, memories of Chicago would be preserved forever. (What a gods-cursed city to remember for all time…) But now, he dreamed of the centuries between the first life and the last.

There were no scorpions, that day in 1918. Sgt. Dorff was cut off by the German advance. Altair al-Adhur never saw the end of that fight: the Germans deployed flamethrowers. In his long, long life, it had been the first and only time Seth had burned alive. He had awoken in his shabti cache in New York with tears streaming down his face.

A scorpion might mean many things. The gods were obscure. But to dream of that day, and to see scorpions instead of fire…

This was an omen. He knew it.

He hadn't dreamed since ancient times. Now, after Theo had planted his own heart in his chest again and said the sacred words over him, he dreamed his old memories once more. It was a connection that couldn't be ignored.

Rolling over, Seth took his battered cell phone from the floor. He fired off a message to his personal assistant: *Round-trip ticket to New York, first thing tomorrow. Two tickets coming back.*

CHAPTER 7

I will remember you said this, and I will not forgive it.

—Graffiti in the private diary of Ralf Swann of Berwickshire,
author unknown, c. 1434 ACE

"Morning," Aki said. He sat on the floor, leaning back against one of the sawhorses as he tapped listlessly at his tablet. Printouts of a murderously long PowerPoint littered the ground around him. Theo spotted the tell-tale warm, earthy palette and flattened perspective of Spanish Joy.

She silently handed him a double espresso and watched as he drank it down without stopping to breathe.

"This doesn't look fun." Theo nudged one of the incriminating printouts with her toe. "What is it?"

"Publicity caught me." Aki slurped the last of the coffee and wadded up the cardboard cup with one hand, pitching it away. "I didn't know you got Publicity people shittier than ours, but these Heritage guys are really going for it. Rush job on the pitch deck before I even *think* about something that actually makes them money. You're in deep trouble, too."

"What'd I do?"

"You painted sexy women. It's a no-no."

Theo blinked. "What?"

"The banqueting mural." Aki pointed his stylus toward one of the huge canvas rolls still wrapped in plastic. "Someone complained about the dancing girls. Pearls are being clutched even as we speak."

Theo rolled her eyes. In the past, she'd fought passionately to keep controversial elements in her paintings. "That's how it actually was!" she'd shouted, defending her mural of Aztec warriors like a tigress guarding her young. Lately, stress forced her to rethink things. The dancing girls had certainly existed (she could point to a dozen tomb paintings), but losing them in this one case wouldn't change anything important.

"I'll talk to Dr. Harper," she said. "It's pretty easy to fix up that one section for now. I'll go bug them for some paint, too."

"Try asking the big curator. The really happy one." Aki pulled an envelope out from under the pile of printouts. "He left this for you."

Theo opened the envelope and found a key card and a note.

Theodora,
 Here's your new key card! We have the go-ahead to start on the preliminaries, so keep sketching!
 Best,
Dr. Alan Armstrong, Ph. D.
Assistant Curator of Egyptology
The Heritage Museum of History, New York, NY

"Freelancing, huh?" Aki said as Theo folded the note. With the espresso infusion, he was starting to perk up. "Any fun?"

"Dunno." Theo tucked the note and the key card away. "Dr. Armstrong wants proof of concept for a future exhibit. I'm guessing the board doesn't want to authorize it, so they blocked him from using in-house resources. Too bad there's other artists hanging around, huh?"

"If any more special jobs come your way, kick one to me. I'm dying here."

"Depends. What will you give me?"

"Tacos?"

"Done."

Theo waved to Aki as she headed for her station. Out of respect for his stylistic pain, she didn't let her glee show until her back was turned.

The key card! Finally. Now she had full access to Building H and a legitimate reason to be in there. She'd head over there during lunch and see what was going on.

And if the red mist turned out to be dangerous...Theo's hand went to her heart. The scarred tyet was the symbol of life and renewal. It had protected her from Meren himself: a red will o' the wisp wasn't going to be a challenge.

Still smiling, she checked with Dr. Harper, who was starting to look frayed around the edges. He was arguing with one of the Heritage maintenance people when she found them in one of the back rooms.

"Theo!" he said. "Sorry, but there's bad news. One of the murals is problematic."

"I heard. We're waiting on some spars anyway, so I figured I'd do a quick cover job on it and pull pictures to get the fixes done on future prints."

Dr. Harper looked relieved. "That's what I hoped you'd say. I sent a request to get you into their painting studio, so go ahead."

The head of the Heritage painting studio turned out to be an enormous Ukrainian paleoartist named Konstantin something-or-other. He grunted approval for the materials requisitions from the middle of a half-completed plesiosaur sculpture and pointed Theo to Erika, a skinny BA with blue-green hair and a wary look. Theo showed her the materials order.

Erika eyed Theo. She seemed to be wondering what Theo's angle was.

"Yeah, OK," she said reluctantly. "You can have some stuff. But you need to bring it back, got it?"

Theo nodded. "Look, even I can't use up that much beige in one go."

"Sure. Sure." Erika shook her head. "Look, things are kinda tense around here, and I don't know you. We've all gotta look out for number one. Got it?"

"Tense, huh?" Theo said. "Is it always bad?"

"Some days. If you ever want a good horror story, check out this dump's Glassdoor ratings."

Theo made a mental note. "So it's been like this for a while? I guess you guys definitely don't need some other museum on your turf."

"No, it's not that. OK, not *just* that." Erika waved a hand. "It's just... It's in the air. Ever have one of those days? Where you feel like something's about to explode? It's been like that for, like, a year here."

Someone further down the line shouted her name. "Coming!" she called back. She shoved the rest of the materials into Theo's hands and turned away.

* * *

Theo set up in front of the banqueting mural and got to work. She silently apologized to the dancing girls as she blanked them out. Well, maybe they'd be happy for a night off.

Their unscheduled vacation left a gap in the composition. She extended the shapes of the wall and floor, and filled some of the space with a low table and a cup-and-jug set from the tomb treasures. Not bad!

Normally, she would edit a digital file and have new canvases print-ed, but this was a rush job. She could use reference photos to make a cleaner version of the file later. For now, she worked as lightly as possible, trying not to cake the surface of the canvas.

The texture was definitely damaged. But once the dancing girls were gone, there would be no reason for anyone to look too closely. She kept the details of the background furniture vague and blurry and worked in small, stippling strokes, leaving no visible brush marks.

For two hours, Theo did nothing but concentrate: light, shadow, form, and color. Gentle highlights on the warm curve of the clay jug and the pale gleam on the gold of the tabletop.

Then her phone rang. Again.

"Hi, Mom," she said. "I'm working right now. Can I call you back?"

"Only if you promise you *will* call back," Mom said tartly. "You're so hard to get hold of these days."

"Mom, work is—"

"Never mind. I want to talk to you. If you really are in New York—"

"I am—"

"Don't interrupt me! If you really are in New York, this is a good time for you to break it off with that man. If you're worried about your safety, he's far away right now."

Theo fumbled her paintbrush. A thick streak of beige almost ruined the gold detailing. "Mom!"

"I know, I know. When you're young, it seems like it's perfect." Her mom let out a sigh. "But older men only date young women because women their own age won't put up with them. They like having all the power. I don't want you to get hurt, Dora."

Theo balanced her loaded paintbrush on the rim of a cup and sat down, careful not to bump the canvas.

"Mom," she said, when Amy Rose finally stopped for breath. "Seth isn't like that. I know, he's older than me, but he's not trying to run my life. I really had to work to make him notice me." *Like seducing him in a hidden artifact cache after we bonded over his memories of Cleopatra.* "And I promise, I'm being careful."

"Dora. I know you think you understand what's happening. But someone like that man isn't thinking about long-term with a younger girlfriend. He's thinking about what he can get out of this."

She really, really didn't want to have this conversation. "Mom, I have to go. I'm in the middle of something."

"Don't you hang up on—"

Theo ended the call. The phone immediately rang again, but Theo turned it off and hid it under a pile of drop cloths. Just in case.

In a way, Amy Rose was right. There was a power imbalance, all right: money, age, and magical power. But they were making it work in spite of that. The worst of the weirdness was over. Theo took a breath, let it out, and got back to work.

She feathered out the edges of the painted patch and faded it all back into the softness of the canvas, color-correcting a few other areas to unify the whole piece. Once the paint dried, she took a dozen reference photographs and uploaded them to her Columbian Museum virtual drive.

Her hands and shoulders were a solid mass of cramps. Groaning, Theo stretched out and popped her back.

"OK," she said to herself. "Time to get some lunch."

She came out into the main hall behind an enormous fiberglass stegosaurus. The space hummed with the echoes of voices. Small groups moved through the hall, led by tour guides or escorted by teachers, and a few people just on their own looked up at the vaulted ceilings or paged through guidebooks.

As she reached the security desks, a flash of color caught Theo's eye. She followed it. A man, tall, dark hair lightly streaked with gray at the temples. Broad shoulders, slate-colored tie. Gauze patch on one eye. Skin with blue indigo undertones. If she painted him, she'd begin with purple ochre.

Seth?

He saw her at the same moment she saw him. A slow smile spread across his angular features.

"Theo," he said. "I was looking for you."

"I wasn't," Theo said. "I mean, I was sort of hoping, but—" She laughed. "Sorry, I'm still in work mode. It's good to see you!"

Seth took Theo's hand, squeezing her fingers tightly. His scarred palm felt cool against hers.

"It's good to see you too." He tugged on her hand, drawing her out into the sunshine. "Let's get away from here."

Her heart flipped. Seth was *here*, and she could feel his heartbeat through his fingers. She had the key card, she'd fixed the mural, and now her boyfriend was magically in New York like she'd summoned him. Could any day be more perfect?

She leaned into him, resting her head against his shoulder. Cologne, cloth, spice. She took a deep breath and closed her eyes.

"Theo?" he said. "Are you all right?"

"I'm fine." She looked up at him. "I just...I'm so glad you're here. It's only been a couple of days, but I *really* missed you."

He pressed a kiss to her mouth, a gentle brush of lips that made her breath catch in her throat.

"I missed you too," he said. She leaned her head against his chest.

"We shouldn't stay here," he added. "Unless you want to put on a show for your coworkers."

She raised her head. Oh, right: they were still on the museum steps. Duh.

"Let's go down to the square," she said. She grinned up at him. "There's benches. And grass. And little private corners."

* * *

Manchester Square was ringed with food carts and coffee stalls. The ornamental fountain in the center had been lightly scarred by rioting a few years back, leaving several empty plinths where statues had been removed. There were benches, budding trees, and even flower beds, though those fought a losing battle against the usual city chaos.

It was a beautiful day, too: the vendors were out in force and the crazier parts of the nightlife were sleeping off last night's benders, leaving the scene fresh—if not entirely clean—and lively. The sun peeked out from between piles of fluffy clouds, and the sky was a clear, wholesome Pacific blue, almost too pigmented to be real. (Nature had no sense of color theory sometimes.)

They found a bench under a willow tree. Theo caught hold of Seth's tie and tugged, and he dropped onto the bench and pulled her down with him. She leaned into him and kissed him, still twining the tie through her fingers.

"I'm so glad you're here," she murmured. "I really did miss you like crazy."

"I feel the same. And not just because you've apparently changed your mind about public displays of affection." He dropped his sunglasses onto the bench and threaded his fingers through her hair, stroking her cheekbones with his thumbs. "You look beautiful."

"I look *sweaty!*" Theo laughed. "Last-minute mural fix. Your suit's going to smell like paint."

"It's been through worse," Seth promised. "You're glowing. I haven't seen you like this in weeks."

She wrinkled her nose. "You've seen me sweaty before."

"You're drunk. On your work." He leaned forward. His forehead touched hers, lightly, his lips feathering over her mouth. Theo flushed from head to toe, sudden and complete: the sun felt fifty times hotter on her skin.

"I needed it," she murmured. "But I needed this, too."

She did. It felt good to work, felt good to win, but Seth—he understood. He knew, better than anyone else alive, that art was life. She kissed him and felt him respond, hot and quick and strong.

At last, Theo let go of him and gently pulled back. Seth let out a breath.

"Well," he said. "I suppose we've both been under some pressure lately."

"Work, work, work. I like it, but sometimes I need a breather. What about you?"

Seth shrugged his left shoulder, the good one. "The lawsuits are on-going. Some of the board members are mutinous, but I have them under control."

"The Columbian's directors are like that sometimes," Theo said. "There's something about getting on a board that makes people hate fun. Is that why you're in town? Business?"

Seth frowned. "No," he said. "Something happened. Theo, are you safe?"

"What? Why?"

"I had a dream." Theo's expression must have shown her confusion, because Seth elaborated. "I haven't dreamed in…a long time. But since you gave me my heart back, I dream sometimes. And last night, I dreamed of scorpions."

"OK, that's definitely weird," she said. "Are you feeling all right? Did something happen to you yesterday?"

"Nothing to cause that. Theo. Are you safe? Is anything wrong here?"

His words were tense, sharp. There was a look on his face she hadn't seen in months: the expression of a man on a mission he didn't particularly want.

He'd looked that way when he'd tied her wrists, months ago. Keeping her out of the way while he'd robbed the Columbian Museum of his own mummy and shabtis. She hadn't known that day what he was, but she'd seen him die, and it had left her shaken and haunted. She didn't like seeing that look again.

"All right," she said. "Yes. I saw something. A couple of days ago. But it's not a big deal, Seth."

The lines of his face deepened as his mouth tightened. Strokes of shadow that looked out of place in bright sunshine.

"What did you see?"

"Red mist. In one of the archive buildings on the museum campus. Thataway." She pointed roughly in the direction of Building H. Seth's one visible eye was fixed on her, hard and intense. "It made a few shapes—sort of like hands. And I think I heard a voice."

"A voice. What did it say?"

"'Please don't leave us.'"

His breathing hitched. She wouldn't have felt it if she hadn't been leaning against him: the movement was so small. But it was there.

"Do you know what it is?" she said quickly. "I've been thinking about it, but they're keeping us busy as hell. It's probably not a ghost, anyway, 'cause there's no bodies in that building. Some kind of old curse, maybe?"

"I don't know what it is," Seth said slowly. "There are possibilities. But none of them are...kind."

Theo frowned. "Come on, tell me. I'm not scared."

"Perhaps you should be." His hands tightened on hers. "Theo. I think you need to leave New York."

"What? Why?"

"I dreamed of *scorpions*. A scorpion is a curse of the most profound type. If something otherworldly lingers here, it can only be evil."

"Seth—"

A chill flickered down her spine. Her mother's voice echoed in her head, whispering about men who liked having all the power. *I don't want you to get hurt, Dora.*

Don't be stupid, Theo. He's just worried.

"Seth! I'm fine. I have a job to do, and I can't pack up every time you have a nightmare."

"It wasn't a nightmare," Seth said. "Scorpions mean death, Theo.

Only the gods could stop them. And I've crossed the gods for four thousand years—they might have sent it. You have to leave here, *now.*"

"That's crazy!" Theo's voice squeaked on the word.

Seth feared his gods. Understandable. Theo had seen the magic firsthand, and still carried its marks. But...

Theo pulled away from him and stood. Her head swam. "That's crazy," she repeated. "If they wanted to, I don't know, smite you, they would've done it already. Right? They would've stopped you long ago."

"Then maybe it isn't the gods." Seth stood too. He paced. "There are more powers out there, Theo. You'd call them—demons. Old powers and nameless spirits."

"Demons?" she said sharply. "Then why haven't they tried to hurt me? Maybe possess me? Oh, wait. It was your brother that did that."

"And I will live with that." His jaw was set. "You can recriminate me all you like when you're away from here and safe. But you raised me from the dead, and that forged a connection between us. Now something inhuman calls to you, and I dream of scorpions. It has to be an omen."

"Seth!"

"I've booked us tickets back to Chicago tonight. They'll be sent to your hotel."

"What? Seth, I said no!" She rounded on him. The feeling of wrongness was getting stronger. "I'm not leaving!"

He held out a hand to her. "Theo. Please, trust me. You can't stay here."

"Don't you *dare* tell me what to do!" she hissed.

"Hey, you!" someone hollered. Both of them jumped.

A skinny man on a bicycle had stopped on the path and was watching them. His brows were furrowed, and he had his phone out.

"Leave her alone, pal," the man said. "Or this shit's going on YouTube!"

Seth gripped Theo's arm, but Theo shook him off. "It's fine," she told the skinny man tightly, crossing her arms and staring him down. "How about some privacy, buddy?"

The skinny man slowly lowered the phone. Theo's vision wavered, red-tinged.

Come on, try it. Just try it. See what I do. What I—? Had she thought that? Nothing felt right. As the skinny man backed away, Theo took a deep breath.

She had to calm down. Seth had a point, she told herself. They both *knew* that gods and magic existed and had some power in the world. It made sense that there'd be some kind of mystic bond between them after she created the new body for him. Just because Seth was trying to tell her what to do now—when she'd coped with the last Meren nightmare *perfectly fine*—she didn't even have the nightmares much anymore—and she was *really* not wanting to leave New York right now, not even if he thought there was some kind of curse, because this was really good for her career—

And because there *was* a power imbalance. Damn him. Because Mom's words kept playing in her head.

Seth watched the skinny man until he was out of the square. "Things have changed," he said. "New Yorkers used to mind their own business."

"That's our fault. We can't just argue about ghosts in public. We'll go viral."

"If I had known what would happen," Seth muttered, "I'd have killed the man who invented YouTube. There's no damned privacy anymore."

"Not even in your dreams," she said softly. He nodded, his expression grim.

"At least this time, we had warning," he said. "We can still avoid this, Theo. You don't need to stay here. Not for a damn job." He laid a hand on hers. "If it's money you're worried about, I can help you."

Something detonated behind her eyes. Theo let go of his arm as if she'd been scalded.

"All right," she said tersely. "I get it now."

"Theo—"

"Older man, younger woman, right? It's great until the woman starts doing shit you don't like!"

"Dammit, that's not what this is!"

Her mouth tasted like iron. Why had she ever thought his colors were cool-toned? In the hot sunlight, even the cold man in front of her looked red. "Isn't it?" she said. "I can handle spirit stuff. I have before. Because *your goddamn brother* attacked me!"

Her mother's words played in her head, over and over again. *Older men only date young women because women their own age won't put up with them. They like having all the power. I don't want you to get hurt, Dora.*

"Meren was still *human*. This could be something else entirely!"

"Then I'll handle it!"

She turned away. Faster than any normal man, Seth grabbed her arm. "Theo, wait—!" he began.

Theo saw red.

The world was red, dim red, and Seth was a warped rust-colored shadow in the center of it. He was twisted. He was *wrong.* Something skittered over her, clawing at her, and she swatted at herself with open palms as she backed away.

"Djed," he said gently. Like he was trying to calm her down. Like she was a *child.*

"You can't control me," she growled. She shook his arm off and ran, leaving him standing on the path. The asphalt under her feet glinted red in the noon sun.

CHAPTER 8

The spear of Anhur shall transfix the lion and take the crocodile from his waters. Swift victory without shame or fear shall come to the ones who pray to Anhur. Very effective, a million times.

—Excerpt from the "Book of Commands,"
instruction text for new priests,
c. 2100 BCE, Abydos

Seth found a hotel in a decent part of the city, only a few blocks from the museum campus and near Central Park. Odd, how the city had decent parts now. He left a message with his PA, telling her he'd be out of town for a few more days. If Adler Financial couldn't manage without him for a week, then he'd badly misjudged his current team.

His first instinct was to chase Theo down in the museum and demand answers. She always felt things keenly. Her bleeding heart, her deep-seated love for art that made her reach out even to his shabtis, had proved that a hundred times over. This was a passing frustration—a moment's argument, brought on by hard work and high stress.

But he'd seen something in her eyes when she'd turned to him. Red. Turning black pupils the color of Aswan granite.

Something was wrong.

An abandoned house. No. A hut. An iron pot on the guttered remains of the fire. Rust ringing its lip. Boiled dry days ago, when the place was abandoned.

De Ville's raid on the southern fields. He remembered it. *Blood on his fingertips when he touched his scalp. A cracked skull?*

Seth shook his head. No. He *didn't* remember it. And if he did now, he was damned well going to manage it.

In his room, he closed the curtains and dimmed the lights. He sat on the floor, cross-legged like a scribe with his parchment, and closed his eyes.

Breathe in and out. Slowly. He rested his hands on his thighs and began to murmur his way through the prayers.

As the sun descends towards the horizon and the night, Lord Horus, I beg you to safeguard it throughout the night. Bring us safely to our thresholds at the close of day and close the jaws of the river and the bank. I shall sleep, and the sun shall be born anew at its rising, and I shall be alive and whole.

He was no priest. But if the woman he loved was in danger, the daily prayers were the place to start. This was not an enemy he could defeat with bronze or steel.

His racing heart began to slow. As the words rolled out of him, familiar and rhythmic, the visions began to fade.

Seth let his eyes open slowly. He touched his throat, where the tyet amulet was still hidden by his shirt and tie. No burning: if he incurred the gods' displeasure yet again, they weren't showing it.

His new body, still working its magic. Strong and healthy, despite everything. For the first time in four thousand years, his heart and soul were united again. His mummy was within his grasp, and he had more shabtis than almost ever before.

How strange. If he wanted to leave the Seth Adler identity behind, now would be the best time to do it. He had money and resources, and his tomb treasures under lock and key. Make a clean break from the woman who'd awakened his clay and find another place to spend the next few years of eternity.

He was immortal, and in possession of his own heart. Disease and age couldn't touch him. He was almost impossible to kill. Was this a sign that it was time to rejoin the wars?

Faces swam into view. He smelled the Argonne. Wet wood, cloth beginning to mold, the thick clay-laden mud that clung like a hangover.

1918. Fire in the forest.

Today, he could look up the battle report on Wikipedia if he wanted: 554 men separated from the rest of the army, surrounded by hostile forces. It was hard to believe there'd been more than five hundred other men in those woods: Altair's memories revolved around B Company of the 308th. Schwartz, Liebermann, Napolitano. And Sgt. Dorff—one of the few to survive the war.

Seth had encountered the sergeant again, decades later, when Dorff was an old man. Seth had given him the usual story—claiming to be merely a son of the al-Adhurs, now the Adlers—but Dorff didn't believe it. He'd thought he was being haunted by the ghost of Altair, one of the men he'd failed. That night, Dorff had suffered a heart attack.

Seth blinked. He didn't remember that.

No, he did. But he hadn't remembered it five minutes ago.

He could hear their voices now: casual, pointless talk around a campfire, four days before the push into the Argonne. Napolitano starting an argument over a dirty mess kit. Schwartz and Red Schwartz (no relation) playing cards. Dwyer, soon to be one of the early casualties, laughing at Adder for setting traps—until the first rabbits were brought in that night. Dorff watching them all while he hand-rolled yet another cigarette out of Bull Durham and smeary French newspaper.

Seth hadn't written that in his diaries. It was yet another scene of yet another night, one of millions over the years. But he could see it now, remember it. Hear their voices.

He tried to relax and breathe deeply. He had to finish his prayers.

As the sun descends, Lord Horus—

"Hey! Leave off!"

"Both of you, pipe down! In the army now, got to have some discipline!"

Bring us safely to our thresholds at the close of day—

"Why's Old Man Adder here, anyway?"

"Who cares? We're all here."

"Yeah, but we're young. And stupid. He talks like a book."

"Probably did something. Maybe he was with the Boers and ended up cracked. He's a basket case, isn't he?"

—close the jaws of the river and the bank—

"Yeah, and you're a conchie."

"Che cazzo credi di essere? Say that again, I dare you—"

"Liebermann! Napolitano! On your feet!"

"Sarge—"

"Sarge, I—"

—I shall be alive and whole.

The voices faded under the cadence of the prayer. Seth held up his hands, palms flat, and willed himself to be calm and still. His control held for now.

Was this because of her?

Just when he'd gotten everything he needed, when he'd been ready to be safe for another thousand years—he'd met Theo. She spoke to the clay of his shabtis like a magus or a priest could: unaware of what she'd done, but waking the magic all the same. She had seen him in his real form, trapped as an eyeless, voiceless mummy in a crumbling body. And yet she hadn't turned away then.

So what could make her flee now?

In the park, she'd seemed dazed, torn. Frightened of something she couldn't explain. Then, as she turned away, the red in her eyes. Red pupils within the green.

What had that place done to her?

Anhurmose, son of Merenptah, hadn't been taught about magic. He was raised to serve on the pharaoh's mortal battlefields, not contend on the planes of the gods. His brother Meren might have known what red mist and reaching hands meant, but Meren was dead.

The color red, though. Every son of Kemet knew what red meant. The red desert. Death. *Chaos.*

Chaos clinging to Theo, and scorpions polluting his dreams. Chaos and poison. He was no priest, but he had to do something, quickly.

Prayer helped some. Action helped more. He stood, grabbed his suit jacket again, and went out.

* * *

You could buy anything in New York. Seth found a little kiosk at a nearby art fair that sold handmade pots—lumpy redware, still showing the potter's fingerprints. That and black paint were all he needed.

Finding the spot was harder. There was no clear village border to cast his work outside. There wasn't even a single dump site for all of the unwanted things: instead, a lot of the trash ended up in the river, which was undrinkable and full of cess. That would have to do. Chaos couldn't be allowed to linger.

A mere hour after the argument in the park, Seth sat on a concrete barrier overlooking the river and prayed. The pot and paint rested in front of him. There was a bike path only five feet behind him, but none of the cyclists paid any attention. In his time, they would have avoided him to respect a man's private devotions. In this time, they ignored him because he might be a violent lunatic.

The thought made Seth laugh. Violent, when the occasion called for it. And by modern standards, a lunatic. (Gods? Magic? Get the strait-jacket.) But he was probably one of the safest men in the city.

He prayed over the pot and paint, the rhythm of the sacred words calming him. Then he picked up the brush and painted a few short words.

The curse whose nature is unknown to me, which bedevils Theo.

After a moment's thought, he added the other names he recalled her mentioning before the trip. Even if Theo was made safe, others in her group might be polluted as well.

Once the paint was dry, Seth murmured one more prayer to Thoth and Maat. Wisdom and truth. Then he crushed the jar in one bare hand and threw the pieces over the concrete embankment. They plopped soundlessly into the gray water and vanished.

Thin lines of blood flared on his palm for a moment, where the broken pottery had gouged him. In minutes, they'd be gone.

With any luck, the evil influence that dogged Theo would be gone too.

It wasn't a certain thing. He was no priest, and he'd used the only ritual he knew. This sort of thing was meant to cast out a man, not another curse. But he had to try.

CHAPTER 9

A woman's heart is like unto an egg. For it is filled with
that which is good and golden, and so easily it is broken.

—*Excerpt from the Wyatt Papyrus,*
trans. Dr. A.P. Wyatt

Theo slumped onto a bench outside the Heritage Museum. A hell of a
headache pounded between her ears. She wiped her face and tried to
take deep breaths, forcing herself to think calmly.

"I'm fine," she said to the air. "It's fine."

She went back to her mural. She tapped at the canvas lightly with
the flat of her brush, feeling the texture where the paint was drying. Still
sticky. If she tried to throw more paint on it now, she'd ruin it.

So she grabbed her tablet and began to sketch. Her fingers felt
numb. A loose array of shapes formed under her stylus: a swirl, jagged
hashmarks, a collection of half-loops and half-moons.

She couldn't think.

She couldn't *think.*

Time passed—maybe. She wasn't sure. The headache still churned,
and the shapes blurred in front of her. Her head drooped.

"Hey, Theo!" Footsteps on concrete: soft-soled Converses. Aki had
the exhibition bible in one hand and flipped rapidly through its pages,
making a face. "Are they nixing the dancing girls all over? 'Cause I've still
got them on the 'Party Like It's 1999 BCE' shirt, and that one moved
really fast in—crap. Theo?"

Theo wiped her face. It didn't seem to help. Her mouth twisted as
she tried to keep the sounds behind her lips.

"What the hell?" Aki almost dropped the exhibition bible. "Are you
OK? Did someone try something? Jesus, Theo!"

The stylus fell from her hand. She covered her face and began to cry.

Aki had seen Theo crying before. Usually after too many drinks in art school, when she would rocket right through the manic phase and into the depressed phase. But she never called him for breakups: she preferred to dive into art and take out her emotions on the canvas for a while.

He had no idea what to do with a crying, sober Theo. His hand hovered awkwardly above her shoulder.

"Theo? Come on. It's gonna be OK. What happened?" He frowned. "Did your mom call again? I told you, you need to disown her already."

Theo wiped her face with the back of her hand.

I ran away from Seth. I think I scared him off. And I don't know why I did it!

"Seth is a bastard," she rasped.

Aki nodded cautiously. He wasn't good at feelings. "OK, fine," he said. "But let's talk about it somewhere else, OK? C'mon."

He gently took her arm and tugged. Theo got to her feet and dropped her tablet on the bench. A few of the builders and docents eyed them as Aki steered Theo toward the nearest door. No one tried to stop them, though Theo knew the rumor mill would be getting into gear any second now.

Hell. She didn't care. She *didn't.*

Aki pushed open the fire escape door and nudged her through. Theo half-sat, half-collapsed onto the topmost step and buried her face in her knees, her hands flat on the concrete.

"All right, that's better." Aki toed the door closed behind them. "Head down. We're doing the classic recovery position here. You're not gonna choke on your tongue, right? OK. OK. Cool. Now." He took a deep breath. "Who do I have to kill?"

"Seth! Seth, he—he was being—"

Her throat felt thick. She flattened her hands against the steps, but her fingertips kept curling, scraping against the concrete. Each scratch of her nails shivered up her arms and settled in the back of her spine. Her head still pounded, and she squeezed her eyes shut.

Everything was wrong. Misshapen. She dug harder, tearing calluses off her fingertips.

"Jesus Christ," Aki breathed. He settled into a crouch next to her. When he tried to touch her shoulder, she flinched violently, thumping into the wall. "OK! OK! I'm sorry! No touchy. Theo, talk to me."

"Go to hell," she gritted out. She wanted to scream—no, she wanted to *bite.* "I'm gonna kill him! He doesn't get to talk to me like that. He's not even human. He's not even real!"

She whipped around, hissing her words at a wide-eyed Aki. "He's not real," she repeated between her teeth. "You hear me?"

"I hear you." Aki held up his hands. "But, Theo, man, there's something wrong here. What are you doing?"

Then, in the distance. A snap. Something shattering.

Her headache vanished. Theo sagged against the wall, closing her eyes. All of the anger seemed to leave her in one titanic wave: she felt wrung out, exhausted.

"Jesus Christ," Aki repeated. "What kind of crazy juice did you drink this morning?"

Theo swallowed. Her mouth tasted like pennies and rust.

"I don't know," she managed to say. "But I think it just wore off."

They sat for a minute in silence. Theo breathed slow and deep, trying to maintain her new calm. Aki hovered at her side like a deeply confused guardian angel.

Finally, Theo opened her eyes. Aki sat back on the step and tucked his hands in his pockets.

"Well," he said, "judging by your incredibly articulate and well-reasoned argument earlier, I'm guessing you and Imhotep had a falling-out."

Theo wiped her face with a shaking hand. "I don't know. But...things are getting really weird. And I just went off on him. Everything went red."

"I've been there." Aki shrugged. "Did you hear what they're trying to do with the banners? They want to reset the title fonts. In *Papyrus.* I'm not saying I'm gonna kill someone, but my mom knows a guy who owns a pig farm and isn't gonna ask a lot of questions."

"No, I don't mean I got mad. Aki. I *saw red.* Like a red mist." She swallowed. "There's something weird going on in one of the buildings here, too. There was red mist in it, with hands, reaching for me. And a voice calling to me."

"And you're not taking anything? No fun new prescriptions?" She gave him a look that said *Are you serious?* "OK, no new prescriptions."

Aki tapped his thumbnail against his chin. "All right," he continued. "I want to say something sensitive and helpful and all that shit, but look, I'm way outta my comfort zone here."

"That's OK." She laughed, though her voice shook. "I'm pretty lost here."

"And somehow the spooky shit got you into a scrap with your creepy boyfriend?"

"He's not creepy."

"He's 200 times your age and dead. The high court of Aki hereby rules that that's creepy." Aki mimed pounding a gavel on his knee.

"I tried to tell him about it, but he got weird. Started saying I should go back to Chicago right away and forget about what I'm doing here. He said if it's money I was worried about, he could support me until I found another job…and I just went off on him."

Aki whistled. "Shit. He pressed the 'professional' button."

"Yeah."

Theo and Aki had been friends since age ten. Theo had given him a place to hide when his ex tried to break into his apartment. Aki had held her head when she was throwing up in the bar bathroom after a really bad Halloween party. They understood each other's weaknesses and fears. Aki knew that Theo's job was her life, and that telling her to ditch it would short-circuit her brain.

"Too bad," Aki said after a moment. "A spooky-shit expert would be really useful right now, huh?"

She nodded again.

Aki straightened up and paced down a few steps. He turned, looking her in the eye. "I'm gonna say something, and you'd better not bite my head off. Deal?"

"Deal."

"You fucked up."

A heartbeat. Then Theo nodded. Aki relaxed a fraction and moved down a few more steps. He settled onto a step and stretched out his legs, his head about level with her knee. Shop sawdust dusted his short black hair.

"All right, then," he said. "Lay it on me. What're you gonna do to fix it?"

"I don't know," Theo admitted. "It was dumb to get mad at him. He was just trying to help. But I'm…I'm scared."

"The red mist, right."

"No. I'm sort of...I don't know. Scared of Seth?"

"Come on." Aki nudged her. "He's the last thing you should be scared of. Sure, he's got a bad case of dead. But he's crazy about you. And if he turned into a monster or something, you could magic up a bunch of shabtis and go full Terminator on his ass."

"I don't think they call that healthy conflict resolution, Aki."

"'Cause we're so good at that, right?"

She covered her face with her hands. Her shoulders shook.

"I know," she said. "I messed up so bad, Aki. I don't know why." She swallowed. "I started hearing everything my mom ever said. How I need to go home, give up on painting, and get a degree like my sister. Marry a fucking chiropractor or something. Get a *real* job and join the chamber of commerce. Stop *wasting my time with art.* I don't know. But she said he's bad for me, he doesn't trust me...and then *he* started saying it about my job...ugh."

"Hey." Aki made himself comfortable on the step. "Remember when we met?"

Theo smiled. "Mrs. Farmer's art class. She wanted us to design a building."

"Right. So I get paired with the new girl, the weird one. And I don't want to be there. Art is dumb, right? *I'm* gonna make computer games. But I get paired with the new girl, and I say, 'What're we gonna design?' And the new girl says, 'Let's make a hospital.' And I say, 'Why?' And she says, ''Cause it's easier to draw people lying down.'"

Theo groaned. "I can't believe you remember that!"

"Look, I had to remember it. You missed the point of the assignment so hard that it was sort of impressive. You went"—Aki snapped his fingers—"bam! Right for the tiny detail of *the people we don't even have to draw* and completely overlooked the rest of the project."

"Is there a reason for this cringy trip down memory lane?" Theo said. She was smiling, despite her face still stiff from the tears.

"Come on, I gotta spell it out? You're all about details, but you suck at the big picture." He nudged her again. "That's OK. I suck at not being a dick. Just gotta know *how* you suck. Then you can fix it. Or you can cry on the fire stairs and not fix jack shit."

Theo wiped her face.

"I do remember Greenfield," she said. "I remember this jerk I got paired with who wouldn't come up with any ideas of his own but kept shooting mine down." She grinned at him. "What an asshole."

"He's probably dead in a dumpster somewhere," Aki agreed.

Silence fell, warm and comfortable. Theo took long, slow breaths, swallowed hard, and pushed away the last of her irrational anger.

She'd messed up. She'd lashed out and she still wasn't sure why. But she could wallow, or she could fix it. And sitting here wasn't going to fix it.

"Aki?" she said.

"Yeah?"

"Thanks. I get too much in my head, sometimes."

"Got your back."

Gently, Theo bumped her fist against his.

"Tell you what," she said. "If you ever get around to asking out Sandy from Interactives—"

Aki quickly held up his hands. "Whoa, whoa! Personal-talk limit for the day reached."

"I'm just saying. She doesn't hate you."

"Of course she doesn't. I'm awesome. But seriously, ixnay on the andySay. I don't poke around in *your* personal..." Theo nodded as Aki trailed off. "Kinda walked into that one, huh?"

"Headfirst, Aki." She offered him a hand up. "C'mon. I owe you some tacos."

"Love to, but we've used up our lunch break on the emotional breakdown." Aki tapped his watch. "I've got another meeting. If they keep pushing for Papyrus, there's gonna be a mysterious outbreak of poisonings. You gonna be OK?"

"Yeah. Yeah, I think I am. But, uh, do you have time after work? I think I need to do something."

"Spooky shit?"

"...Maybe?"

"Then yeah, I've got time. If something's cursing this dump, I want to know about it. Later!"

As he slipped through the door, Theo stood up, stretching. He was right: she got stuck in her own head sometimes and lost sight of the bigger picture.

Right now, the bigger picture was that there was something strange going on in the Heritage Museum, and it was enough to scare a man who couldn't die. She'd only known him for half a year: she could read about history all she liked, but she couldn't read his mind. There was still so much she didn't understand. And if it was scaring Seth, then it should definitely be scaring her.

CHAPTER 10

I say to you, [name expunged], I cast out your curse upon
me. I do not fear [name expunged] because he is nothing.
He is dust and sand, which has no power over me.

—*Ancient Egyptian execration text,*
c. 410 BCE

Everything was back to normal for approximately twelve minutes. Theo
was checking on her mural replacement (drying nicely) when someone
tapped her on the shoulder.

"Problem," Dr. Harper said.

"Wasn't me," Theo replied automatically.

Harper laughed. "Technically, it was. But only by proxy." He handed
her a sheaf of scribbled notes. "Panel twenty-two. They want a replacement."

"Twenty-two? That's just more hieroglyphs from the tomb scene."

"A couple of symbols pinged the consultants. Stuff that resembles
religious symbols. How fast can you design a replacement?"

Theo chewed on her lip, thinking. "I can pull some prayers from the
literature and doctor them up. But that'd be a digital painting. What
about the murals?"

"They're covering the gap with panel twenty-six. Make it a digital
and they can print a new canvas from it later."

Theo examined the notes. Some of them contained comments.
"I...wow."

Completely unacceptable!!!

This is what happens when we work with flyover institutions.

Why are we even bothering with this amateur hour stuff?!

Dr. Harper saw her expression and nodded. "Some of the folks here aren't too happy about us."

"I've noticed some tension." Theo remembered the glaring paleo-artist and the edgy Erika. "What do you think's going on?"

"I don't know. Our job is to modify this exhibition ready for their needs, not solve their personnel problems. Think you can do it?"

"The panel? Yeah. For the rest of it, though, it sounds like they need a therapist."

Dr. Harper was too professional to agree out loud, but from his expression, he was definitely thinking it.

Theo grabbed her tablet and headed out to look for a quiet spot to work. With the limited space for the exhibition build, there wasn't a lot of space to find: everyone was moving furniture, building frames, haul-ing pieces, and running wires.

Finally, Theo found a broken sawhorse in the corner next to a paint-stained tarp. The smell of sawdust and chemicals filling the area made it feel more like the loft at the Columbian. She got comfortable and began to sketch.

This was the best part of her day. Her happy place. Light and color and form and shadow—the pools of dark and edges of light that built the world—were always there, asking to be noticed. The glow of sunlight in steam on a cold afternoon, turning the billowing clouds fiery orange and making flame without heat. Rain warping light on the glass, chilly blues and grays with a single streak of hot magenta from the neon signs across the street.

Colors could be anything. Sometimes, they were even sounds.

Theo closed her eyes and imagined a ribbon of colors. Emerald green, gunmetal, cinnabar, English lavender, goldenrod, Eton blue...each one felt different to her, each one with its own sound. By pinning a sound to a color and memorizing the contrasts of the resulting stripes, she could remember long strings of sounds in a language she didn't speak. Like ancient Egyptian.

Almost two hours passed. The symbols flew past under her fingers: crooked sticks and proud birds and the bent-kneed shapes of seated gods. She curled over her tablet, head cocked at an angle, tongue between her teeth as she focused.

This was where she lived. Little pieces of the world bent and reshaped under her fingers, and she smiled as she worked.

* * *

Dr. Armstrong found her again around two o'clock. He bounced into the gallery and darted from station to station, looking at everything, making notes in a leatherbound black book. When he saw Theo at work, he skidded to a stop. Today's Hawaiian shirt was, if anything, even more hideous.

"Hi!" he said. "What's on the agenda, Theodora? Anything good?"

Theo looked up, suddenly aware of the ache in her neck. She'd turned herself into a pretzel while working.

"Panel replacement." Theo turned the tablet to show her work. "I drew a prayer from Budge and doctored it up a bit."

Dr. Armstrong peered at the tablet. "Wow," he said, and began to read the hieroglyphs aloud. "'May these Watchers never gain mastery over me, and may I never fall under their knives! Who are these Watchers? They are Anubis and Horus... May I never fall under the knives they use to inflict cruel tortures! For I know their names, and I know the being who is among them, though he is hidden...' That's pretty neat. Do you write Demotic too?"

"Uh, no."

"Too bad." And Dr. Armstrong moved on, happily oblivious, while Theo looked at her tablet and *knew* that wasn't the passage she'd picked.

"What are you trying to say?" she asked the tablet.

A reddish shadow passed through the gallery. Theo flinched, looking for more, but there was nothing there.

One of the assistants on the other side of the room straightened up. He glared at the man next to him, who'd been helping him run cables a second ago.

"I still can't believe you treated me like that," he said.

"What?" the other man said. Keiran, Theo vaguely recalled. He and his friend—David, possibly—were doctoral candidates from one of the local universities. They'd been civil all morning. Now, though, Keiran looked ready to snap. "Is this about your thesis again?"

"Yes! You said it needed work! You *know* I worked hard on that research—"

Keiran snorted. "You call it *research?* Konrad Kujau called, he wants his 'sources' back—"

"This from someone who cites *Wikipedia?*"

"I did not! I did not! Shut up!"

"What's wrong? Don't have a crowd to source your arguments for you?"

David apparently decided that the best thesis defense was a good thesis offense and took a swing at Keiran. The two would-be doctors flailed away at each other, grappling awkwardly. David managed to launch a loogie at Keiran, but it landed on the floor between them. Keiran had a fistful of David's flannel but couldn't seem to actually push or pull him.

Silence spread across the hall as people turned to watch the show. Someone coughed. One of the carpenters took the opportunity to step out for a smoke. Everyone else just sort of watched as the two pawed and slapped at each other, grunting out threats.

Eventually, David got Keiran in a headlock, and someone decided to intervene. In this case, the someone was the enormous paleoartist from yesterday. He growled something in Ukrainian, pulled them apart, and shoved them both out of the gallery. Theo could hear them hissing insults as they left.

"Holy shit," Aki said. Theo looked up to see her favorite partner-in-crime carrying a pile of hard drives, his expression curdled. "That was pure cringe."

Theo nodded. "I never wanted to see octopuses fighting over a limp noodle, but the universe provided."

"I was going for eight-year-olds wanting the bigger fruit cup, but I think you're onto something." Aki leaned on the sawhorse next to her. "What started the fight? Someone tread on someone's blue suede shoes?"

"I don't know. Everything was fine and then one of them just went off."

"Weird." And Aki wandered off again, his duty done.

Yeah. Weird. Theo looked back at her tablet and wondered.

If someone else was hearing and seeing red mist, they weren't mentioning it, but people seemed to feel its presence. The whole place was slightly off. Theo was no curator, but she knew what a healthy museum looked like, and this one boiled with tension.

A wisp of red touched the corner of her vision. She whipped her head around, trying to follow it, but it vanished into the hallway after Keiran and David. Theo stood up off her sawhorse perch, hesitating, before sinking back down. Gone.

Quitting time came too slowly. But finally, finally, the clock crawled toward quitting time and she packed her tablet bag and headed for the door. To her complete lack of surprise, Aki fell in beside her.

"Tacos first?" he said hopefully.

"Magic first," Theo replied. Aki's face fell. "I'm going back to Building H. I need to figure that place out."

"What about Imhotep?"

Theo hesitated. The memory of how she'd reacted that afternoon made her face flush. She wanted to talk to Seth, apologize, and explain—but she also hated thinking about how she'd acted. Right now, sticking her head in the sand sounded like a good idea. Or going to check out a building full of fakes and magic mist.

Was this why the Scooby-Doo gang was always getting into trouble? Maybe they all had significant others they were hiding from.

"Give me a minute," she said finally.

Aki hit up the vending machine down the hall (he still had some blood in his caffeine stream) while Theo pulled out her phone. The voicemail icon blinked accusingly at her. Six missed calls from her mother. None from anyone else.

Calling was a no-go. She didn't trust herself to keep her voice steady. She slowly tapped out a series of texts.

[6:09 PM]

Hey, Seth. I know it doesn't mean much now but I'm sorry. I'm stressed out & I took it out on you.

[6:11 PM]

Im going back to where I saw the red. Building h, 1222 Bolton. Maybe I can figure out whats going on.

[6:12 PM]

Meri tje. Have a good flight.

Aki returned with a Monster in each hand. "Put it on silent, or you'll be checking it every five seconds," he said. "Don't wanna be reading texts when we should be running away from magic bullshit."

"Who's 'we,' Statler?"

"We be 'we,' Waldorf."

Theo shook her head. "You do realize there might be creepy stuff," she warned. "You didn't respond great to that last time."

"Look, I love a good car crash." Aki hitched up his backpack. "And I told you, if weird shit is happening around here, I wanna be in the know. I wasn't last time, and I ended up having to stab someone."

"Should I be checking you for sharp objects?"

"I plead the fifth."

Theo snorted and headed for the door. Aki trailed behind, letting her hurry ahead. He probably knew what she was thinking.

The sun wasn't even on the horizon yet, but the late afternoon sun was a rich gold, beginning to warm toward the orange of sunset. The parkland campus between the museum buildings was a sprawl of dappled greens, with low bushes and shade trees beginning to show paler yellows and browns where the heat of summer dried their edges. On the healthy plants, the sun struck hard white highlights.

The asphalt paths were ribbons of muted black that radiated heat. Humid air laid a thick, wet blanket over everything, and Theo could feel the sweat trickling down her back. It was a relief to pass into the dense, dark shadows of each building.

Students and museum workers hurried from building to building. It felt like a college, except that some of the speed-walking figures were pushing carts full of skulls. One elderly man with his polo shirt covered by a rubber apron had a large bubble-wrapped jar in his arms. It made sloshing noises as he inched past, careful not to drop it.

Theo shaded her vision as they drew closer to Building H. Nobody seemed to be coming or going: just the stoic shapes of the misshapen gargoyles and the red dot of the security camera aimed at the door.

As they approached the entrance, though, Theo paused. Someone was moving behind the glass doors. A tall, heavyset man in a Hawaiian shirt.

"Crap," she said. "Hide!"

Aki didn't ask questions. They ducked behind the hedge, crouching down, as the door opened and Dr. Armstrong strolled out. A broad grin decorated his face, and he carried a file folder bulging with papers. From the glossy edges, some of them were high-quality printouts. He waved goodbye to the security guard and whipped out his phone with his other hand, already texting someone.

Once he disappeared around the edge of the next building over, Theo gave the all-clear signal.

"Hate that guy," Aki muttered.

Theo shot him a sideways glance. "Seriously? Why?"

"He was in the design meeting this morning." Aki glared at Armstrong's retreating back. "He's one of those guys who took half an art class and thinks he's one of us. He actually used the phrase 'fellow creatives.'"

"Well, right now, he's hiring me to sketch his pet project, so I like him. And he doesn't know the building's full of magic, so *come on.*"

They strode briskly into Building H like they had an appointment. Theo swiped her badge at the security desk, and the guard barely glanced up. He was different from the morning man, and Theo felt herself relax at the sight of his five o'clock shadow and rumpled uniform. They were well into the two-to-ten shift, and she'd called it right: this guy didn't care much. He barely looked up as the pair walked past.

But something was different today. As they moved down the corridor toward the main hall, the air felt thicker. Theo blinked hard: the colors had shifted.

"Hey, Aki?" she said.

"Yeah?"

"What color would you say the light is?"

He glanced up at the buzzing fluorescent panels. "Uh, pale blue. Tiny bit of green in it. Maybe...ultra-desaturated pastel cyan. Don't ask me about the Pantone number, though. Why?"

The light was purple. Shading to red.

"Either I spent too much time on the tablet," she said, "or it's happening again."

She led the way into the main hall. Aki whistled at the sight of the cases filled with gleaming gold and muttered something about Howard Carter rolling in his grave. "Look at all the *shiny,*" he said approvingly.

Theo could barely see the gold. Red mist filled the hall.

Before, it had been swirls and eddies. Now it was a fog. The cases seemed to pulse as rippling redness poured from them in waves. Clouds tinted brick, rust, and carnelian clung to the concrete.

As she watched, the mist streaming from the cases shifted. Long, searching fingers grew out of the formless clouds. Once again, transparent hands groped their way across the floor and pawed at the world around them.

"It's awake," she said.

Aki muttered something, but she couldn't hear him. At the sound of her voice, an answering chorus rose from the cases. Discordant voices hissed and shrieked.

Broken.

It hurts!

Help! Help!

Make it stop!

More words were lost in the chaos. Theo clapped her hands over her ears.

"Stop! Stop!" she called out.

Aki jumped. "What the hell?"

The voices surged again. Pleading. Terrified. Plumes of red shot up, desperately trying to form coherent shapes: a suggestion of a head or a slumped figure would pull itself into existence for a bare second before collapsing back into nothingness.

Theo leaned against the nearest case, squeezing her eyes shut and trying to draw breath. In. Out. In. Out.

Hurts so much—

Hungry, hungry—

Don't want—

Makeitstopmakeitstopmakeitstop—

Was that her or them?

She could hear Aki saying something, but she couldn't focus on him. "One at a time," she ground out. "One. At. A. Time!"

The pressure eased for a moment. She pried her eyes open again to see Aki crouching down next to her, his eyes huge in his paling face.

"What the fuck!" he blurted out. "What is this *Poltergeist* shit?"

"I don't know." She took another deep breath and touched her hand to her heart, tracing the shape of the tyet. "But something or someone in here is scared, and it's not just us."

"Great. New friends." Aki raked a hand through his hair, tousling the gelled mass into hedgehog spikes. "So, what would Imhotep do?"

Something cautious, probably. Seth liked to look before he leaped. But Theo was mortal, and the rising mass of mist still roiled and pulsed in the center of the room.

"Here." She handed Aki her phone and tablet bag. "I'm gonna try something. If it goes wrong, call Seth, OK?"

She wiped her face with the back of her hand and strode forward before she could change her mind. The rough square formed by the old display cases was almost completely carpeted with the sickly, sticky mist, and she tried not to wince as she stepped into it.

Maker, the voices whispered. One whimpered. Another let out a high, thin cry, as piercing as the scrape of chalk.

Theo dropped to one knee in the middle of the square and fumbled in her pockets. No chalk, and Sharpie would leave marks that others would question. Lip balm would do. Squinting through the obscuring mist, she bent down and began to crudely sketch hieroglyphs on the concrete.

Six months wasn't enough to learn ancient Egyptian, even if she didn't have a full-time job already. But she had her color code, and she'd memorized a few things.

First, the tyet. Life and stability. In front of it, the double cone: *give.*

The voices rose again, babbling frantically. Theo couldn't understand individual words now. She bent over her work, focusing through the noise. Another double cone and an upright pillar, the *djed:* stability, perseverance. Just like Seth called her, sometimes.

She didn't feel very stable right now. A short laugh broke from her as the mist thickened.

The hands were all around her now. They clung with insubstantial fingers to the back of her hands, seemingly desperate to hang on as she shaped the sacred symbols. The smell of dust and old wood was growing deeper. Damper.

"Hold on," she said. To herself or to them? Not sure. She kept working.

The ankh, the flame, and the folded cloth. *Ankh, wedja, seneb.* Life, prosperity, health. The most pervasive of the ancient formulas, studding every pharaoh's monument, now lined out in grape lip balm on pitted concrete. The little tube was almost empty.

The grasping fingers finally caught. Theo gasped and lost her hold on the lip balm. Pain shot through her fingers as red-and-purple bruises flowered down the backs of her hands.

The sound of shattering broke through the chorus of voices. The mist convulsed. Shards of broken glass landed on one of the cases and bounced, skating across the concrete. Theo looked up.

Seth was already halfway down the staircase. Glass flecks clung to his hair and clothes. The jacket knotted around one forearm was cut deep.

He dropped down beside Theo and wrapped his arms around her, pulling her to her feet. Theo panted for breath as she was drawn up out of the mist.

"Djed." His voice was a deep rasp in her ear. "Say these words."

Breathless, she nodded. He began to recite in a low, rolling chant.

"Behold your provisions." She repeated the words after him. "Behold that which is given to you. Oh eldest one, foremost of the upper house, you give bread to Ptah. Give bread and beer to the ka. Their breakfast is a calf bone and a loaf of bread. Ferrymen of the Field of Reeds, bring them to the head of their waters…"

Theo recited the words, mimicking the rhythm of the chant. As she spoke, the swirling mist began to lighten. Some of the voices faded.

"Did it work?" Seth said.

"A little." Theo relaxed an inch. "What was that?"

"A spell from the Book of the Dead, to quiet spirits. It seems the old words have some power here."

"Thank you," Theo breathed. She kissed his uncovered wrist. For a few heartbeats, they stayed there, breathing together. His arms were tight around her.

Finally, Theo looked up at Seth again. He'd exchanged his suit for plain jeans and a black t-shirt, and in the red-tinged light, he stood out cool-toned again.

He'd removed the gauze patch. Spiderweb scars ringed his injured right eye and the iris was clouded, but that side wasn't blind—only weaker than the left. He wanted to see clearly now, even if it meant shedding part of his everyday disguise.

"Hi," she said softly.

"Hello." His hands were gentle on her bruised skin.

"How are you here?"

"Climbed the west side of the building." He paused. "I may have broken a window."

"I think I guessed that." She turned in his arms and reached up, carefully picking a small shard out of his hair.

"I was looking for you."

The same thing he'd said earlier, when they met in the museum hall. It had been so good to see him. Theo squeezed his hand.

"I was looking for you too," she said. "Listen, Seth—I'm sorry. I was freaking out. It was a personal thing, nothing to do with you, and I let it…I let it get in my head."

"It wasn't just you." He cupped her chin in one broad hand and tilted her head back, looking intently. "Your eyes aren't red anymore."

"It was in my *eyes?*" God. This just kept getting bigger. "Wait, you could see it? Can you see it here now? The red mist on the floor?"

Seth looked around the room, but shook his head. "Not here. Only in you. We are connected now, djed."

"I just felt so crazy earlier." She groaned. "I wanted to lash out. This thing, whatever it is—spirits?"

"Spirits, or echoes, or essences...difficult to explain in this language."

A polite cough broke in. Turning, Theo and Seth saw Aki standing at the edge of the square of cases, still holding Theo's phone and bag.

"Not that I don't appreciate the floor show, but I'm really friggin' lost," he said. "Theo, help a guy out. Is it safe now?"

The red mist still lingered, but the grasping shapes were gone. Theo looked up, searching the catwalks above. The shadows had gone almost completely blue-gray and dim. Tinges of purple lingered in the deepest recesses, but... "The red's calmed down."

"Great. Let's figure out a way to keep it like that." Aki shuffled over, careful not to step on the lip-balm hieroglyphs, and nodded to Seth. "Karloff."

Seth nodded back. "Cannon fodder."

"Boys." Theo took her bag and phone back. "Thanks, Aki. Seth, do you think we've solved it?"

"No. The spell won't work for long." Seth's jaw tightened. He followed her gaze up into the catwalks, his stare hard as if he could force the ghosts to reveal themselves to him. "Offerings and prayers must be constantly renewed. Be cautious."

Theo raked a hand through her sweaty hair. Her fingers twinged. She looked down at her right hand and frowned: the bruises were deep, with red-speckled edges.

"Well, we know they can affect us," she said. "They tried to touch me while I was drawing, and they left marks."

Seth caught her hand. "Are you sure?" he said cautiously. "This bruise looks hours old and deep."

She nodded. "See where it is? My stylus rubs against those two fingers. I'd have noticed it before."

Seth ran his thumb over the markings. "Deep bruising, moving un-commonly fast. Djed, I know what they are."

So did she. "Ghosts."

The thought had been there for hours now. Voices, hands, humanoid shapes. New York was old: any kind of dead spirit might be hanging around on any patch of ground.

But Seth shook his head. "Ghosts or spirits, but perhaps not as you know them. Most never visit the living. The ones that do are *heqer*—

hungry. The unquiet dead."

She swallowed. "You mean like poltergeists?" He did say the scorpions were a bad omen. But she'd read a lot of books on ancient Egypt in the last six months, and she didn't remember anything about evil ghosts.

"In a manner of speaking. It wasn't often discussed outside the priestly castes."

His thumb traced mindless symbols against the back of her uninjured hand. His pulse still rabbited against her skin, but his tone remained low and level.

"The soul has many parts. The name, the shadow, the breath, the essence. But the unquiet dead are shattered. Part of their soul is damaged. Their mummy destroyed, their names forgotten, and so they are malformed. Wherever they go, their presence is marked by misfortune. Disease, bad luck, withering...*Ukhedu.* There isn't a word for it in English. Something like inflammation, rot, but deeper. Entropy."

It sounded crazy, but she'd already seen golems and the walking dead. She'd signed up for crazy when she fell for him. The problem now was in fitting the idea into her head: crazy was a lot nicer when it was all in the past. It was comforting to say she *saw* zombies, not that she *was seeing* them.

"What about the red mist?" she said.

"Red is the color of chaos. The red desert is the place all madness comes from. You're seeing their influence, Theo."

Red. Chaos. *Ukhedu.* No wonder the whole damn museum seemed to be red-tinted: the ghosts' influence was poisoning everything around them.

Including her. She'd been seeing red, literally, and every time she did someone was losing their temper.

"How do we help them?" she said.

"Wait a second!" Aki interjected. "I've seen a few documentaries. Entropy is a bad thing. It's like 'all existence decays into chaos'-type stuff. And I've seen a *lot* of fantasy movies, and anything that's part of magic chaos is bad news."

"He's right." Seth said it completely bluntly.

Aki grimaced. "Did that feel wrong to anyone? Felt wrong to me."

"'Even an idiot can find an arrow,'" Seth quoted. It sounded like vaguely insulting folk wisdom. "But he *is* right. Unquiet spirits are harbingers of disaster."

"How does this even happen?" Theo said. The alien swirls of red mist were looking more pathetic by the second. Like ants trapped in a death spiral. "Thousands of people die in the city every year, and a hell of a lot of them are 'unquiet.' The murder rate is insane. So how come I haven't seen these things before? There must be more to it than just screwed-up ghosts."

"Theo—"

"Seth. Please. Help me understand."

"Gods help us," he said, but relented. He paced forward, flattening his hands against the case of pottery skulls, and looked up again. Searching the shadows for the things he couldn't see.

"Your people once had a saying: 'Man's not dead while his name's still spoken.' Among mine, it was different. Man stays dead while his name is spoken. Neglect the care of the dead, and parts of their souls go hungry. *Heqer.* And they become withered, impure, sick. *Ukhedu.*"

"But it's not their fault?" Theo asked.

A darkly ironic smile crossed his face. "No. Just as radium isn't at fault for cancer."

"But there's things you can do about radium. Like lead shielding." Theo crossed her arms, hugging herself. "That spell helped. So is there another spell? You know the language—"

She lit up. "The language! Of course. Colors and shapes and magic, all tied up in the language. The image of the thing is the thing, right? Like your shabtis. But *the thing* is even better than the image of the thing, because your shabtis never perfectly replicate a human body." He used to bleed clay, after all. "So you saying the spells in your language, the original language, should help more. Maybe there's something in the Book of the Dead that can help. There's tons of those in museums, with lots of different spells." She turned back to him. "What do you think?"

"I think we need a priest," he said softly. "And you're the closest thing we have, djed. If you want to do something for them, it will have to be your words. Your hands."

Her heart sank. "You're not going to help?"

"I don't want to," he said bluntly. "No more than I'd want to help you walk into a nuclear reactor. But..." He shook his head. "I can't stop you, can I?"

Theo bit her lip. The answer was no, of course.

Six months ago, she'd created two shabtis of her own. She had used roadkill and papier-mâché, but she'd said the right words and they'd come to life on her parents' kitchen table. A man and a dog: a hunting pair to guide her to where Seth was being imprisoned. Once their purpose was fulfilled, they'd crumbled into dust.

She'd named them Al and Lucky.

They'd been alive for an hour or so. Alert, thinking, speaking. But they had been something beyond Theo's grasp, and she couldn't give them real life.

Sometimes, she thought that they were more of a loss than Meren. Meren had his chance and chose to use his immortality to hurt people. Al and Lucky didn't hurt anyone, and they didn't even get to live a whole night.

She'd gotten through that. She could figure this out. She *had* to figure this out.

"They're in pain, Seth," she said.

He cupped her chin in his hand. "Gods bless you for a charitable heart, love," he said gently. "But you can't save everyone."

She met his eyes. "I'm not trying to save everyone. But whatever's happening here—these voices—they're hurting. Scared. And no one else can even see them."

"…So be it, then." He released her and scanned the room, one more time. The mist remained low, but the rust color was beginning to deepen in the shadows.

"It's coming back," she warned.

"Then we should go while their influence is still subdued."

"But—"

"Theo, your hand is bleeding."

She looked down. Her whole middle and ring fingers were bruised purple now. A shallow cut glimmered carmine red in the darkest part of the skin.

"That's new," she said. She hadn't even felt it.

Seth wrapped his handkerchief around her injured fingers. "They'll be here tomorrow," he promised, low-voiced. "They have no other choice. But until we can protect you from them, we shouldn't linger."

* * *

Seth had taken rooms in an old hotel on the far side of the park. It was slightly faded 1920s glamor: golden Art Deco sunray decorations and a glittering lobby tiled in crisp black-and-white marble. The staff paid no attention at all as Seth led Theo and Aki through the main hall—Aki in his tasteless t-shirt and Theo with a bloodied handkerchief wrapped around her hand.

But then, most of the clientele looked fashionable, artsy. Someone was having an evening photo shoot for Instagram by the poolside. A couple of slim, long-necked women with the too-smooth look of artful surgery hurried past, high heels clacking on the marble, each towing a rolling clothes rack with garment bags on it.

Aki whistled. "Doesn't look like your scene, Imhotep," he said.

"It used to be," Seth said wryly. "When it opened."

His suite—this was the kind of place that had *suites,* not rooms—was on the plainer side for Art Deco, with wide open spaces and broad chairs in sleek dark wood. Seth urged Theo to sit down and retrieved a medical kit from his luggage.

"I thought you have an X-Man healing factor," Aki said as Seth helped her clean and bandage the damaged fingers. "Why are you carry- ing a first aid kit? You don't bleed."

"I do now," Seth said shortly.

That was true, but it wasn't why he had the medical supplies. The fight with Meren had injured both of them. Seth's wounds had been worse, but his new body still recovered much more quickly than a normal person's. Theo's burns had taken longer to heal.

They'd traded silly injury stories as they'd sat on the edge of her hospital bed. Seth had told her about falling off a chariot at the Battle of Two Wells and discovering that, yes, his shabti body could definitely get a concussion (albeit under circumstances that would kill anyone else). Theo had told him about the time a badly designed mixed-media instal- lation fell off the wall while it was still curing, plastering her with half- cured chunks of clay that ended up needing to be shaved out of her hair. They'd shared a bottle of water and a laugh over the ridiculous places life took them. Seth had promised he'd show her how to treat her deeper burns at home.

He'd kept medical supplies for her. To a veteran painter who'd injured herself on every type of toxic art supply known to man, that said romance.

Seth met Theo's eyes as he taped up the cut. She didn't need his help handling such a minor wound...but he wanted to, and she liked it when he helped her. Theo squeezed his hand with her good one. When he squeezed back, she could feel her cheeks warming.

"Guys?" Aki said. He leaned into Theo's view, waving like a party clown in a pointed attempt to remind them he was there. "Spooky shit? Chaos?"

"Look, if you didn't want to see this, you shouldn't have tagged along," Theo pointed out. "And I'm still buying you tacos later."

Aki considered that. "And a quesadilla."

"Deal."

Aki flopped down in one of the armchairs and laughed. "Too bad we can't solve ghost problems like that, huh?" he said. "Hey, Imhotep. What did you bribe people with back in the day? Gold? Honor?" He waggled his eyebrows. "Beautiful maidens?"

"Beer," Seth said.

"*No shit.*"

"None whatsoever." Seth cleaned his hands with an alcohol wipe and discarded the used gauze packaging. "Bread and beer. The traditional offering to the spirits of the dead. Sometimes honey for purity, if you have it—not everyone did."

"Should we do that?" Theo asked.

"Not yet. We still aren't certain of their nature. Giving them the wrong offering would only make things worse."

Unfortunately, that made sense. Theo looked up at Seth. His brow was still furrowed, and she could feel the edge of tension still thrumming through him.

"How did you figure it out?" she asked.

"I didn't," he admitted. "But I began to guess. When I saw red in your eyes, I knew something chaotic must be dogging you. I made a curse jar this afternoon, to break any spells on you and your team—including the child here," he added. Aki gave him the finger. "But the scorpion dream—such a profound symbol of evil couldn't point to any ordinary threat. When I came through the window and saw you there, struggling with something invisible, I gave you the most potent spirit-calming spell I could remember."

"Fast thinking. I was trying to calm down whatever they were, but I don't think the djed and the tyet did anything."

"Not for shattered spirits," Seth said. "One must isolate the disease before treating it. If you plan to help them, be their priestess, then we must learn more about them."

Theo Speer, priestess? Mom would have a screaming fit. Very much *not* in her plan for the Speer children and their journey to the upper middle class. Religion was so...*déclassé.*

"Um," she said. "I don't think I'd call myself a priestess. I haven't, uh, passed any trials or anything. Studied any sacred text."

"And yet you spoke to the spirits of the dead and the dispossessed. Acknowledged my shabtis' nature and knew it well enough to awaken them. Put my heart in my chest and spoke sacred words over me. Made me whole." Seth touched his throat where the tyet still hid. "You've done the duties of a *sem* priest, Theo. One who cares for the funeral and the dead. The ghosts will respond to that."

It made a strange kind of sense. Images were her life's work. And she had knelt over him in the graveyard, reciting the incantations that brought him back to life.

Priestess. Not a comfortable thought. But she could feel...*motion* in it. Life for her was never static: she sought motion, change, depth, the same way she tried to make her painted figures look alive and moving on canvas. Being comfortable wasn't part of it.

"OK," she said.

Aki snorted. "Just 'OK'?"

"I've had my scheduled freakout for the day." She looked back at Seth. "How do we 'isolate the disease'? All we know so far is spirits in Building H."

Seth leaned forward, resting his elbows on his thighs as he thought. "Whatever the ghost or ghosts are, they seem to be connected to these fakes. You're certain that they *are* fakes?"

Theo nodded. "The museum had them X-rayed years ago. Just pig bones and papier-mâché. One's a mannequin."

"Then there must be something about these fakes that drives the ghosts to haunt them. Perhaps one of them had some connection to these fakes in life?"

Research. She could definitely do that. "I've already got the in with Dr. Armstrong. I'll hit up the archives and see what the paper trail looks like. Maybe someone got murdered in that building back in the day."

"And I'll pursue the fakes themselves from a different angle. I know an antiques dealer who specializes in forgeries like these. He might know something."

Aki perked up. "A forger? That sounds like fun. Can I come?"

"No." Seth looked up at him. "You'll need to help Theo here. Gossip with the museum workers and see if you can discover any more signs of the spirits' influence. Remember—disease, bad luck, corruption, madness, chaos."

"C'mon! Theo can do that."

"Definitely not," Theo said. "You're better at schmoozing than me. The last time I tried to schmooze, shabtis started coming to life. It was a whole thing."

Aki snorted. "Seems to have worked out pretty good for you."

She glanced up at Seth. Despite the frights, the red mist, the spirits… "It sure hasn't been boring."

CHAPTER 11

A scholar is a man who thinks about everything and does nothing.

> —*Graffiti written on a scribe's hut, Dendera, c. 50 BCE*

Theo dreamed of the voices that night.

Help us, they murmured.

Maker, said one.

Tearing, said another.

Help us. Help us. Help us.

Don't let him have us.

Who? her dream self tried to ask, but the babble of voices filled her ears and drowned each other out. She woke half an hour late with a fuzzy head and a feeling like she'd slept on a pile of rocks.

As soon as she clocked in for the day, Theo "borrowed" a copy of the museum directory from an unlocked office and quickly found the name she needed. Dr. Mallory H. LeDieu, head archivist—specifically a specialist in early-twentieth-century documents. Theo managed to get through to her office and scheduled a meeting for five o'clock.

While she was poking around, she looked up the history of Building H too. The museum's "History of Our Institution" page had a gratifyingly in-depth summary. Building H had been built in 1890 as a bank, which folded in the Panic of 1893. The building did a brief stint as apartments before being sold to the Heritage Museum. It served for a few decades as a classroom annex, but a change in city codes required that the building be gutted and updated—which would be expensive as hell. The insulation was flammable and the wiring was out-of-date. It was a firetrap, which explained why the fakes were stuck there. Nothing particularly valuable would be lost if it all went up.

Otherwise, it was mainly used for storage and long-defunct records. A perfect place to lose something for a few decades.

Or maybe a good place for a dead priest to steal another body. She wondered if Meren had been there, too, and left a ghost behind.

* * *

She knocked off right before five o'clock and went looking for Dr. LeDieu. A docent pointed her toward the basement.

The subbasement, to be precise. Despite the carpeting and insulation, a damp chill radiated from the concrete.

Dr. LeDieu herself was an imposing figure of about six feet, swathed in a colorful print caftan, her graying hair gathered up in a scarf that almost but didn't quite match. Books filled her office, overflowing the shelves and stacked on the desk and chairs, almost to the point of hiding the computer. Their pages bristled with red-and-blue reference tabs. A hand-woven tapestry on the wall showed the characters of Linear B, the prehistoric script, in stark white on black.

"Thanks for meeting me, Doctor," Theo said. The two women shook hands.

"Not a problem." LeDieu was brisk, businesslike. "I hear you've been doing provenance research. This is about the exhibition build?"

"Yes and no," Theo admitted. "Some of it is just personal interest."

At that, LeDieu flashed a narrow slice of smile. "Chasing the rabbit?"

"You know how it goes. Start on potsherds, end up two hours later on eighteenth-century pirates."

"True. But my archivists say you were visiting one of Alan Armstrong's pet projects."

"Well, the Heritage teams are busy. And he knows I'm interested in mummies."

"You understand that there's a question of appropriate behavior. This isn't your museum or your resources."

Ouch. But not unexpected. Scholars could be *really* territorial.

"I know," she said. "And I wouldn't get involved." She raised her hands in a 'What can you do?' shrug. "But when it's a curator asking…"

"I understand," Dr. LeDieu said. She sat down behind her desk and moved a stack of books, gesturing for Theo to sit down. The seating provided was a deep, awkwardly shaped folding chair covered in more fabric, black-and-white with a heavily textured pattern.

"So what specifically are you looking for?"

Theo made herself comfortable. One advantage to pretzeling herself constantly: she could get comfy in just about anything. "Names," she said. "Dr. Armstrong's fake mummies are fascinating, but I really don't know anything about where they came from or who made them. No one's been able to tell me anything. Is there a file that your archives would be all right with sharing? Things like who acquired them, when and where exactly they came from?"

"Hmm. You'll understand if I don't have that data on hand. We handle hundreds of thousands of records related to the collection."

"Oh, definitely."

"And I may not be able to help you." LeDieu frowned. "Certain artifact records are frustratingly incomplete. Several records were retyped in the 1960s, and the originals discarded. And there was an archive fire in 2006—probably thanks to celluloid film strips stored with papers. I wasn't in charge then, but it's common knowledge that someone should have been fired."

From the look in her eye, she had a pretty pointed idea about who that *someone* was, and she'd tell Theo all about it in a heartbeat. Now really wasn't the time to hear about departmental grudges. "What about microfiche copies?" Theo asked quickly.

"The museum didn't start microfilming records until 1955. And digitizing the microfiche is still an ongoing project. Budget concerns."

Theo's shoulders slumped. "So it's a dead end."

"Possibly." At the sight of Theo's visible disappointment, though, LeDieu relented. "I can give you a one-time pass. For Dr. Armstrong's *special project.* You'll be monitored, of course."

"That would be incredible. Thank you so much, Doctor!"

"Yes, well. Anything to ensure that one of Alan Armstrong's projects actually gets followed through."

Another comment with a bite. This woman really, really didn't like Dr. Armstrong. Theo wondered who had swiped whose sources.

Dr. LeDieu made out a temporary archive ticket and handed it across. "Better go now," she said. "You never know when people will change their minds."

CHAPTER 12

The writing is finished. It took one thousand, four hundred
and twenty-two days. Now for Christ's sake, give me a
drink.

—Scribal commentary in an illuminated manuscript,
11th century

The ticket got Theo into the main reading room of the archive. It resembled a library from a Scooby-Doo episode: windowless, a maze of tower-
ing shelves and stacks of files in various stages of preservation. Huge
daybooks and tiny, fragile chapbooks were carefully wrapped in sterile
paper, while spiral-bound catalog records bulged with fading transpar-
encies between fingerprint-smeared plastic covers. And those were just
the documents allowed to be in semi-public view.

Theo was escorted to a heavy Edwardian desk with a green-shaded
banker's lamp and a chair whose leather was sagging and worn from
decades of researcher behinds. The tall, curly-haired research assistant,
who resembled a Greek statue of Young Apollo Counting the Minutes
Until Quitting Time, brought her a pile of books and papers and then
disappeared into the stacks. Probably to nap.

But then, this *was* an archive. Archivists were the mad wizards of
the museum world. Theo carefully pulled the pile toward her, knowing
that eyes were still on her. A pair of security cameras winked from the
corners of the room.

Judging by the condition of the yellowed folders, the preserva-
tionists hadn't gotten to some of these yet. Shreds flaked off the pages.
Theo brushed away a few of the flakes, which stuck to her hands.

The documents themselves were pretty short. They began with a
handwritten receipt dated May 1913, for "Lot of 6 mummified specimens

in fair condition, late of private collection in Bristol, donated by the gracious wishes of Col. Jason W. Wolff (ret.)."

Donated, not bought. That explained why they hadn't been examined too closely when they were taken in. A notation scrawled in spiky handwriting had been blotted and scraped, leaving behind only a few legible words: "Split lot...Brother Priest to..., funeral wares to...of Kowloon."

Kowloon. Hong Kong? Theo made a note.

The next papers in the file were from January of 1926. Two of the mummies—"The Minister" and "The Priestess of Serqet"—were examined by Dr. F.W. Shaw-Cross, who pronounced them to be Seventeenth or Eighteenth Dynasty. The good doctor's notes: "The unusual and varied nature of the wrappings & artifacts can be justifiably ascribed to the flowring of art under Khuenaten...Lovely specimens." The paper said that they were "returned to storage."

The complete collection of "3 full bodies, 1 partial torso & artificial legs, 2 heads (male)," went on display in October of 1946. They were shown for less than a year before being returned to storage as "unsuitable for the public, owing to concerns of taste."

"Someone must have sniffed a fake," Theo murmured as she turned a page.

The elaborate mummies should have been on display—and on souvenirs. Museums bled money, and a glamorous body draped in gold would be a star exhibit. Unless someone higher up the food chain suspected something rotten in the state of Denmark.

Eight years ago, the department had re-translated the "Priestess of Serqet" tablet and formally identified her as one Princess Penedjmet. However, the study was truncated after the initial work: "some doubt about the findings," wrote the head of the study. Two years later, the princess and her fellow lot-mates were X-rayed and pronounced by Dr. Armstrong himself to be turn-of-the-century fakes.

Overall, a pretty undistinguished career. Except...

Serqet was the scorpion goddess.

Theo turned back to the 1946 pages. Penedjmet hadn't been Penedjmet yet. Something had made them call her a priestess of Serqet.

There: buried in the body-condition photos. A glimpse of the underside of the mummy's golden plate, half obscured by the hands of the examiner.

A scorpion.

A really *bad* scorpion.

"Do not pass Go," Theo said. "Do not collect two hundred dollars. *Damn.*"

Some attempts had been made to add finer detail on the scorpion's shell and segments of the tail, but the lines had been etched in the under-lying material—probably wood or clay. When the material was electro-plated to give the illusion of solid metal, most of the detail work was muddied or lost. A good way to disguise bad hieroglyphs.

But the profile! Half of the legs were tucked underneath, hidden beneath its shell. The angle of the tail was almost three-dimensional, and the hook of the sting obscured part of the body. No ancient Egyptian drew a scorpion that way.

Theo walked briskly to the shelves and grabbed several thick refer-ence volumes on ancient Egypt and art forgery. Back at the table, she piled up books, scanning texts as she "accidentally" blocked the camera's view with the collected works of Wallis Budge.

Under cover of covers, she slipped her phone out of her bag and took a few quick shots of the pages.

Her pulse raced as she flicked through the rest of the documents. The information was limited, but something was there. And her brain—the thing that constantly forgot her own Social Security number but remembered the exact shade of the crayon she was holding during one project fifteen years ago—was screaming at her about misshapen scorpions.

She'd seen them before, and not just on Penedjmet.

When Apollo came back, Theo practically shoved the documents into his arms and raced for the door. A quick sprint took her across campus to Building H.

(Ever since Meren, she'd been working on her running. Next time she was chased by a screaming, melting clay golem, it wasn't going to get nearly so close.)

Building H was practically deserted. The evening security guard was playing a phone game and barely looked up as Theo swiped her pass. She pushed through into the vast exhibition space and raced over to the Minister.

"I knew it," she said to herself. "I *knew* there was something about that scorpion."

Crouching down, she tilted her head, angling to get a closer look at the underside of the fake's propped-up sarcophagus lid. There it was: the same scorpion, with the same strange angles and mismatched style.

That one hadn't been in the archives. Nobody would have seen it if they weren't staring hard at the hieroglyphs for hours. But Theo had seen it—and more like it.

She walked the circuit of the room once more, checking them off. On the Other Woman's footboard, the scorpion symbol replaced a vulture in one of the lines of hieroglyphs. Hai-Ti's wrappings included a faded drawing of a scorpion under the left leg. Even one of the fake heads wore an earring shaped like a scorpion's tail.

The same image, again and again. All on different fakes, modeled on different eras.

"Thanks, guys," she murmured. "I knew there was a connection."

She snapped photos of the scorpion markings on the Other Woman, Hai-Ti, and Tilamentu, and texted one of the photos to Dr. Armstrong.

This wasn't in the provenance, she tapped out. *If we can date the tool marks, it may give us a better time frame for the pieces.*

That was the first message. Theo began to type the second, but the phone rang almost immediately.

"You found the marks!" Dr. Armstrong said happily. "I was wondering when you'd ask me about them."

Theo's heart dropped. "You know about them?"

"Yes, of course. We think it's the mark of a turn-of-the-century forger. The literature calls him the Unknown Master."

"But...I didn't see anything in the documentation about it. No name or anything."

"Well, no, we don't have his name," Dr. Armstrong admitted. "He didn't leave his ID or anything. But we know he was working in the northeast around, oh, 1905—some of the materials point that way. Are you sure you didn't see it in the papers? You should have full access."

"Maybe I missed it," Theo admitted. "I should look again."

"Well, maybe there's a few papers Dr. LeDieu's people didn't find for you," Armstrong said. "You should ask Dr. LeDieu about the Unknown Master. Make sure you mention that it's for my project. She loves being involved in my projects!"

Which was either total ignorance or a sneaky show of passive-aggression from the otherwise cheerful curator. Maybe the *ukhedu* was powerful enough to affect even him. Theo thanked him and hung up, mentally cursing inconsistent documentation.

She ran her fingertips over the edge of the nearest case. Princess Penedjmet looked almost peaceful. As Theo touched the case, red mist bubbled up through the bandages.

"The Unknown Master," she said aloud.

Something about this forger's works attracted shattered spirits. She leaned over Penedjmet's case, studying the sculpted face and thick yarn wig with its gilded beads.

Whoever this forger was, he'd worked hard. He'd made his creations with care. It didn't matter that they were fakes and that selling them was a crime: he had layered onionskin paper into fine folds and soaked it with lacquer to make it set over the plaster skull. He'd *made* it. If she looked, she could probably find his hundred-year-old fingerprints in the layers of papier-mâché.

Theo knew about the power of the artist. She'd done the same when she built Al and Lucky, sitting there at her parents' kitchen table.

Maybe this Unknown Master had found the wrong hieroglyphs somewhere. Something from the Book of the Dead or a tomb painting: he'd certainly slathered his creations in symbols. But the ancient words had power, especially combined with the strength of an artist who loved their creations...and now wounded spirits clung to them. Stuck. Radiating chaos and poisoning the whole museum. Even taking the form of his maker's mark.

When she thought of it like that, she sympathized with the Unknown Master. She hadn't planned on raising the dead either, when she fell in love with the shabtis. But now she had to unriddle his work, or the contamination would only get worse.

Seth was on his way to New Jersey tomorrow morning. Apparently, it took time to get in contact with a "completely legitimate businessman" in the antiques business. Theo grabbed her phone and texted him about her findings. If this Unknown Master used the scorpion as a signature, it might just be the thing that helped them unravel this mystery.

CHAPTER 13

History is a gallery of pictures in which there are few originals and many copies.

—*Alexis de Tocqueville*

Seth left early the next morning. His contact was in Princeton, and he said he'd be back that evening. He carried printouts of the pictures Theo had taken in the archive, but he didn't say what he was going to do with them. Probably an "If you need to ask, you don't need to know" kind of thing.

Once he was gone, Theo couldn't get back to sleep. It wasn't quite six a.m., and she didn't have to be at work until eight-thirty. She spread out her own notes and began to flick through them.

So. The fakes had been donated to the museum in 1913 by "Colonel Jason W. Wolff." (Google hadn't turned up anything on him, though it had helpfully informed her about an influencer in Massachusetts with the same name.) Dr. Armstrong believed the fakes to be the work of a single faker, the Unknown Master, who'd been working somewhere in the eastern United States. The Unknown Master used a scorpion as his symbol. Now the only living dead man in the world was dreaming about scorpions, and ghosts clung to those same fakes.

Theo chewed on her pencil. The museum was definitely haunted. *Disease, bad luck, degeneration, and withering:* fights breaking out and tension in the air. And that red haze over the building the day she'd arrived.

The notes weren't giving her anything new.

Damn. It had frozen.

There's always a point when a project goes wrong. Theo called it *freezing:* that moment when she'd drawn and re-drawn a piece so much that the flow of the original linework was lost and the figures turned blobby and flat. When a painting froze, she needed to change something up. See the problem differently.

She gathered up her notes and tucked them into her laptop bag, along with the beer and bread offerings for the day. With any luck, she could talk Dr. LeDieu into letting her have another look at the archives.

As she passed a coffee shop on the way toward the campus, Theo had an idea. She swung in and bought a tray of espresso brownies. Every archive department ran on insane amounts of caffeine, and she was betting the Heritage Museum was no different. A little bribery to grease the wheels.

The sun didn't reach the archives. No light wells down in the subbasement: that would risk daylight damaging the historical documents. Theo balanced the brownie tray and knocked on Dr. LeDieu's door, shivering as the concrete's chill seeped into her.

Today, LeDieu wore a long dark-blue dishdashah robe with embroidered neckline and sleeves. It had been carefully patched at the hem, and paler lines showed where the dye had faded over the years. She looked up sharply as Theo opened the door.

"Morning!" Theo said cheerfully. "Sorry to bother you. I wanted to swing by and say thanks again for letting me have a look at the archives. It was really helpful. Brownie?"

She held out the tray. LeDieu studied it for a moment, like an archaeologist examining a particularly concerning artifact, before delicately taking a single half-brownie.

"Thank you," LeDieu said crisply, "but this isn't necessary. I was doing my job."

"Yes, but you still took the time to help me. I appreciate that. Things seem a little tense around here, so it was nice to meet a friendly face."

LeDieu gently toed a small garbage can out from under the desk.

"Is that what you're doing?" she said. "Being friendly?"

"Well, yes, I guess. I mean, I don't want to be *un*friendly." Theo shrugged. LeDieu's stare felt pointed. "I mean, you can't go wrong with brownies."

LeDieu dropped the half-brownie into the garbage can. She took a tissue from the box on her desk and wiped her hand thoroughly.

"Miss Speer, let me make something clear," she said.

The chocolate-smeared tissue followed the untouched brownie into the garbage. LeDieu leaned forward.

"I'm well aware of who you are and what contacts you've made at your home museum," she said. "Not all of us can afford to be *friendly,* whether with security guards or wealthy donors. Some of us have had to work for what we have, particularly in an underfunded and underappreciated department.

"I let you have access yesterday because it's in my best interests to work with Dr. Armstrong's pets. You see, I have to work with him after you leave. But you get one free. That's it."

Theo blinked hard. Red touched the corners of the world. LeDieu's blue dishdashah fell in deep wine-colored folds.

"Now," said LeDieu, "get out of my office. And take your cheap coffeehouse pastries with you. I recognize the label on that tray, and I can't believe you think I'd eat that crap."

Theo mumbled an apology and skittered backward out of the office. The shadows in the corridor were bruise-colored despite the harsh blue-white lights above.

"Honestly," she said to herself. "The brownies aren't *that* bad."

* * *

She headed up into the main museum complex. LeDieu might not have been bribable, but that was her loss. Theo left the brownie tray on a workbench in the exhibit, and the brownies were gone in ten minutes. She spotted two carpenters with chocolate smears on their work gloves, and that made her feel better.

Theo found a corner and settled in with her tablet, working on the day's project. Another emergency panel redraw: someone in PR was worried about the dotted patterns on the hieroglyphic boat being a seizure trigger. While her hands worked, her mind wandered.

The archives were definitely closed to her now. The inter-museum gossip network loved a juicy story, and last December's theft-and-arson spree had spread far and grown a lot of extra details in the process. LeDieu had probably pegged Theo as a bimbo sleeping her way into better jobs. For a woman dedicated to her profession, that was repulsive.

Theo respected LeDieu for that. Even if the archivist was dead wrong.

Unfortunately, that meant problems for the investigation. If she needed more on the fakes' provenance, she'd have to find a way to work around the head archivist.

When her break came, she took her bag full of printouts outside and sat on the museum terrace next to the steps. The noon sun was baking the city, and she basked on the hot marble like a crocodile on a sandbank.

Theo fanned out her pictures from the archives and held them up to the sun. She leaned back and unfocused her eyes. The third-hand pictures of the fake mummies softened into shapes and lines. The text from the catalogs and records turned into gray squares.

The lines…the shapes…

Huh.

Theo blinked, and the shapes came back into focus. The text turned into text again.

But something was definitely wrong.

"Professionally set," Theo murmured. "These *should* be even." But the paragraphs were slightly crooked on the page, and the font didn't quite match the one on the opposite page. Palatino versus Palatino Linotype.

Someone had tampered with the records! They'd replaced a whole page, but they hadn't perfectly matched the details. Forged documents to go with the forged mummies.

Hell yeah.

But she'd jumped the gun before and ended up getting nowhere. Think logically. Who could have altered the books? And why?

The documents were only available through a reading-room request…or by being a member of the archive department. Getting a list of reading-room requests just wasn't going to happen unless she spent about a year bribing Dr. LeDieu and company. And if she wanted to bribe people, she'd be in Publicity.

But she did know her way around museums. Now she had an idea of exactly what to look for.

* * *

Dr. Armstrong was happy to sign another archive request form. He probably didn't realize just how much Dr. LeDieu resented him. That was one person, at least, who seemed immune to the tension in the air. The only thing red about Armstrong was his shirt: he sported a Starfleet security officer's shirt under his blazer. He beamed when Theo noticed it.

With a pre-signed authorization form from an assistant curator,

Theo could bypass Dr. LeDieu and go straight to the reading-room staff. Once in, she settled into the same spot and pretended to focus on a photocopied newspaper article. The handsome Apollo of an attendant was still there, looking no more engaged with his job than yesterday.

In a few minutes, Apollo was bored and stopped paying attention to her. She quickly flipped to an exhibition catalog from 1946, when the mummies had supposedly gone on display for a short time. The pages had been unbound and preserved under plastic before being slipped into a ring binder. Theo found the page mentioning the fakes and gently slipped her fingertips under the plastic.

The other pages were heavier, clothlike—almost like watercolor paper. It was the real stuff, crumbly at the edges. But this paper was wrong: too smooth and glossy. Modern.

Yep. Someone had put a fake page into the records.

The rest of the catalog gave her nothing. But now she knew that the information had been tampered with. And that opened a whole lot of interesting possibilities.

She flipped back to the early documents: Wolff's handwritten be-quest and the intake notes. They'd been fully laminated and she couldn't touch the paper, but now she knew what to look for.

"Split lot…Brother Priest to…, funeral wares to…of Kowloon."

Split lot. And there were no Egyptian funeral wares in the collection, just the fake bodies. So there'd been other items in the same collection, but they were separated out. Who was the Brother Priest? Another mummy?

Theo peered closely at the paper. Brother Priest to where? Someone had scraped away the words (deliberately?), but she could see the marks left behind.

Geltner. Brother Priest to Geltner.

She didn't have time for a trip to Hong Kong. But Geltner? She knew that name. The Geltner House Museum was an independent Staten Island institution specializing in medical history. Small museums without endowments might have stumbled and bought a fake.

But why would this one specifically go to Geltner? Why separate this one out of the lot? Was it too lousy for the Heritage Museum to buy?

Theo grabbed her phone and had the Geltner House website and phone number in seconds. She dialed.

"Hello, you've reached the Geltner House Museum of Medical History. Please leave your message, and a docent will return your call as soon as possible."

If Theo could get a look at this Brother Priest, she could match it to the others. Getting to it would be a problem for a no-name artist with no connections. But she did have a connection, and he had connections of his own.

As soon as she left the archive, she called Seth.

"Is everything all right?" he said. Theo smiled.

"Nothing's on fire, anyway. But listen. I rechecked the provenance. The exhibition catalog was doctored with modern tech—probably Photoshop. Just the pages with the fakes on them."

"So these things could be…"

"Modern," they said together. Theo nodded. "If they're really from 1913, there's no reason for someone to put fake provenance in the archives a hundred years later." She tugged on the end of her braid, thinking. "But I don't know why anyone would make a fake look like an older fake. It's confusing."

"Chaos and deception," Seth said. "My contact may have more information. I have a meeting in an hour. Keep your head down, love, and I'll call as soon as I'm finished."

"Be careful. Please don't hurt anyone."

"Don't worry. His mafia connections aren't worth much anymore."

"You have a weird life," Theo informed him.

"Mm. Remind me to tell you about the time I was killed by a hippopotamus."

CHAPTER 14

Thank you for your last communication, Mr. Bestuzhev. My father would be grateful to be remembered as your enemy. However, despite your advice, I have not buried him with a stake through his heart. The funeral director did not offer that option.

—*Excerpt from a letter from Seth Adler
to Pyotr Bestuzhev of La Belle Epoque, Inc.,
on the occasion of the "death" of Seth Adler's "father"*

La Belle Epoque of Princeton, New Jersey, had a reputation. You heard the rumors: a questionable acquisition, a strange deal, a rare artifact going for a suspiciously low price. Veteran antique dealers shied away from it. Well-established experts hinted that their clients should look elsewhere.

But the rumors hadn't affected business much. On a bright summer morning, the air-conditioned showroom was full of people.

Small groups passed to and fro, speaking in low voices. Several were guided by experts, shabby-looking men in rumpled suits. Their patrons were wealthy, over fifty, casually dressed, and following an internal script that made no sense to a dedicated historian. Leaning on a cane, Seth watched a pair of gilded twelfth-century Byzantine icons being purchased by a woman who said they would go with the chandelier.

Icons were only the appetizer. Seth saw William-and-Mary bed-posts, Tang Dynasty vases, late Ottoman glassware, a Spanish altar cloth labeled from the sixteenth century, Kamakura painted scrolls, a carved Inuktitut seal figure ("Authentically spiritual!" the chandelier woman said), Etruscan statuettes, Minoan snake-goddesses, a Xhosa leopard skin...and everywhere, Kemetic artifacts. The floor displays were in overlapping rows, making it impossible to see all the way through the maze. Each one was roped off and guarded.

Seth's own personal collection was the detritus of his past lives. Theo had balked when she'd first seen it: a jumble of glass cases filled with scraps and bits of cloth and metal. But each of the objects had meant something to him in a past life, and so he kept them. That shabby tunic or segmented Spanish *real* was a part of him, like the diaries and the memories. That which is not remembered, not recorded, is not real. So the priests once knew.

In this showroom, Seth saw a collection of a different kind. The flashy, the exotic, the rare, the colorful, and the enticing were all gathered here, in a carefully curated mix of art and objects to give it the sheen of authenticity. The showroom was a honey pot for collectors and the wealthy. Seth spotted four fakes in two minutes.

But the fakes were what he was looking for.

In 1972, Pyotr Bestuzhev was one of the best-known names in the international antiques business. Seth—then Faruq—had contacted him, searching for shabtis. What he found was forgery.

If you must have enemies, then know where they are. Wealthy as the Adler "family" was, its international connections were limited, and 1972 was a bad year for a supposed American to be picking a fight with a nominal Russian. Bestuzhev knew that Faruq had figured him out, but Faruq only wanted specific shabtis. Weeding out forgery wasn't his job.

Ever since, Faruq/Seth had kept one eye on the Bestuzhev operation. The men even exchanged a few letters when Faruq "died" and Seth stepped into his shoes. By that time, Bestuzhev was in his sixties and still keeping one hand in the game.

Always respect an old soldier and an old liar. The sloppy ones don't last.

Now Seth was here again, in the showroom of La Belle Epoque. Proprietor, Andrei Pyotrovich Bestuzhev. Time to see what the new management had in stock.

He passed easily through the showroom, skirting the antiques. Here, a good suit was an exception rather than the norm: today's millionaire collectors tended to be celebrities and entrepreneurs, not bankers or stockbrokers. A man with no pet expert was a browser, not a buyer.

At the back, offices and conference rooms served the business part of the operation. Clients would come here to hash out details, sign checks, and wait while their experts argued with La Belle Epoque personnel on what each piece was or wasn't worth. Occasionally, someone mentioned forgery. That person was firmly escorted out and told to return with a better attitude or a lawyer.

Seth had an appointment. He presented his business card to the concierge, who showed him to one of the smaller reception rooms. Refreshments, he refused. He sat, hands folded on the pommel of his cane, and listened with sharper-than-human hearing to the buzz of conversation in the rooms around him. A security camera's glass eye winked from a decorative screen.

Eventually, he was shown into the back office. The current Bestuzhev believed in living an aspirational lifestyle. He favored Zen-inspired Orientalist designs, and everything was new. He did not furnish with his own wares.

Andrei Pyotrovich was of an age with Seth's supposed self. He might have stepped off a yacht that morning: with a deep tan, an open-necked polo shirt, boat shoes, expensive sunglasses, and a gold chain, he was pure twenty-first-century money.

"Seth Adler," he said, smiling and showing perfect white veneers. "It's great to finally meet you. My dad always said your old man was the sharpest tack he'd ever met—no bullshit. And in this business, that means something. Sit down, sit down! Take a load off. Drink?"

"No, thank you." Seth leaned the cane against the side of his chair. "Mr. Bestuzhev—"

"Call me Andy."

"Mr. Bestuzhev. I need your cooperation."

Some of Bestuzhev Jr.'s goodwill slid away. "If you have a problem," he said, "we supply full provenance before purchasers decide. La Belle Epoque is not responsible for upkeep. Otherwise, you should be talking to our legal team."

"Never mind the merchandise. Have you ever handled forgeries by the so-called Unknown Master?"

His words stripped Bestuzhev's amiable persona right off. The other man's gaze turned hard.

"That's a nasty accusation, Mr. Adler." Bestuzhev stood. "And I don't like your tone. We're done here."

Seth stood as well, without the cane. Bestuzhev was taller by an inch and on his own ground, but Seth had millennia of practice and young Andrei didn't have Pyotr's spine. He fell back a step.

"Get out," Bestuzhev said. He fumbled in his pocket for his phone.

"You sell forgeries," Seth repeated. "We both know it. *Put the phone down.*"

Bestuzhev hesitated. Seth took the phone and crushed it. Wisps of smoke threaded between his fingers as the battery collapsed. Bestuzhev reached for the desk phone, but Seth leaned forward an iota, and the younger man flinched back.

"If I yell," Bestuzhev said, "I'll have five guys here inside thirty seconds. You'd better make a good case fast, pal."

"Your father founded this operation in 1964. He had workshops in Los Angeles, Kolkata, and Rome, and occasionally acted to launder money for certain criminal interests out of Odessa. You're still maintaining the Rome and Kolkata workshops and have added production facilities in Valencia, but you've cut down on the number of personnel to keep things quiet and mostly detached from Odessa. Your father preferred artifacts from the first millennium at the latest. Coptic manuscripts and Roman glass. But you like furnishings from the sixteenth century onward."

Seth tucked one hand into his pocket, concealing the wounds left by the broken shards of phone case. Already half-healed. Bestuzhev was listening, maintaining a casual expression, but Seth could hear the other man's heart racing.

"So what is this?" Bestuzhev said. "Is this the point where you try to blackmail me? It's been tried."

"I don't give a damn what you're forging. But you also move other forgeries. Right now, I need provenance on some fakes."

Seth pulled Theo's sheaf of printouts from his jacket and spread them on the desk. Pictures of the provenance documents and the sketches she'd made of the delicate, crumbling fakes. Bestuzhev peered at them and then looked back at him, baffled.

"That's it?"

"That's it," Seth confirmed. "They're supposed to be from a forger headquartered in the northeastern United States. A man supposedly called the Unknown Master. They were sold as 1910s vintage, but the provenance documentation has been tampered with and they could be modern."

Bestuzhev pulled on a pair of nitrile gloves before picking up the printouts.

"Looks authentic," he said after a moment's examination. "You're wasting your time."

"Look again," Seth said. "I know you keep files on workshops and contractors. Give me what you have on the Unknown Master, and we're done here."

"Why the ever-loving *fuck* would I do that?" Bestuzhev queried politely.

"I've recently become invested in an artists' consortium," Seth told him. "My investment is in danger of being exploited. La Belle Epoque is one of the best in the business when it comes to tracking forgeries."

Bestuzhev nodded. "I get that," he said. "But I'm not hearing about why I should help you. My dad did some shady shit, but La Belle Epoque is proud to be completely legal and aboveboard."

Seth knew then that the gods weren't watching them. If they had, Bestuzhev would have been struck with white fire for the sheer enormity of that lie.

"If you're legal, then you have no reason not to help me. While my firm can't publicly endorse yours—based purely on the past and the behavior of your father, of course—I know many collectors and enthusiasts who could be directed towards your showroom."

That got a snort from Bestuzhev. "You think I can't get 'em in here by myself? I need you to pimp my business?"

"Yes," Seth said bluntly. "The museum circles don't trust you. But I know a dozen wealthy donor families who notoriously ruin pieces they buy. They hire designers to repaint things, turn them into art pieces and social media fodder. They won't go to you now, but they will with the right word in the right ear."

And ruin antiques with no real value. Neither said it, but it hung in the air between them. Bestuzhev could clear a multi-million-dollar profit off a handful of sales. Getting an entry back into certain fashionable circles would mean a record earning year for him.

The two men studied each other. Seth was old-school, formal, and apparently disabled; Bestuzhev was new-school, trendy, and capable. Each spotted the character the other was putting on, inventoried it, made their guesses as to what game each was playing. This was business.

Finally, Bestuzhev grunted. "We might have something," he conceded finally. "Making La Belle Epoque legitimate was always my goal, but we still keep files on the forgeries we saw in the old days. You said the Unknown Master?"

"Yes."

Bestuzhev sat down at his desk. "That's bullshit," he said. "'Unknown Master' is what you call the random guy who painted a fifteenth-century Dordrecht altarpiece. Not a forger."

"Is there a reason for that?"

"When you have a known but unidentified forger with a signature, enough that he gets noticed, then he's called after his best work. Like the St. Joseph Confession Forger or the Nailhead Casket Forger. Only Oxan Aslanian was ever called 'Master,' and he was one of the greats. Special case." He shrugged. "Too bad he got caught. A real craftsman. His Amarna stuff…shit."

Theo and Bestuzhev should never meet. It would either end in a murder or an elopement.

Bestuzhev woke up the computer. Seth sat as well, hands on his cane. Perfectly harmless if anyone came in: just the boss chatting with some businessman. His hand was already healed.

"I'm going to bill you for the phone," Bestuzhev said conversationally as he typed. "That model isn't even on the commercial market yet."

"Send me an invoice," Seth replied. "And buy something else. It was cheap."

"It was *carbon fiber.*"

Indeed? The carbon fiber hadn't given him much trouble, then. And Bestuzhev was shaken by the gesture—not only by the gesture itself, but the ease of it.

Seth waited while Bestuzhev worked. Occasionally, the man frowned at the computer as he typed, not bothering to hide his expression.

Theo would like this scene. She could rhapsodize about color, light, form, shadow, and contrasts between this and that. It was a language he didn't speak, but he knew the sound of. She could find pleasure in the turn of a head or the fold of a cloth.

Bestuzhev was still typing. His brow furrowed as he worked: he ignored Seth now, intent on his task.

"Huh," he said.

Seth craned his neck to look at the screen. "Problem?"

"Could be." Bestuzhev was leaning forward now, flicking through files onscreen with a click of the mouse. "You said an East Coast outfit?

1910s to today?"

"Correct. New England, supposedly."

"Well, I'm not seeing anything on this guy. Too broad. Any other info? What kind of stuff did he make?"

"Egyptian mummies."

Bestuzhev whistled. "You're out of luck, then. Mummy forgers are harder to pin than a Hollywood pervert. For a time frame that big, you're looking at outfits in Milwaukee, New York, and LA, at minimum."

A vague memory flickered in the back of Seth's mind. A board building on a scrubby lot, backing onto acres of nothing but arid California desert. Rachid al-Adhur with a cane of his own in hand...elderly...1908? A man saying, *The sun bakes 'em dry, a hundred years in a day...*

"I know that museums are still finding them," he said, shaking off the memory. "There's money in mummies."

"Nah. There used to be." Bestuzhev was typing again. "The bottom dropped out of the mummy market about fifteen, twenty years ago. Egypt's been cracking down on the international trade."

Museums couldn't risk alienating the Egyptian government. But museums weren't the only ones in the business.

"That leaves private collectors," he said. Bestuzhev glanced up. "That's always how it goes. When something is harder to get, only the rich and the criminals have it."

Bestuzhev nodded. "Supply and demand. Mummies go to rich people who want something cool and don't bother X-raying the thing. And the forgers do everything they can to fuck up the provenance."

Once more, a memory stirred. Seth didn't try to chase it. He remained seated and let the thought come to him.

"All right." Bestuzhev turned the monitor. "This is what I'm getting."

The screen showed a pitiful specimen. It was lumpy and misshapen, its exterior shedding flakes like onionskin. The mismatched sockets had never held eyes; there was no place for the optic nerves to pass through. It lay, half-unwrapped, on someone's dining room table.

Something prickled at him. The jaw had a sharp line, almost ridged. The feet and legs were different: the bones were all mismatched, one femur shorter than the other. Understandable when you were making a mummy out of soup bones and paper, of course. But why take so much time with the jaw and not even bother making the legs the same length?

"You didn't sell that," Seth said. It would have destroyed any dealer who tried.

"Ya think?" Bestuzhev pointed to the dates on the screen. "Twenty years ago. Offered by a collector who claimed he'd inherited it from an uncle. Supposed to be an Egyptian priest from the New Kingdom. Bought in 1899, passed down through a bunch of relatives who didn't have much paperwork for it...same old, same old. My dad turned him down, but not before opening a file on the deal."

"What was this collector's name?"

"Come on, Seth. You know I can't say that."

"It's on the damn screen, Bestuzhev."

Bestuzhev shrugged. "And if you read it while I'm not looking, then that's an accident and I'm not responsible for a breach of privacy."

Point taken. Seth flicked a glance toward the screen. The crude fake had been offered for sale by one Jason Wolff, then aged twenty-eight, of Windward Harbor, Massachusetts.

"Of course." Jason Wolff. A relative of the Colonel Jason Wolff in Theo's notes? Or the modern maker himself using a pseudonym? "But it doesn't look like any of the Unknown Master pieces."

"I know. Didn't make much sense." Bestuzhev tapped a key. The screen flickered and moved forward to the next file: a photograph of the exact same specimen, now older and very much the worse for wear. Its forearms had been fully unwrapped, revealing highly detailed bones under papery skin. "This is Specimen 47-FFB. Offered for sale to us by *Mike* Wolff, a few years ago. After my dad died and the business changed hands. Now being billed as a turn-of-the-century fake by the 'Unknown Massachusetts Master.' Completely different provenance."

"So it is modern," Seth said.

Bestuzhev nodded. "That's what I'm guessing. The Wolffs—if that's their real name—probably know someone that's been at this for years, making mummies in the garage. When La Belle Epoque changed hands, boom, the old junk gets polished up and sent to us again. We didn't take it then, either, but it's the only 'master' I could find in the mummy game."

"Interesting," Seth said quietly. "Interesting indeed."

He leaned forward in his chair, studying the images. It wasn't only time that had damaged the mummy. He could spot subtle signs of repair and restoration, particularly around the face and hands. This work was finer, cleaner, than before. The bones looked real.

A stroke of genius, to offer it as a historical fake.

He said as much, and Bestuzhev chuckled.

"No kidding!" he said. He seemed delighted by the concept, or was very good at pretending he was. "I mean, I'll shut the fucker down if I find him, but you gotta give credit for balls."

"And the Wolffs? Nothing on them?"

"Not even a phone number." Bestuzhev tapped the screen. "Dad told them he didn't want anything to do with it. Marked a complete DNC."

Seth had liked Pyotr Bestuzhev for reasons such as that. The man had been a forger, a smuggler, and a professional liar, but he'd had some standards about the things he forged and smuggled.

No, La Belle Epoque would never have sold this kind of product. It was too clumsy in its first iteration and too questionable in its second. Yet it almost might have passed as a real thing.

"I need those pictures," he said. "At least one copy."

"Why?"

"To prove something to a woman."

At that, Bestuzhev laughed. "Divorce, huh?" he said. He hit Print and copies whirred out of a photo printer. "Shit, you should've said so. She better be worth it."

She was. But Bestuzhev didn't need to know that. Seth made a non-committal noise.

"That's all I can give you." Bestuzhev closed the window on the screen and pushed back from the desk again with an air of finality. "There's some connection to what you were talking about, but you're gonna have to do the legwork yourself from now on. We don't handle cheap fakes."

"Thank you, Andrei." Shaking off the phantom, Seth stood and offered the man his right hand. Bestuzhev hesitated for a fraction of a second before they shook on it.

"Hell of a grip," Bestuzhev said. "What're you taking? PCP? Steroids? Don't mix that shit."

"Clean living and cross-training. Are we square?"

Bestuzhev didn't believe him for a second. "We're square," he said. "Now listen. When you're done fucking around with *clean living*, give me a call. I've got some pieces that would look great as accents in an Instagram reel—mid-eighteenth century, the first Japan craze. Inlaid snuffboxes and ivory fans. Tell your rich buddies."

"It's a deal."

Seth nodded to Bestuzhev and left the office. He would hold up his end of the bargain. If people insisted on buying and destroying antiquities in the name of fashion (and he could name several of them), then they could buy from Bestuzhev, who always had more where those came from.

CHAPTER 15

Ptahhotep is a liar. No one will work with him unless they are drunk. He owes me 12 deben.

—Graffiti from a workman's hut, Dendera,
c. 50 BCE

Disease, bad luck, withering. Theo had an idea.

On her lunch break, she tracked down Erika from the Heritage art department. After a few days on the job, she had a pretty good sense of the flow of the place, and finding one artist wasn't too hard. Erika jumped when Theo appeared beside her workstation.

"Crap!" she said. "You're sneaky. Is that a Chicago thing?"

"More like a 'get out early on a Friday' thing." Theo leaned against Erika's half-cubicle wall. "Listen, I wanted to say thanks again. You helped me out with the paint." She hesitated for a moment, making a show of wavering. "And, uh, I guess I wanted to say you were right. This place is *tense.*"

"Seriously?" Erika's blue-and-green eyebrows shot up. "Wow, you *are* serious."

"Well, yeah. So I wanted to say thanks. You were one of the only people who's been even a little bit friendly."

"Well...thanks." Erika's shoulders unbowed. She put down her stylus and leaned back in her chair. "Things are just like that, though. I bet you guys deal with the same stuff."

"Kind of." Theo smiled. "Have you ever seen the Museum Fights feed?"

"Duh, yeah." Erika returned the smile hesitantly. "Everyone here has."

"One of our Fabrication guys runs it."

"Yeah, right!"

"I can prove it. He's here right now. If we get into an argument in front of him, it'll get posted five minutes later," Theo promised. "It's all like that back home. So I guess I just wanted to say...I get it."

"Thanks. Not a lot of people around here would actually try to be nice. C'mon, sit down. I need a distraction."

Theo perched on the edge of Erika's low filing cabinet. They chatted for a few minutes, sharing gossip and agreeing how much better the world would be if they ran it. Theo could tell Erika was working up to something, so she kept it light and stayed put, hoping for the right moment.

"So," Erika said finally. "This is kinda weird, but are you...uh...are you the one from Chicago who had that thing happen last year? With the crazy security guard?"

Not really what she'd hoped for, but it was an opening.

"Yeah," she said. "That one's pretty high up on my list of 'weird stuff that happens at work,' but not actually the weirdest."

"What's the weirdest?"

Theo laughed. "Probably the sacrificial altar."

The legend of the lost altar was a running joke at the Columbian. Someone in the 1890s had taken in a marble building block from a fallen temple at Delphi. The block itself was badly cut and never actually finished. But on seeing the unusually deep hole in the center, some Victorian genius had decided that the block was an altar for human sacrifice and the hole was a drain for blood. The item was stored as such and forgotten until a few years ago, when it was supposed to be part of an exhibit on Delphi.

A whole team went looking for a sacrificial altar and found a marble block. So what did they think? Did they think that the initial item was mislabeled? Or did they tear half of Oversized Storage apart, looking for a phantom altar and calling the Storage teams idiots for losing such an important artifact?

Erika laughed out loud at the story, and her face lit up. For a moment, she looked—Theo blinked—cooler-toned. Like her reds were less red.

It's affecting her too. It must be affecting all of them. Does it fade when someone is happy? Or are happy people harder for it to affect?

"At least you figured it out!" Erika was saying. "We lose shit here all the time and no one ever finds it. And do the curators care?" She rolled her eyes. *"Hell no.* They're too busy with their stupid power games. Who *cares* who slept with who?"

"Oooh." Theo leaned forward. "Juicy secrets?"

"No juice left in those. Dr. LeDieu slept with some married guy a million years ago and it turned into this feud with her and Dr. Armstrong. Someone said someone's judgment was compromised, someone said someone else was trying to get a better position. Now she blames him for everything that ever happened, including that archive fire a million years ago. Lots of he-said-she-said."

"Bo-ring." In the backstage world, sex was barely anything. If Dr. LeDieu had stolen credit for someone's journal article, then that would be juicy. "Is that all? I thought it'd be way worse."

"I know! It's a big nothing. But nobody listens. Did you check those Glassdoor reviews?"

"Sure did. Two stars out of five. 'Stay away, they hate you.'"

"Yeah," Erika said. She ducked her head, fiddling with her stylus. "Now imagine the stuff that isn't getting posted. Or gets taken down 'cause the museum complains."

Theo let out a breath. "Is it really that bad?"

"I don't know." For a moment, Erika looked lost. "I don't remember. I think it's always been like this."

* * *

Seth's last message said he was back from New Jersey and had more information. He didn't have a key to her room yet, but Theo wasn't at all surprised to find that he'd gotten in anyway.

But he didn't look too good. Seth sat in the corner, bolt upright. His eyes were open, but his gaze was blank, and his pupils darted as they followed something Theo couldn't see.

She knelt down next to the chair and gently said his name. His current name, anyway. He blinked and focused on her.

"Theo. What time is it?"

"A little after six. You were zoning out." She touched his forehead. It was hot and fevered. "Do you get sick?"

"No. I was remembering." He caught her hand, but gently. "I'm fine. What did you learn?"

"You know, Seth, a shrink would call that a diversionary tactic."

"I've been certified sane by the best psychiatrists my company could bribe. What about the ghosts? Did you find anything else?"

Theo dropped the subject (for now) and brought out her notes. She sat on the armrest of Seth's chair, leaning against him, and they read through the papers together.

"Interesting," Seth said. "The Geltner House. Why would one fake be sent there, when the others were slipped into the Columbian's collection? False bodies don't have medical conditions."

"Maybe that one was really good?" Theo guessed. "Good enough to pass a small museum's inspection, anyway. No one would do X-ray diffraction on a mummy unless they were sure it was a fake."

"We should have a look at it. I'll call them and arrange a visit." Seth drummed his fingers on his thigh, thinking. "You should come as well. I'll tell them you're my expert consultant."

"I can't get the time off. We're doing more panel redesigns—"

"I'll call Dr. Van Allen. He'll call Dr. Harper."

Oh, right. What the donor wants, the donor gets.

"Must be nice to control the world," she said wistfully.

"Not yet," Seth said calmly. "But soon."

Theo looked down at him. His face was perfectly impassive, but there was a spark in his eye. Theo groaned and dropped her head against his shoulder. "Oh my God. Your poker face is incredible."

"Plenty of practice." He nudged her gently, a small smile curling the corner of his mouth. "Don't fall over, Theo. What else did you find?"

"I got some inside information from the Heritage art department. You were right about the wrath and the chaos—they all hate each other, though no one's sure why. Petty problems get blown up huge. Oh, and Dr. Armstrong and Dr. LeDieu have a nasty, gossipy history. Now Dr. LeDieu blames him for everything that goes wrong."

"How so?"

"There was an archive fire back in 2006. Old celluloid film sets off paper, that kind of thing. Lots of damage. According to the art department, LeDieu blames Armstrong for it."

Seth frowned. "So the archives were compromised. That would have made it easier for the forger to insert his provenance. Do LeDieu and Armstrong have any particular reason for being at odds?"

"Sex. Not with each other, but someone did something, someone else said something about it...the usual stuff. Not much we can do with that. But it's sure not helping the whole 'chaos' thing." Theo made a disgusted noise. "What about you? Did your contact say anything else?"

"You have to let me up first," Seth said. Theo sighed and moved just enough. Seth retrieved a file folder from his briefcase and showed her.

When she saw the photos, her breath caught. The thing on the table was unmistakably one of the Unknown Master's pieces.

"Holy cow," she said. *"Look* at it. Someone's put it through the wringer. The bones are amazing, and the face is great, but the rest of it's just a mess. It looks like acid stripping and staining."

"Yes." Seth hesitated. "The bones."

She looked at him. His expression was distant. "Seth, what's wrong?"

"I had a suspicion, djed, but I wasn't sure until I saw these pictures. I think I know why the fakes are followed by ghosts."

"Oh, no. You don't think they're...?"

"Real," he said.

Theo swallowed. The thought had almost been there—niggling at the back of her mind, like something stuck between her teeth—but she'd tried to ignore it.

"Look. The old photos show more of the skeleton." He turned over a page. "If I saw this thing lying in the dunes, I'd know it was a body."

She craned her neck to look. The bones were good, all right. Too good. If she took them away and only looked at the workmanship on the rest of the mummies, she'd call the Unknown Master an amateur. The fake flesh looked half-finished.

But some of the bones were good. Some were obviously pig, and some were plaster, but some of them were *perfect.*

"So what do we do?" she said softly.

"The plan hasn't changed," Seth told her. "The ghosts are lost and angry. Worse, they've been dishonored." His expression darkened. "If they were only bodiless, haunting the museum, then we could continue to speak to them as the nameless dead. But if these fakes contain real body parts, then those parts have been separated from their true bodies and patched together under different forms and names."

"The parts of the soul," Theo whispered.

Seth nodded, grim-faced. "The name—lost. The heart—lost. Body torn apart. Gods only know what's become of their *ka* and *ba* spirits. No wonder they've gone mad."

Theo jumped up and started to pace. The papers crackled in her hands. "There has to be a bigger story here. We have to get into Geltner and look at that seventh mummy. We *have* to."

"We will."

His voice was calm and steady. Calmer than she felt right now, that's for sure. She rocked back on her heels, trying to burn some nervous energy—trying not to think about ghosts and bodies and bones that were all too realistic.

"Come." He stood and held out his hand. "Let's make a plan, djed."

* * *

An hour later, as Theo went over her notes again, the door banged open.

"Theo!"

Theo looked up. Aki stood in the doorway, his laptop bag slung over his shoulder.

"What?" she said.

"I'm bored. C'mon, let's go get a drink."

That sounded good. Theo's back creaked as she straightened up. Beside her, Seth murmured something as he turned over another page of photocopied notes. One broad, warm hand gently rested on the curve of her back.

"Sorry," she told Aki. "I still owe Dr. Harper two panels."

"Aw, shit. More replacements?"

"Yeah. They don't like number seventeen. One of the hieroglyphs looks like it's making a face."

Seth chuckled. "It *is* making a face," he said. "It's Bes. God of the good life. They should be happy he's wearing clothes."

"All right, finally some magic bullshit I can get behind." Aki hitched up his laptop bag. "I'm still heading out, though. Hey, Imhotep, you wanna come?"

Theo gave Aki a sharp look. He was shifting in place, moving from foot to foot. His fingers tapped nervously against the strap of his laptop bag. He looked like he had something on his mind and he didn't know how to say it.

Seth and Theo exchanged a look. From his expression, Seth saw what she'd seen too. But he gave her an understanding nod and stood.

"It must be time for the official art-department hazing," he said.

Theo laughed. "Probably. But if he tries anything, you can take him."

"You won't be angry that I hurt your friend, then?"

She pointed her stylus at Aki. "We've been friends since grade school. I know for a fact that if anything goes wrong, he started it."

Aki nodded. "She's not wrong," he said. "C'mon. Let's go get hammered. I found this place just around the corner that's way too shitty for this neighborhood. It's probably a front for something."

Seth kissed Theo gently, running one long-fingered hand through her loosened hair. Theo leaned into him for a moment.

"Be safe," she said quietly. Seth's eyes were warm.

"Finish soon. You'll need to bail us out in a few hours."

She grabbed his hand and dropped a quick kiss on his fingertips. "I'll get your lawyers on speed dial. Have fun."

CHAPTER 16

In vino, veritas. In wine, truth.

—Anonymous

The bar-that-was-probably-a-front-for-something was called Dan's. Its windows were blacked out and the signboard outside hadn't been cleaned or changed.

A long wooden bar showed years of scars; racks of glasses hung above; middle-aged men and women lined up on stools, drinking and talking. A few feet behind the bartender, a grill sizzled. The smell of frying onions competed with the smell of old carpet. In the corner, a TV was showing a rerun of an MMA fight.

Aki Lee swaggered in as best he could, not bothering to check corners. He hollered "Hey, bro!" to the bartender, who gave him a flat look, and elbowed past two heavyset MMA watchers without noticing the glares they shot him. Seth followed in his wake, bemused.

They found a table in the corner, away from most of the noise, and Aki waved over a waitress.

"Tequila, *por favor*," he said. "One bottle, two glasses, and a metric fuck-ton of limes."

"Sure thing, boo," the waitress said with a wink. Aki grinned after her while Seth muffled a laugh.

"Dude!" Aki said. "I know a I'm-not-laughing cough when I hear one. What is it?"

"Nothing."

"I'm gonna tell Theo you're being a shithead."

"This is hardly a new development."

Aki made a face at him. "Touché," he said. "What's going on with you guys, anyway? I half expected to walk in on something NC-17. And instead, you're hot and heavy with the paperwork."

"Ghost research. We're going to the Geltner House Museum tomorrow. They have a mummy that might be from the same collection of fakes."

"That is the lamest thing you could have said."

The waitress returned with tequila and a bowl of lime slices.

Two shots in, the world didn't look much different. Tequila wasn't Seth's usual drink, but it went down smooth and burned satisfyingly. He turned over the shot glass and examined his reflection in its bottom, wondering if it was even possible for this newest body to get drunk.

His old shabti forms had been built in a land where alcohol was often safer than water. A general was required to hold his liquor, but drunkenness was a part of life and even expected in the afterlife. Charms on tomb walls guarded the spirits of the dead against otherworldly hangovers.

On rare occasions in the past centuries, he had managed to reach drunkenness. A large amount of an unusually potent poison could affect him, and modern humans had certainly distilled drinks of greater power than ever imagined in his time. But in his new form, who knew?

A single shot of tequila only seemed to make Aki talkative. More so than usual.

"I hate my job sometimes," he informed the world. "Meetings. We had a ninety-minute meeting about PowerPoint formatting. But hey, now there's drinks." Aki burped. "And wings. Should get some of those, too. Soak this stuff up before the night ends too early."

Seth downed his third shot. He refilled his glass and pushed the bottle toward Aki. "You clearly need this more than I do."

"Ha ha ha." Aki downed another shot. "You suck. What *was* so funny, anyway?"

"What?"

"Before. When she was over here and you started laughing."

"That word she called you. In my language, *bu* means *dog.*"

"*Seriously?*" Seth nodded, and Aki considered that. "Wait. So if I call someone my boo...then I'm saying they're my bitch?"

"Technically correct."

"The best kind of correct! This calls for wings."

* * *

Aki was three shots in. Seth was at twelve.

Wings, it turned out, were fried chicken pieces in a spicy sauce, eaten with the fingers. Consumed with alcohol, they served the vital purpose of making someone able to drink more.

"Ah," Seth said, when Aki explained. "Zakuski."

"Gesundheit."

The MMA fights on TV had wrapped up. The men at the bar muttered and grumbled to each other, swapping cash and complaining about the outcomes. The television switched to a Las Vegas poker tournament, adding the click of chips and the terse statements of "Raise" and "Call" to the background noise.

Seth tapped his fingers against the tabletop. The scarred wood was slightly sticky, and every touch left fingerprints behind. The aroma of someone's vape pen mingled with the smells of old carpet, cigarettes, and fried food, adding an unsettling note of artificial raspberry to the general miasma.

Aki was talkative and red-faced but still coherent. He rolled his empty shot glass between his fingers, looking as pensive as a man can while his hands are covered in orange sauce.

"All right," he said, when the wings were half gone. "I'm gonna get good and fucked-up soon, so I better say this now before everything starts spinning. It's important."

"I'm sorry about how you feel, but I'm spoken for."

Aki almost snorted his tequila. "Ow, fuck! In the nose! Argh!" He wiped his face and laughed. "Sorry, not my type. But you do get points for having an actual sense of humor. No, this is the 'I have a shotgun and a shovel' kind of talk."

"And you'll kill me if I hurt Theo."

"Nah. I can't kill you. I've seen the healing mojo you do." Aki put down his glass and fixed Seth with an attempt at a menacing glare. "But I can ruin your life."

Seth considered that while Aki poured himself another shot and grabbed a lime slice.

Theo and Aki had been friends long enough for her to be like his sister. Heretofore, Seth had mostly tolerated the young man: clever, immature, and harmless. But now said man was attempting to act *in loco fraternus*. Or *loco shotgunus*, anyway.

"I assume you have a plan," he said.

"Damn straight." Aki pointed his lime slice threateningly. "And it's one you'll never see coming."

"Hrm. You can't physically harm me. I have more in the way of fiscal and legal resources than you do, and my influence outstrips yours. However, my public profile is also larger, making me a high-value target with multiple angles of attack."

Seth tapped his shot glass on the table. "So you'd target me with satire and word of mouth. Public shaming. Phony social media posts, perhaps, but someone with my resources could trace that. Ultimately, you would try to ruin my reputation. Give the scandal six weeks to percolate and you could possibly see me lose a great deal."

Aki's mouth hung open. *"Whatthefuck."*

Seth took another shot. The eye-watering effects of the tequila were almost gone, leaving nothing but a pleasant warmth. "I've done it," he said.

"Wait. Seriously? When?"

"A long time ago. The technology changes, but the techniques don't." Seth refilled his glass.

"Uh, OK." Aki rallied. "So...no hurting Theo. Even if she's crazy sometimes." The lime slice was brandished for emphasis. "Get it?"

Seth dipped his thumb in the tequila and drew Maat's feather of truth on his mouth. "In the name of my patron goddess Neith and Montu of Thebes, I swear it," he said. "I mean no harm to Theo. Let it be written and known."

Aki shifted in his seat. "Uh, yeah. That's...uh...that's what I was going for. Fucksake, you're dramatic."

"I said that for me and her. Now let me say this for you." Seth leaned forward. "Don't persuade yourself that I'm helpless. I've forgotten more dirty tricks than you can learn in a dozen lifetimes. If you attempt to harm me or mine without good cause, you will suffer. And you will live long enough to see that no one will believe you."

He raised his shot glass in a toast. "Do we understand each other?" he said quietly.

"Jesus Christ. Yeah." Aki poured himself another shot and finally chomped on his slice of lime, his eyes watering. Now that he'd done his duty and delivered his "shotgun and shovel" talk, he seemed unsure of what to do.

Seth watched him in fond amusement. Akeela Lee was almost like a child. He'd never stood in the line of combat, tilled a field, hunted for his meals, or been held to even the most lax standards of behavior and responsibility. His food came from machines and his life was spent staring into one screen or another.

But the man was loyal. It was a strange, juvenile sort of loyalty, like seeing a boy of five trying to defend his mother. In the old days, that meant the boy would grow up well.

Aki burped and stole the last of the wings. "New round!" he proclaimed. "Your turn to buy. And you'd better have one of those black cards, 'cause PowerPoint bullshit makes me thirsty."

Of course, the old days got some things wrong.

* * *

Aki was at five shots. Seth had slowed down once he'd reached fifteen.

"OK," Aki said. "Free association. I'm gonna say something, and you say the first thing you think of."

That seemed sensible enough after fifteen shots. "All right."

"French Revolution."

"Which one?"

"Oh, right, the *Les Misérables* thing. That movie sucked. First one—the big one."

"Doomed. Too many fuzzy ideas, not enough solid planning. And killing an anointed ruler always spells disaster."

"Figures the monarchy guy doesn't like democracy. OK. What about, uh, aliens? Do they exist?"

"Yes." Seth ate a lime slice whole. Aki squinted at him blearily, not sure if he'd seen what he just saw. But there was no point in wasting good food, and modern limes were much sweeter than they used to be.

"That's it?" Aki said. "Just yes? Wait a minute, did aliens actually build the pyramids?"

"No. But if the universe is so vast, and the gods' power is so great, then aliens have to exist. Even if only as bacteria."

"Hang on, hang on, hang on." Aki made a face. "But you guys didn't know about other planets, right? How could your weird gods do anything with 'em?"

Seth shrugged. "We also didn't know about germs. Didn't stop them from existing."

"Weird," Aki said after a moment's thought. "You guys could do the"—he wiggled his fingers vaguely—"the woo-woo, spooky undead shit, but you didn't know all this other stuff. It's like having superpowered wizards who don't know about the law of gravity."

"Your point?"

"It's lame. Guys who know one big secret should know lots of other big secrets too." Aki glanced around, looking for a prompt. On the TV, Tiger Woods was advertising something. "How about golf?"

"A waste of good farmland."

"Ha! You're just pissed that they wouldn't let you play back in the day."

Seth blinked. "They wouldn't?"

"Uh, yeah. It was a WASP thing. And you're not white, not Anglo-Saxon, definitely not Protestant."

"Country clubs, right? I'd forgotten. Only my last life played, and most of the bans were gone by that time."

Aki grimaced. "You must have a *lot* of money if you can forget being treated like shit 'cause of skin."

"If the WASPs want to ban me from playing golf, then fine. The British wouldn't have wanted me joining their Everest expeditions, either, and I'm fine with that as well."

"*Dude*," Aki said. "Why wouldn't you climb Everest? If I lived forever and had a shit-ton of money and healing powers, I'd be on top of the world. Literally!"

"I've never died from cold. I don't intend to start now." Even the thought seemed to chill the air. Seth refilled his glass.

"So you're chicken."

"Yes."

"Fucking weak."

"I've died too many times to enjoy it. I'll face it again if I have to, but I won't go looking for new ways to kill myself."

"Huh. What's the weirdest way you've ever died?"

"Weird to me or weird to you?"

"Either one."

"Six months ago, I had to drink paint thinner to escape security guards controlled by my murderous brother."

Aki groaned. "No fair! I already know about that one!"

"It was still unpleasant." Seth winced at the memory. "Pour yourself a glass of *maison du acetone* if you don't believe me."

At that, Aki held up his hands. "I'm good, bro."

* * *

The shot count stood at seven and eighteen, respectively. The wings didn't seem to be helping as much. Seth could feel a vague sense of imbalance, a consciousness of altered state.

Which was ridiculous. He was Anhurmose of Waset. He had lived since the dawn of mankind, the glory of many empires behind him and under his command. Alexander the Great was a pauper by comparison. Seth might have said so at one point.

Glory. The thought bothered him. Honor and glory. Great things. He'd gone to war for them. Honor and glory meant power in times past, and power meant...power. And shabtis.

"You know..." Seth leaned forward, elbows on the table. Things seemed softer now. More distant. "I remember the sun god. The prophet."

"What?"

"The prophet of the sun god. At the Horizon of the Aten. I was there. When the prophet overturned the old gods for a few years. I lived in the barracks by...Ahmose. Ramose. The general."

Aki refilled his glass. He only spilled a little on the table. "Aw, you had a friend!"

"I don't even remember his name—you think we were friends? No. We were all in the barracks by the great way. The king's road." Seth took the tequila bottle from Aki and refilled his own shot glass. They were on their second bottle. "I saw the chariots going by. The king had a good team. Matched horses with gold on their bridles."

"Did you guys really do that shit? Like in the movies? Gold on everything? Like, solid gold chairs and stuff?"

"Not solid. And not any of us—the soldiers. But yes, a lot of gold. He glittered when the chariot went past. Royal disco ball."

This time, the tequila went all the way down. Aki coughed up half a shot and narrowly avoided burying his face in the lime bowl.

* * *

Aki stopped at those seven shots. Seth stopped at twenty-five.

That wasn't planned. The bartender cut them off when they emptied the second bottle of tequila.

"Laaaaame," Aki slurred. He was having trouble with the concept of "vertical." Seth paid the tab while keeping a firm grip on Aki's hoodie.

"You can drink," the bartender said.

Seth nodded. "High tolerance."

"Uh-huh. Well, if you're on something, don't bring that shit in here. Got it?"

Aki giggled and swayed. Seth valiantly resisted the urge to drop him. He left a generous tip and dragged Aki out, leaving the eagle-eyed bartender watching them.

Seth was *not* drunk. He hadn't been properly drunk in decades. But he'd wasted enough time on this diversion.

Outside the bar, Seth stopped and looked up. The sky was deep purple, only turning black at the very height of the dome, and marked with a weak handful of stars. Scorpius was nowhere to be found. He hoped it was a good omen.

Aki had trouble walking in a straight line. Seth held on to the hoodie and silently promised himself that he would remember this the next time one of Theo's friends had a bright idea. If Aki had been alone, the young man would be in serious trouble.

Perhaps that would be a profitable line of business. Bodyguards for inebriated artists. They clearly weren't capable of looking after themselves. Hire former Secret Service members and ATF agents, and reward them based on the number of graphic designers they saved from walking off bridges...

Hmm. Maybe he was *slightly* drunk.

The crowds on the streets had changed. As clubs and bars began to eject their first problem patrons of the night, knots of partygoers drifted out onto the pavement. A tired-looking young woman exhaled a cloud of smoke as they walked past, and Aki got a lungful.

"Good shit," he mumbled.

"I've had better," Seth said dryly. "Focus. We're almost there."

Aki shrugged off Seth's hold. "I'm fine," he said. He turned around, trying to get his bearings, and promptly stumbled into a group of young men.

"Watch it!" one said. Another added a pejorative term for Asians.

"Sorry," Aki said. "Guess clown college got out early—guh!" Seth hauled him backward by his hoodie again.

The young men spread out, squaring up. Three of the four were armed. One carried a handgun in his trousers, while two others had knives.

Aki was still talking behind him. Seth regretted this entire chain of events, but he ignored the artist for now. All of their potential aggressors were doubtless carrying phones. One, otherwise unarmed, had a phone in his hand.

That was where the real danger lay. Being caught on film would kill this identity more effectively than a hail of bullets.

"I apologize," Seth told the leader of the group. He had the gun, anyway. "My friend is drunk. Please let us through."

"Please let us through!" one of the young men mimicked in a squeaky voice.

"Shut up!" the leader said, shoving the mimicker. He kept his eyes on Seth. "You're on our streets. Say you're sorry. Like you mean it."

Ah. They were trying to humiliate and intimidate the outsiders. He knew his own abilities and would be saving these idiotic young mortals a great deal of trouble by conceding. It was the sensible thing to do, for both Seth Adler and for Anhurmose. Not to mention charitable.

However, the tequila also had a vote.

"No," Seth said.

"Say you're sorry." The leader pushed himself into their space. He was shorter but made a valiant effort to loom. Seth stepped forward, ensuring that he was between the young man and the incapacitated Aki. "Say it!"

"No. Go home."

The leader faked a punch at Seth's chin. Seth didn't flinch, but the leader smirked as if he had won a point.

"Fuck off, old man," he said. "You're not gonna like this."

He turned away, grinning at his friends. His narrow shoulders tensed. Then he whirled back again, his expression gleeful, and punched Seth in the stomach. Seth grunted as he absorbed the blow. All right, then.

He grabbed the leader-boy by the collar and dragged him off his feet. The leader squawked as his shoes flapped in midair. Not yet fully grown: broken bones now would be a disaster. Seth threw him into the closest wall, but gently, only knocking his wind out. The boy fell across the sidewalk and landed half in the gutter.

"Get him! Get him!" someone yelled. Two of the young men launched themselves at Seth. The boy holding his phone raised it.

Never mind the others. Seth knocked the phone out of the young man's hand. It struck the wall and cracked, components bouncing off the brick and landing in the gutter with the wheezing leader.

"That's assault!" one of the geniuses contributed from the back.

"That's assault! Knock him down!"

The boy who'd lost his phone hesitated, but the two others were already on him. One had a knife; the other was lashing out like he was trying to swat a wasp on Seth's shirt. Not trained.

Seth caught the knife and twisted the young man's hand. Bone cracked. The knife slipped from spasming fingers and hit the ground. Seth caught it under his foot and kicked it back, sending it skittering past Aki into the darkness.

The one in his grip let out a strangled cry. There was a smell of urine and a dark spreading stain on the boy's clothes.

Seth drove a low blow into the boy's stomach, just below the ribs. The breath exploded out of him. At the same time, Seth let go of his now-damaged wrist. The disarmed attacker staggered back and sat down hard.

The other one clawed at Seth with his fingernails. Seth kneed him in the gut, knocking his wind out too, and dropped the second on top of the first.

The leader crawled out of the gutter, digging in his pants. Grabbed the gun.

Seth twisted to the side. The first shot cracked past his ear, sending chunks of broken brick spraying out. The second shot didn't miss. One in the shoulder, hard. Something deep inside split as the lead went through.

Two shots was more than enough. Seth tore the gun away. It was a Hi-Point, barely worth the scrap. He ejected the magazine, fired the chambered round into the ground, and ripped the slide off. His fingers left marks in the thin metal.

Blood already oozed from his shoulder. An irritating end to a busy day.

"Go home," he said to the young men.

The leader clutched his wrenched hand. Seth had sprained three of the boy's fingers when he'd pulled the gun away. Now Seth tucked the damaged weapon into his jacket, knowing that his fingerprints were all over it. (Forensics had made his movements much harder to hide over the past hundred years. Of all the things for mortals to improve.)

"Fuck you, man!" the leader shouted. "You fucking assaulted us! We're gonna find you and tell everyone! You're never gonna work again! You son of a bitch!" Two of the three were digging for phones.

The first one to pull out his phone found it taken from his hand.

Seth snapped it in half and dropped it, careful not to use the pads of his fingers where the fingerprints would show. The second one dived behind his leader, trying to protect his property, but Seth grabbed him by the collar of his jersey. The phone didn't even have a case. It practically collapsed in Seth's hand.

"Now yours, please," he said to the leader.

"Fuck you!" the leader spat.

Well, if he could admire Aki's loyalty, he could at least acknowledge this young man's courage.

"Give me your phone," he said. "Or I'll take it."

The leader hesitated. He was young, dumb, and defiant, and all of those things could be strengths. But his eyes flicked to Seth's open hand. Crushing the phones had cut skin, and blood dribbled down Seth's arm from a dozen small wounds. Shards of plastic slowly slipped out of the flesh.

Wordlessly, the boy gave him the phone. Seth crushed it.

"Go home," Seth repeated. He crouched down to help Aki up. The artist, at least, seemed unaffected by the brawl. Seth put an arm around the staggering Aki and turned away, helping the younger man walk.

Something pinged off the streetlight. One of the boys had tried to throw a knife and missed.

"Put your hood up," Seth told Aki. "There's cameras everywhere."

"We're gonna fucking find you!" the leader roared from behind them. "Pig! Pig! Pig!"

"Go home!" Seth called back to them.

They kept walking. The young men followed them at a distance, but the fight had gone out of them. Two were injured and two remained slumped on the concrete half a block back. When Seth and Aki turned down a side street, the boys didn't follow.

They limped along for another few blocks. Seth changed direction several times, looking left and right to spot cameras that might pick them up.

"Shiiiit," Aki slurred. "Thought you were kidding about the bail thing."

"I never kid."

There was a short pause while Aki's sodden brain processed that. They walked another block.

"OK," he said. "I approve."

"What?"

"You're allowed to date Theo. But I still get to make fun of you."

"I don't think I could stop you. Or you could stop me."

Aki stumbled and wiped his mouth on his wrist. He was going to have a hell of a hangover tomorrow.

"Go home?" he said. "Was that seriously your best line?"

"What should I have said? They wouldn't respond to a lawsuit."

"No, no, no. Come on." Aki prodded him, or tried to: his bodily coordination seemed uncertain at the moment. "It's like a rule. The one-liner."

"The what?"

"The one-liner. The good line. Right before you lay the beatdown on them. Like Arnold. 'Give me your clothes, your boots, and your motorcycle.' Come on. Haven't you seen any movie ever?"

Seth had indeed seen movies. Occasionally. "I don't use one-liners."

"Well, you should. Come on!" Aki prodded him again, harder this time. "You're a literal movie monster. How do you not have a one-liner?"

"You're drunk."

"Yeah. Feels nice. Everything is a lot…fun. Funnier. No. Wait. It's not like ha-ha funny. It's funner. More fun. But it's good. And you're stupid, 'cause you could do shit I would *kill* for."

"Ask for someone's motorcycle?"

"You have *powers.* You could be a superhero. Money like Batman, powers like Superman. The original Superman. That one couldn't fly."

Aki slumped against him. "I mean, if I could do that? I wouldn't be paying student loans. I would've ruled the world, like, five years ago. Why aren't you ruling the world? Or did you? Were you Genghis Khan? He ruled the world and had, like, a thousand kids. How many kids do you have out there?"

"I don't have any children anymore, Aki. Take a deep breath. You're going to vomit."

"No, I'm not. I'm doing f—urgh—"

Aki threw up.

Hmm. Ruling the world. At the moment, he was doing his best to stay out of the splash zone as an intoxicated artist voided hot wings and too much tequila. He handed Aki his handkerchief.

"I thought about it," he said as Aki cleaned himself up. "Ruling the world. Or a kingdom or two. I was a general and a noble at times, with estates and lands of my own. Once or twice, I was a prince. But I wasn't

Genghis Khan."

Aki offered him the soiled handkerchief. Seth shook his head, and Aki threw it into the nearest dumpster.

"Seriously?" Aki slurred. "You can live forever. Rule the world already! Why not?"

"You said it already. I'm a coward."

Aki made a face. "Bullshit."

"Not at all. When you know the gods are real, and what power exists in the world...you hide from them. Or try not to anger them." That was the tequila's opinion, anyway. "They're always watching. I bowed to the gods of the lands I traveled through, but I couldn't be a priest or a king for them. Not when mine..."

Seth looked up at the night sky. It was velvety purple, red-tinted, and spotted with a few weak stars. The vast unknowable beauty of the universe and chaos itself, framed by the brick walls of an alley with a nauseated t-shirt artist next to him.

"My brother discovered that," he said. "This existence. It defies the gods and natural order. How far are you willing to go, when gods are watching?"

"Dunno," Aki said. "This far?"

He gave the sky the finger.

Seth snorted. "You wouldn't have lasted five minutes in my time."

"Yeah, well, your time sucked. It sucked so bad you decided to live until they invented tequila."

"Yes, and waiting for tequila accomplished nothing." Seth steadied Aki again. "Except for getting me shot again."

"Sorry, would you like some cheese with your whine? Enjoy your healing factor and shut up. I'm gonna be so fucked-up tomorrow, and you can be smug then."

* * *

By the time he dragged Aki back to the hotel, his drinks had worn off. Dawn was only a few hours away, and he could feel the nighttime half-death replacing the artificial bravado of the tequila. He needed rest.

After dropping off the drunk artist, Seth went up to Theo's room. Light still leaked under her door, but the heartbeat behind it was slow and steady. Asleep...

...in the chair, as it turned out. Her head was pillowed on her folded arms, the stylus tucked between her fingers.

Seth murmured her name as he picked her up. She blinked sleepily up at him.

"I smell booze," she mumbled. "And blood."

"No bail required, but it was a near thing."

"Wait. Wait. You're bleeding again." Theo roused herself as he set her down on the bed. "Why are you bleeding? No. Wait. It's half healed. You were hurt? Seth, *what?*"

"Aki started a fight. I finished it."

"Did Aki stab you again?"

"No, I was shot. And it wasn't him. Go back to sleep."

"Seth, you can't just drop 'by the way, I got shot' and not expect me to freak out!" Theo clambered to her feet. Seth caught her hands as she reached for him.

"Theo," he said. "It was shallow and low-caliber. The bullet's already been pushed out. It's fine."

She peeled back the torn cloth. The bullet wound was half healed, the skin drawing together. She let out a sigh and dropped her head against his unwounded shoulder.

"I'm sorry," she mumbled. "I just...I don't want you to get hurt."

"Accidents will always happen. For my part, I plan to keep them to a minimum. But this is nothing, djed. Go to sleep."

Theo reluctantly nodded and fell back into bed. Seth stripped out of his ruined clothes and washed off the remaining blood. By the time he was finished, she was already asleep again.

Dark circles marked her eyes, and her features were drawn and tight. In sleep, she barely relaxed. Seth passed a hand over her face, touching her cheeks and forehead, feeling the tension there. She leaned into his touch.

Strange, still. To have someone who knew what he was and accepted it—even while worrying about things she couldn't change. Who said, "It doesn't matter if you can survive this; I wish it wouldn't happen anyway." Because she didn't want him to hurt.

He fell asleep with his arms around her and her head against his shoulder. He slept deeply and did not dream.

CHAPTER 17

It shall be that the Evil One shall fall when he deviseth a
plan to destroy thee, and the joints of his neck and back
shall be hacked asunder.

—*Excerpt from The Papyrus of Ani,*
trans. E.A. Wallis Budge

The Geltner House Museum was housed in a Gilded Age mansion
plopped awkwardly between two apartment buildings. The Staten Island
neighborhood was honeycombed with similar oddities: here and there
were patches of old worlds, preserved in the thirties or the sixties or the
nineties, while every other piece of land moved with the times. Geltner
House, with its turret and widow's walk, had looked at the twenty-first
century and decided it didn't want any of that nonsense.

Theo had, of course, gotten their brochure.

"Augustus Wilhelm Geltner, born March 4th, 1860, in Munich," she
read aloud as Seth parked the car. "Committed some unnamed indiscre-
tions—wonder who she was—that led to his family sending him as far
from Bavaria as they could afford. Ended up in New York at age sixteen.
Studied medicine and began collecting medical manuscripts. When he
died in 1919, he willed his entire collection to the city, along with his
entire fortune...on the condition that they make his collection available
to the public. No museum, no money. So the city got stuck with his junk.
Uh, phrasing. His stuff."

"Unusually honest, for a brochure."

"I read between the lines," she said, flapping the brochure at him.
"Don't make fun."

"No, I prefer your style." Seth grinned across at her. "I wish their
lawyers took the same tack."

"Do you have a number on it yet?"

"They'd never show their hand so fast. At first, they want to confirm my sincerity. And liquidity."

Seth had called the Geltner House that morning, giving his credentials and hinting that he wanted to donate to the museum. An hour later, his office called from Chicago, confirming that Geltner had contacted Adler Financial to verify his identity and movements. Geltner then phoned Seth back, acting as if they hadn't been checking on him. Seth, of course, pretended he didn't know they had been checking on him, and an initial meeting was set up. The museum mating dance.

That's what Theo had called it, anyway. Sitting on her motel bed, wrapped in a sheet, she'd listened to the exchange of phone calls. Watching Seth seduce a respected New York institution with the power of money. "If you were a peacock, you'd be showing off some serious plumage," she'd said.

Now Seth was in character (and a nice suit) as the wealthy donor, and Theo was his on-call expert. She wore a t-shirt, capris, and a blazer, and carried a tablet and a shoulder bag, the costume of the professional-but-artsy type. The shoulder bag hid bread, beer, honey, and paper plates. Everything needed for an emergency offering to the dead, just in case.

She had her museum IDs to show off if anyone tried to interrogate her about her professional contacts, but Seth would be running interference on that. He'd get them behind the scenes with the promise of money. Then it was up to Theo.

One fake instead of six. Perhaps whatever ghost or ghosts clung to them could be heard more clearly alone. And if the red corruption lingered here too, Theo would see it. And they'd know how far the rot spread.

* * *

The museum smelled like age. The glass cases were wood-framed in the Victorian style, with finger-polished rails and claw feet. The floorboards creaked underfoot. There were no docents, just a teen at the front desk selling t-shirts.

As they climbed the narrow marble staircase, they passed portraits of great advances in medical history—Hippocrates, Paré, Semmelweis—and medical curios on plinths. There was an enormous death mask of an acromegaly case, and another of Napoleon Bonaparte; some kind of steel corset, an early back brace; and a collection of nineteenth-century surgical instruments under glass.

Passing the death masks made Theo's spine tingle. Napoleon's eyes were closed, and his jaw was loose. He looked like an actor in low focus, playing a death scene. The acromegaly case seemed sad and tired, weighed down by his own overgrown flesh and heavy bones.

The curator met them at the top of the stairs. She was about fifty years old, a square-shouldered, square-jawed woman with streaks of gray in her red hair. A good sense of herself and her colors: jade-green top with white slacks and a silver necklace. The summer tan ran uninterrupted up her forearms, showing that she never wore watches or bracelets. In a curator, that meant either a minimalist or a hands-on professional. Theo was betting on the pro. A nice change from Dr. LeDieu's fabulous but impractical caftans.

"I have to say, Mr. Adler, this isn't what I expected when we opened this morning," she said. Her tone was light, self-deprecating. An opening gesture in the ritual. "You won't be too happy with the state of things here."

"I don't care if the paperwork is alphabetized, Dr. Ferrara." Seth stopped two steps down from the curator. She was shorter than Theo, and Seth would tower over her if he stood on the same step. This way, they were eye-to-eye. "Dr. Geltner's collection is what matters. Thank you for agreeing to meet me."

"Luckily, there was a hole in the schedule." Dr. Ferrara descended another step. "It's a pleasure, Mr. Adler. And this is…?"

Theo held out her hand. "Theodora Speer, Columbian Exposition Museum."

Dr. Ferrara flicked a glance at Theo. Something in the set of her mouth said that she'd heard the same rumors LeDieu was listening to. Standard donor research would have turned up a lot of gossip.

But Ferrara played it cooler than LeDieu. "It's a pleasure," she said, shaking Theo's hand. "We heard all about the Heritage Museum getting *Treasures of the Middle Kingdom.* You're in town for the pre-show build?"

"Just helping out. The Heritage Museum is giving *Treasures* its first out-of-town shakedown. But Mr. Adler knows the Geltner collection deserves attention, and he asked me to advise."

Seth expertly picked up the thread. "I've been interested in history for many years," he said. "It's a family passion. When I learned about the specimens you hold here, I knew I had to be part of it."

A few fine lines crinkled in the corners of his eyes, hinting at suppressed amusement. Theo hid her own smile.

Nobody, of course, would be so *crass* as to discuss money right off the bat. Everyone pretended that the donor was a fellow expert and a student of great truths—and not a walking checkbook looking for a tax break. They pretended that the institution was an heir to Plato and Alexandria, in no need of petty worldly things like money—and not perpetually in the red, praying for one big show on dinosaurs or Jack the Ripper to balance out all those potsherds that didn't earn a dime.

Dr. Ferrara took them on a tour of the collection. Augustus Geltner had specialized in medical ephemera, and there was plenty to see: surgical instruments, Ayurvedic drawings, an iron lung (new since Geltner's day), and an Assyrian panel illustrating paralysis in lions. Laid out under glass, it was all civilized and easy to digest.

Seth was in his element. Theo would never call him a nerd, but he knew a thing or two about battlefield injuries.

"The work of Brother Theodoric, now," he was saying as they paused in front of a medieval folio. "He had the courage to discard his ideas when faced with new evidence. Not many doctors of the era could say the same."

Dr. Ferrara was charmed, and expressed it the way academics usually did—by starting an argument. "Too simplistic. Medical history is full of innovation and innovators. Theodoric was remarkable, but not unique."

"If not unique, then rare. If there had been many more like him, then we might have re-evaluated Galen centuries earlier and saved millions of lives."

"But before the printing press—"

The discussion lasted through the medieval artifacts, across the hall into a room of prosthetics, and through a tiny exhibit on the history of eyeglasses. Theo mostly hung back: backing Seth up, always kicking the ball back to him when drawn in.

She rarely saw him in business mode. The Seth she knew existed in stolen moments, consciously removing the mask before joining her. Now she was seeing him with the mask on, and it surprised her how well the costume fit.

By serpentine methods, Seth led Dr. Ferrara toward the topic of the mummy. Finally, she bit.

"We do have a mummy here," she said. "Nineteenth Dynasty, according to the provenance. But there are some doubts. We're collecting funds for testing, but it's a slow process."

Theo could almost feel the satisfaction from Seth. It was like watching a cat's fur ripple before it pounced.

"That's a worthy cause," he said. "Are you accepting contributions for the project?"

Dr. Ferrara paused. "Why, yes," she said. "But the scope of the work... We haven't even begun on the solicitation schedule."

"I'm not surprised. High-level donors tend to ignore smaller institutions, even when their work is equally important."

Move and countermove. If Seth pushed too hard, he'd seem overbearing—a bad move with a female curator accustomed to holding her own against chauvinists. But he was there to make an offer, and both of them knew it. This time, Dr. Ferrara stepped neatly into the gap.

"It's true," she said. "Though I must say, it's a pleasure to speak to someone who understands that. Perhaps you could recommend someone for us to approach?"

Seth nodded. "I can think of a few names," he said. "But before we make any lists, Ms. Speer should look at the mummy. She recently led a team studying Middle Kingdom specimens and may have some insights."

That was a lie, of course. In the museum pecking order, an artist was slightly under the guy who vacuumed the entrance hall. But if Ferrara had heard the rumors, she would assume that December was simply promoting May's career. If she hadn't, then the donor was subtly checking on the behind-the-scenes setup before he invested.

"Absolutely," Ferrara said. "This way."

* * *

Backstage, Geltner House was still out-of-date. But someone had put in the work where it counted. Theo saw spotless lab tables, neatly labeled and organized specimens, antique books wrapped in sterile paper.

What they didn't have was space. They'd taken over an adjoining building and turned it into their archives and storage, but for every object on display, there were twenty packed away. Viewing the carefully stacked crates, Theo flashed back to hours wasted in Tetris-knockoff phone games.

The mummy, labeled as Brother Priest of Serqet, had been removed from deep storage recently. Right now, the Brother Priest was wrapped in sterile plastic and kept in an opaque, airtight crate.

Two gloved assistants opened the crate and carefully laid out the shrouded form on a paper-covered table. Dr. Ferrara watched keenly. She and Seth would wait down the hall in her office, discussing Geltner House's "needs," a.k.a. how much Seth would be paying for letting Theo examine this find for fifteen minutes. Theo rocked back and forth on her toes, trying to hide her excitement.

The assistants cleared out. Dr. Ferrara stepped to the door. Seth rested a hand on Theo's shoulder.

"Are you certain?" he said. With his back to Ferrara, he shielded both of them from the curator. Theo looked up and squeezed his hand.

"I've got it," she said.

"I'll be down the hall. If you need me..."

"I've got it, Seth."

He gave her a long look. No more needed to be said. Seth could face magic and death, but the sight of a mummy would never be easy for him.

After a moment, he nodded tightly. The lines around his mouth deepened. He turned toward Dr. Ferrara's office, and Theo was left alone with the Brother Priest.

She set her bag down. The examination room was almost bare. A single security camera winked from its place in the corner, but Theo could see a few blind spots where she could put her offering vessels. She casually shoved her bag under the table with one foot.

Slipping on a pair of gloves, she lifted off the plastic shrouding the form.

It was a small, wretched-looking thing, enough to make the gorge rise if you looked at it too long. Bones bulging under papery skin, blackened teeth exposed.

In the cracks and gaps, redness surged.

Theo's breath caught. The Brother Priest was soaked with red mist. It lingered in the open mouth, leaked from torn bandaging, wisped from each eye socket.

"I'm sorry," she whispered. She gently touched the top of its head. "I'm so sorry."

With an effort, Theo focused on the specimen itself. It showed long, clean lines. A well-formed skull: skulls were hard to get right. Amateurs always made the jaw attachments too solid. This jaw hung loose. The teeth were stubs, and the eye sockets bulged around their funerary pack-ings. A scorpion amulet rested in the hollow of its withered throat.

Theo knelt down next to the table. The mummy's head was twisted, and on one knee, she was eye-to-eye with it. She took out a magnifier and a mirror, angling them so she could have a closer look at the mouth.

The teeth had been ground down to mimic ancient wear and tear. Two perfect teeth bracketed a stained nub.

"That's weird," Theo murmured.

The air stirred. A chilly draft blew into Theo's face, carrying a stale smell, and ended as quickly as it had started.

"Hello," she said.

The air stirred again, faintly. And that was all.

Laying down the mirror, she slowly circled the table, taking in the details. The more she looked at it, the less *together* it seemed.

She recognized this feeling. It had prodded her before, when looking at Penedjmet's plate. Then, she'd ignored it. The experts said these were hundred-year-old fakes, so she'd listened to them. Now she listened to the feeling and looked closer.

Something winked in the depths of the fake's mouth. A metallic object, embedded in one of the stub teeth. A flat chip of gold.

Theo moved the magnifying glass into position. Sweat made her palms slick, and she wiped her hands on her thighs. The chip of gold wasn't a chip. It was embedded deep in the bottom of the gouged-out tooth. There was a deep line scratched into it, and into the tooth on either side.

The tooth had had a gold filling, but the metal was gouged out. The whole thing filed down to hide it.

They were modern and real. And someone had gone to a lot of trouble to hide the signs.

"I'm sorry," she murmured to the thing on the table. "I'm so, so sorry."

As she drew the plastic back over it, something brushed against her hand. A breath ghosted against the back of her neck.

Maker, a voice murmured.

"Maker," she repeated. "Who made you? Do you know?"

Maker. Maker is with me. Another light touch ghosted over her shoulder and brushed against her neck. *Maker return.*

"I'm sorry, I can't understand you," Theo told it. "The spirit must be weak. "I'm going to figure out a way to help you. All right? I'll be back in a minute."

She poked her head into Dr. Ferrara's office. The doctor was folding away a slip of blue paper, and Seth capped his fountain pen. Museum mating ritual complete, for now.

"Mr. Adler?" Theo said. "Can I borrow you for a minute?"

"Of course," he said, standing. His tone was cool. "Dr. Ferrara?"

"Go on," Dr. Ferrara said mildly. "If you need me again, just page for me. When you're done, tell Sam at the front desk. She'll take your badges."

Seth took his leave in a gracious manner and joined Theo in the corridor. He seemed genuinely regretful, as if a reunion with a childhood friend had been cut short.

Inside the lab, though, the mask dropped. "What news?" he said tersely. "Is it...?"

"Yes," Theo said simply. She uncovered the mummy's head. "Look."

Seth flinched back. "He struggled."

"How...?"

"Look at the neck."

Theo knelt again and peered more closely at the mummy. "You're right," she said. "Cracked vertebrae, like a broken neck. And the stain goes all the way in. It happened before he was turned into a fake."

She drew off the whole sheet again.

"He isn't complete," she said. "The stuff still wrapped has the wrong proportions. Probably pig bones. But the head, the arms, the chest, they're real. And they gouged out his gold fillings."

"Hiding his identity," Seth said.

"I don't know. Not all of the teeth are messed up. But it'd be a lot harder to get dental patterns...I think." Theo shivered in the cold lab. "I don't, um, I don't know much about that stuff."

Seth reached out. His big hand cupped the back of her neck, his thumb sweeping over the line of her jaw. "We have what we came for, at least. We know this is another body from the same group."

"Yeah..."

Maker. Maker. Reach out. Please.

"He's trying to talk to me," she said. "He's calling for his maker. I think he's in pain."

Something flickered in Seth's eyes. Trapped in a mummy body, lost, in agony—he'd been that way in Meren's hands not so long ago. "We need to be cautious, Theo," he warned. "This man is still the unburied dead. His spirit may be angry."

"Maybe. But he's talking more than most of the others already. If we feed him, we might be able to get some useful information."

"Perhaps," Seth conceded reluctantly.

She squeezed his hand. "Please. It'll just be a minute. You can wait outside—"

"*No.* I'll be here."

"Thank you," she said softly.

Stepping back, she unpacked the offering vessels. The air conditioning had chilled the can of beer, making her fingers sting as she handled it.

Seth tucked his hands behind his back, features stony as he watched her work. Like a guard. Or a statue.

Theo opened the beer and began to shred bread onto the paper plate. The chill nipped at her fingertips and clawed its way down her back, but she ignored it.

"An offering which the king gives to Osiris, the Lord of the West, the Lord of Abydos." Seth shivered at the words. "One thousand offerings of bulls and birds and every good and pure thing, on behalf of the one who is beloved of Anubis-upon-his-mountain. One thousand offerings of linen and honey and everything the god loves for the revered one, the one here called the Brother Priest."

There were more words, and they rolled from her tongue, but the world began to dim around her. Her arms felt heavy, and every motion came with the weighted dignity of a slow turn underwater. Her breath echoed loudly in her ears as the lights faded.

Her knees gave out. The floor rushed up to meet her. She was vaguely aware of a pair of strong hands catching her, words shouted in her ear, but they faded. Formless, without substance, she drifted into the black.

At last, she opened her eyes again. She leaned against a wooden workbench.

Hands. Hands in front of her, on the bench. Hers? No. *His.* A man's hands, square-nailed, pale skin sun-tanned, marked with calluses and stained with paint.

"You'll need better paperwork than that." A man's voice reverberated from her chest. Broad coastal accent. New England?

"I'll get it." Another man's voice, behind her. To the right. No, the left. Similar accent.

Dimness remained. She made out only thin shapes: the lines of a steel shelf, the gray of concrete underfoot. An echo as stone and metal threw back the voices.

"I don't fucking care!" said the voice from Theo's chest. "Pack it up. We're done."

"Jay—" the man behind them began.

"I'm not making another one!"

"We're not making another one. We just have to finish the ones we've got going. You hear me?"

The knuckles whitened as they gripped the edge of the workbench. "Who the fuck's gonna buy them? The Egyptians are gonna have our asses. It's not *worth it*."

"Art is always worth it, Jay."

"It's gotta be worth at least fifty grand apiece. And it won't be. Not until the government backs off. We can't *move* these things anymore, Al!"

Footsteps. "You have to be patient. Investments take time to pay off."

"I'm not investing shit. You know you can't do this without me. I say it's over. Right now." The speaker's throat felt tight.

"The investment *already* paid off. So what's the problem with doing it again?" The voice was soothing, calm. Reasonable. Friendly, even. "Come on. A few days of work. Then you take a vacation, and I'll make some calls. You could pay off your mortgage."

"God fucking dammit!" She whirled, knocking a shadowy shape off the bench. It clattered to the ground in an echo of distant metal. "I can't *do* it anymore, Al!"

The outline of a man moved in the corner of her vision. A broad, solid shape. Dark hair, solid frame, thick middle. She tried to turn, to look, but Jay's attention was fixed on the shrouded shapes beyond him. Lying under sheets of plastic. White and formless in the dim world of memory.

"Three days, Jay. Three days and we're looking at a six-figure profit."

Theo felt the agony roil in the man's chest. More butchering! Bones splintering as he sawed at them. Lifting severed hands and arms from a tub full of curing salt.

"No," Jay said. "Finish 'em yourself. I'm done."

"Jay—"

"I'm done. And if you say another fucking word, I'm calling the cops. They can deal with you and the fucking Egyptians."

Silence from the shadowy man. Theo's broad hands swept another shape from the bench. It landed with a splintering crunch.

Something shifted in the dimness. A black line flashed across Theo's vision, held in white-sheened hands. *Gloves,* she thought, and then the cord whipped around her neck.

Jay reeled and thrashed, but the cord only wound tighter. He clutched at his throat and gulped for air. A voice spoke in his/her ear, dispassionate.

"I'm sorry, Jay. These things happen."

Breath crushed out of her body as the rope tightened. She struggled for freedom with weakening muscles. Deep inside her throat, a crunch, a snap—and darkness fell.

For a time, there was peace and silence.

Then, separation. Her mind began to part, the consciousness of the right and the left drawn apart. Pieces broke, split, died as they were diminished.

Theo screamed for them to come back. She clung to her pieces, begging them to not leave her, but they were taken. With each one, her self was lost.

They were all in her, somewhere. An *us* and a *you* and a *me* that made up the *I.* One by one, they winked out. Layers stripped away. Words lost their meaning. Nothing remained but terror, animal in its power. The howl of a frightened dog.

Clarity. A piece came back. Another. A sense of hope crept out of its hiding place.

But the edges didn't fit. The pieces weren't hers. Two things stitched together, ordered to become one. She clawed at herself, trying to tear away the intruding flesh, but hands tacked these pieces into place and sewed her mouth shut.

Trapped. Trapped. Killed and cut to pieces, broken, rewritten, patched together by the alien hands of a maker she hated more than anything—

Those hands were on her now. The hands of a maker.

She shook. Rage boiled up inside her, desperate. Hungry. A maker, a maker was *here,* doing something to her. Rewriting her. Distorting the world around her, changing the rules, changing the names and shapes of souls.

Wrong. Misshapen. Evil.

Kill the maker.

Yes! Kill the maker. Stop the unmaking, and the lost pieces would come back. She reached for the maker's throat.

But the maker fought back! Even as she squeezed, she felt her own throat close. Suffocating again. Pressure on her neck, pain in her chest, and the strength in her own hands as she crushed the maker's life away. Even as she choked, she felt the terrible, brutal satisfaction.

Kill the maker. Kill the maker!

Someone calling her name. Strong fingers pried hers open. Air rushed into her lungs as despair raged through her. No! The maker must not live. The maker must *suffer*. She fought the outsider, raging, choking, biting.

The taste of blood filled her mouth. For a second, the rage was overwhelmed by the physical. A man's voice, chanting.

"Be sated and be silent. There shall be no wrath, the watchers shall not overwhelm you. Blind Horus and Anubis shall not turn their knives upon you."

The words broke through the haze. Theo was suddenly aware of a man's arm around her, of a man's hand gripping hers.

Kill the maker! the voice cried, but Theo knew it now. It wasn't her. She gasped for air, loosening muscles that strained toward her own throat.

"Seth?" she called out. "Seth—I can't see!"

He passed a hand over her face. Low-voiced, he recited a spell for the opening of the eyes. At last, the world swam into view. The lab. They were in the lab, and on the table—

Theo recoiled. Seth held her tightly, and she buried her face in his chest and sobbed. He clutched her to him, one hand tight against her back, the other cradling her head. His breath ghosted over her as he prayed, desperate, stumbling over his own words as he struggled to fill each second with protective magic.

She didn't understand most of the next few minutes. She vaguely heard fabric rustling as the remaining offerings were shoved into her bag, and felt pressure on her arm as she was guided, stumbling, out of the museum. Seth saying something to wide-eyed volunteers in passing, claiming she'd had an allergy attack.

Kill the maker. It was only memory now, but it clung to her mind like mold on a rock, staining everything it touched. She could feel the terrible driving need, the animal joy as fingers tightened on the maker's throat. On her throat.

Seth half carried her to the car. She lay limp as a doll as he lifted her into the passenger seat. Her throat ached. Her chest still burned.

But she had her answers.

Seth got into the car and closed the door firmly. As he turned, Theo was already reaching for him again. She kissed him breathlessly—needing that warmth, needing that *life.*

"Djed." The word left his lips in a low groan. Theo held tight to his shirt as she kissed him. His hands swept down her back, pulling her against him, surrounding her with his solid warmth.

Kill the maker. This maker lived, fiercely and completely.

At last, she let her head drop against Seth's shoulder.

"I should probably let you go," she said breathlessly. "Some weirdo's gonna take pictures."

"Doubtless." Seth cupped her chin. "Djed, what happened? You went mad. Tried to strangle yourself."

"I saw him," she said. "Who it used to be. His name was Jay, or someone called him that, and he was making them—making the fakes. Helping. But he hated it."

In a halting voice, she told him. About the argument, and the cord around the neck. About choking, and the wrong pieces being grafted back on. The howl of the agonized animal in every fiber of her body. And the terrible, vicious, bone-deep hatred for the makers. For the ones who put it back together wrong.

"He was murdered," she whispered. "Pieces of him are missing. They're *all* missing pieces. And they've been put back together wrong, and they're screaming, Seth. It's driving them insane."

CHAPTER 18

I shall not speak of the railway, for it is like any other railway—I shall only say that the fuel they use for the loco-
motive is composed of mummies three thousand years
old, purchased by the ton or by the graveyard for that
purpose, and that sometimes one hears the profane
engineer call out pettishly, "D—n these plebeians, they
don't burn worth a cent—pass out a King;"—

—*Mark Twain*, The Innocents Abroad

Theo slumped in the passenger seat, her head on Seth's shoulder.
Exhausted by her ordeal. Already, her own fingermarks darkened into
bruises on her throat.

Even as Seth held her, his mind was drawn back. He saw a brutal
day in the height of summer, when the souk's tents weren't enough to
protect you, and the sensible Egyptians took their midday rest while the
British and French soldiers broiled alive in their high-collared wool
uniforms. Smells of cooking meat, burnt flour, and tea essence lingered
even when the stoves were cold. In the souk at high noon, no one marked
the tall Egyptian in English clothes.

He was only lightly affected by the heat. These bodies still did what
they were meant to do, and he was probably the most comfortable in the
entire souk. But he was not here for pleasure.

His funeral goods had been plundered, his tomb now the property
of the British and French. A world away, at work in America, he'd felt the
scrape of broken clay as the shabtis were taken from their chests. Many
times he had escaped that tomb, breaking out. But the invaders had
broken in.

He had come to the corner of the Khan el-Khalili souk where the antiques scalpers worked, to find and purchase his own corpse.

And there were corpses to buy. A long double row of the dead, upright in broken coffins, half unwrapped or fully exposed to curious passersby. Their wrappings were torn, rifled for the exotic amulets the foreigners liked so much. Here and there, a fly lighted on a flattened slit of a nose, inspected the empty hollow of a dried eye socket.

The man who called himself Rachid al-Adhur did not pray as he passed. These dead were nameless, divested even of the charms that pre-served their last self. They would not hear his prayers.

Some had never had those charms at all.

He halted before one coffin. A woman's body lay there, thin and withered as a bundle of dry sticks. Skin leathered to the color of oak.

Clean skin. No markings on the face where a bandage had flattened or bound her. Long hair, still in the remnants of ringlets.

Perhaps if he looked closer, he would discover how she had been killed. The fellahin of Egypt were no different than men of any so-called "civilized" nation, and men of any color would not blink at making their own stock. Perhaps she'd been a prostitute or an unwanted wife or daughter.

That nameless woman lay in Rachid's memories, locked away, until the flood was undammed. Now, as he stroked Theo's hair, he thought about dusty ringlets.

Men had made false mummies before. They cheated tourists however possible. It was all good business. But Theo's vision meant that someone in today's world—the enlightened, modern, civilized (hah) world—was still building their fakes with homemade corpses.

And not just corpses. Victims. Murdered men torn apart, helpless as they choked.

Anhurmose remembered that sensation. The tightness in his chest and binding in his throat as he gasped for air, gripping the reed mat underneath him. The vague shape of his wife, wide-eyed with fear but thin-lipped with the strain of keeping a calm face, as she ushered the children out of the sickroom. No need to show them their father's last agonies.

Choking. Helpless. Just as he had been, that first death.

Beside him, Theo pressed a hand to her mouth and muffled a cough. The sound was raw and dry. Seth cupped the back of her head, cradling her as she coughed.

"Deep breaths," he murmured into her hair. "Deep breaths. You're alive, Theo. Breathe."

"It's real," she said. "Oh God, Seth. It *hurts.*"

A murdered man. Perhaps many more, meeting their death in those strangling hands.

Theo rested her weight against him and let herself cry in safety. Seth murmured wordless comfort and kissed her again, one hand smoothing over her hair, the other pressed to her back as if he could gather her into him to shelter there.

Slowly, slowly, Theo began to come back to herself. The green eyes were red-rimmed, but she took deep breaths, swallowing the last of her tears.

"Thank you," she said. Her words were still raw. "Thank you, Anhurmose."

She tried not to speak that name. He was Seth in this lifetime. But today, when he had protected her from dark magic and spirits, he was Anhurmose to her.

"I'm sorry," he said. "This should never have happened. If I had acted more quickly..."

"No. The way things are, something crazy was going to happen, no matter what." Theo turned her head and rested her cheek against his heart. "Now we...now we know."

"We do." Seth shot a glance at the building. "Can you still hear it?"

She sighed. "Nothing now. Maybe it needs more."

More offerings? *Never.*

Fear crawled down his back at the thought. He'd always been taught that it was a good thing to honor the dead, to feed the forgotten spirits, but he'd seen what had come over Theo as she stood by the mummy.

As the last word of the prayer had left her lips, she'd stiffened, eyelids fluttering half-shut. The bread had dropped from her frozen fingers. She'd shaken, muttering to herself—and then, slowly, inexorably, her hands had fastened around her own throat.

The Brother Priest had received her offerings and tried to kill her. Let him starve.

Yet the memories she'd seen painted a terrible, clear picture of why the spirits screamed. Murdered—one man for certain, perhaps all of them. Their bodies taken apart, used to build the different fakes. Given a new name, a new piece of soul, and grafted together like a Frankenstein's monster.

And the mentions of the Egyptian government? Bestuzhev had said the mummy market had become less profitable when the Egyptians had cracked down. Twenty years ago, perhaps, these forgers had found their mummies were suddenly hard to sell. One of them had refused to work any more, seemingly exhausted by the butchering.

"He threatened to call the police," Seth said, "and his partner killed him."

"Murder." Theo's voice faltered. "I hoped it wasn't."

As had he.

"Now what?" she said.

"Now we plan," Seth said. He tucked a strand of blonde behind one of her ears. "Did you see the murderer? Hear his name?"

"A little. Jay called him Al. And he's a big guy, dark-haired. Sort of a northeastern accent—you know, 'pahk the cah.'"

"Bestuzhev mentioned the Unknown Massachusetts Master. It could very well be the same man."

"Yeah." She breathed out slowly, trying to calm herself. "It's just…Al. I called my shabti guide Al, last year. Should've given him a better name."

Her shoulders shook. The words forced themselves out past her strangled throat.

"I made him, and then he died," she mumbled.

She blinked hard. Tears streaked her cheeks.

Then she lifted a hand to his face. She traced his features: the line of his nose, the faint frown marks in the corners of his mouth, the shape of his brows. The spiderweb of scarring around his right eye. A touch as light as a breath.

Learning the work she had made. It wasn't what she'd wanted or planned for. But it was what she'd done.

She kissed him again, gently. A mere brush of lips, almost as light as the gentle exploration of her fingers. It felt like a goodbye: not to him, but to something else she had looked for.

"I'm going back to the fakes," she said. "We know more about their maker now. I can feed them and ask them better questions. Will you help me?"

Ghosts. Ghosts and the shattered dead. Every fiber of Anhurmose rebelled against the thought of them.

But Anhurmose had died, choking. Rachid, Altair, Maximilian, and all of the other names and faces he'd worn over the centuries were dead, and so many of them had died hard. Just like that demented corpse on the table.

"I'll help you."

And the gods help them both.

CHAPTER 19

If you can give me nothing else, then give me the honesty
of your hatred. Better the red meat of hatred than the gruel
of heartless understanding and perfect condescension.

—Excerpt from the letters of Mme. Eugenie Moreau (1753–93),
to her sometime lover, M. de Faudrieul.
No response is recorded.

Having Seth help was a godsend. Gods-send. Whatever. They were still
figuring out how to be together, but there was nobody she'd rather find a
body with.

(That one never seemed to get asked on dating sites. Or maybe she'd
just been on the wrong ones.)

Theo stepped into Building H just after five o'clock. She had a copy
of the prayers for the dead in her pocket, but this was strictly a fact-
finding mission. She had to see the fakes with fresh eyes, now that she
knew what to look for.

The guard at the front desk barely glanced up as she swiped her way
through. The cold of the AC prickled. Seth's tyet amulet, the same one
she had given him, rested under her shirt. "Keep it," he'd said when she
tried to hand it back. "Indulge me, djed."

She was alone in the main hall of the building. Light filtered down
from a few high windows on the third-floor catwalks, barely touching
the specimens below. Dust motes swirled in the shafts of sun, illuminated for brief moments before the air circulation swept them out of the
spotlight. Plastic draping fluttered in the artificial breeze. The deep
shadows were touched with bruise purple.

Something stroked her cheek.

"I'm here," Theo promised. The fluttering touches grew stronger.

One pulled a strand of hair from her braid, making Theo's scalp sting.

"Not nice," she told them gently. It felt almost like grade school, when kids would pull hair to get attention.

But she'd set the tone, after all—talking to them, visiting them. Maybe they were hoping for a snack like their angry, crazed brother at Geltner.

Or maybe they sensed a change in her. Bodiless hands tugged at her clothes and pawed at her hands, seemingly looking for touch. They had more awareness now, more strength.

Man stays dead while his name is spoken. Well, she didn't know their names, but she and Seth and Aki had been speaking of them nonstop. Perhaps that was enough to calm them a little.

In the vast central hall of Building H, nothing had changed. The stacks of crates, twice as tall as Theo, creating freestanding walls within the gutted building. The collection of old-fashioned glass cases set to the left, gold glinting atop linen and papier-mâché. Behind it all, the fire escape stairs that led up past the cored-out second story to the third and above. The space echoed as she paced the circuit of the cases.

Six fakes. Hai-Ti, a nearly complete mummy shape and fully bandaged. The Minister, the supposed Ptolemaic court official with his misshapen face. The Other Woman, a legless torso. Tilamentu and Khnumwaset, heads sitting in a case along with Aztec chocolate pots and a phony Greek vase. Princess Penedjmet, with her golden plate and bead-trimmed wig—the beauty who would have been on postcards if she'd been real and whole.

The Minister was partially unwrapped, which made him a helpful starting point. Pieces of his skeleton were subtly mismatched in a way she'd ignored before. *I spy, with my little eye, something that begins with…sternum.*

The folded arms almost covered it, but now that she was looking for it, the clues were there. The awkward, blocky limbs now made her think of plastic Halloween skeletons. But certain body parts couldn't be sourced from Party City, and a premade rib-and-chest assembly never looked right.

Testing would be needed. Lots of testing. But if the Minister had real bones in his body, Theo was betting on the chest.

She moved to the next case. Then the next.

Help us, the voices murmured.

The Other Woman was easy to analyze. Hands and forearms,

shockingly real, protruded from a body like a bag of laundry. Theo had thought it was the forger prioritizing, focusing on what could actually be seen. Now she looked at it and wondered if those parts had been under the sheet when Jay had died.

The two fake heads had real teeth. Tilamentu sported a real jawbone, or part of one. Now that she'd seen the remains of fillings in the Brother Priest, she peered close enough to see metallic flecks in the bottoms of the ground-down teeth. Khnumwaset's human teeth were filled out with carved animal bone, probably sheep, but Tilamentu was all human.

She checked each angle and scrutinized the sketches she had taken. She remembered making these drawings, noting what was right and what wasn't, compensating for this flaw or highlighting an unusually skilled area. Now, looking at the fakes, Theo could see the difference. Not a group of artists with uneven skills, but a single creator using real body parts to fill in the gaps.

Six specimens. Teeth, fingers, orbital bone.

With Jay's bruises still on her throat, she saw them more clearly. A matched set. The same techniques used again and again—techniques that never appeared on their absent seventh member. The angle on the ground teeth was coarser, less like a metal file. The papier-mâché and onionskin layers blended more cleanly. This artist wasn't great, but he was better than the one who'd made the Brother Priest.

Jay made them, she thought. *And then someone else made him into one of them.*

The back of her neck prickled again. She flinched. Fingers brushed her hair and spine, still tugging at her braid, gripping the back of her shirt.

Something snatched at the strap of her bag. Her makeup, wallet, and tissues spilled over the floor. Unseen hands pawed at the fallen things, looking for offerings that weren't there.

Theo scrambled to scoop up her things. A tube of lip gloss skated away, swatted by an invisible touch.

"I'm not playing!" she snapped, grabbing for it.

Footsteps behind her. She finally caught the lip gloss and stuffed it back into her purse. Footsteps crossing the display area, from carpet onto concrete.

"Theodora?"

Theo scrambled to her feet. Dr. Armstrong stood there, hands in his pockets.

"I thought I saw you down there!" he said. "Is it Friday already? That's usually when people hide from me."

"Aw, you caught me!" Theo said. "I was hoping to sneak out early."

Dr. Armstrong laughed at that. "Not a chance," he said. "I've seen how you look at this collection. You've spent a lot of time here, haven't you?"

"I didn't know you were having me followed," Theo joked back.

"I can't help it. These guys are my favorite. How's the work going? Are they talking to you?"

In more ways than one. Theo opened her notebook, showing him some of the sketches she'd made. Dr. Armstrong made approving noises as she pointed out a scene she'd drawn of a forger's workshop.

"Beautiful," Armstrong proclaimed. "Absolutely amazing. I can't wait to see these on the walls!"

"Well, it's easy when you have good material to work with." Theo kept her tone light, almost wistful. "He made some interesting stuff, didn't he? The Unknown Master."

"Indeed he did. Do you relate to him, then? As an artist?"

Yeah. He could say she'd gotten up close and personal with him.

"In some ways," she said. "I'm not a full-time sculptor, of course. But I've been developing…theories, I guess."

Dr. Armstrong reacted to the word "theories" the way Dr. Ferrara reacted to "Theodoric." He practically lit up. "I love theories! Tell me!"

"Well, I was thinking about the inconsistencies," Theo said. "In the sculpting and the choice of materials. After I dug into the provenance, I started thinking about who the Unknown Master might've really been. You know, why he made those mistakes."

Dr. Armstrong tilted his head. "Mistakes?"

"Yeah. The mistakes that got his fakes caught. And honestly—I think I know who he was."

To her surprise, the doctor frowned slightly. "No one knows who he was," he said. "That's part of the mystery. The *allure.*"

"Well, yes. It'd be impossible to know his real name." Not until they chased down Jay and Al's identities, anyway. "But I've been thinking about the techniques. Or, well, lack thereof."

Armstrong's frown deepened. "Explain."

Not in the mood for theories after all? Theo mentally put her guard up. Cranky curators were bad for her career prospects.

"Here." She moved to Princess Penedjmet's case. "Look at the skin. The surface stain isn't evenly distributed. See the pooling? It collected in a pocket between two layers of the onionskin, and then when the pocket burst, it went straight down to the skull and stained too dark."

"Well, accidents happen," Armstrong said reluctantly. "That doesn't mean anything."

"But look over here." Theo moved to the Minister's case. "The sculpting is rough as heck. The sternum area is great, but look at that face! Really inconsistent. I bet there was more than one guy working on this."

Armstrong nodded sharply. "I'm sure you have plenty of ideas," he said with forced cheer. "That's why I asked for an artist, after all."

"But it isn't just the quality of the work. The intake specialists fell down on the job." Theo shook her head. "How the heck did *anyone* think Penedjmet was Seventeenth Dynasty? You know, I really dug into the provenance—"

"Did you." Armstrong's tone was definitely chilly now.

Theo blinked. The friendly, happy curator looked like he was ready to read her the riot act. His jaw was tight and his pale eyes were hard, unblinking. A change had come over him.

And he wasn't red.

Red mist still filled the cases. Theo could see it swirling around the Minister's broken chest, inches from her fingertips. But not a single wisp of it clung to Alan Armstrong.

Whatever was going through his head now, whatever sudden mood moved him—it was all his. The power of the *ukhedu* madness wasn't driving him.

"Well, yes," Theo managed to say, struggling to pick up the train of thought. "You gotta do the research, right?" She forced a smile. "The paperwork was pretty messy, too. I think they tried to recreate some of it after the fact. Dr. LeDieu said something about an accident?"

A muscle ticced in Armstrong's jaw at the mention of LeDieu. "A fire in the archives," he said. "2006. A workplace accident. Someone spilled some linseed oil near an electrical closet."

"Really? She said it was celluloid."

Silence.

"You were mistaken," he said finally.

The façade of the friendly eccentric had completely dropped. Armstrong never raised his voice, never took a step forward, but the look on his face still made Theo's skin prickle.

His eyes flickered over her face. She could feel his gaze probing, searching her.

"You really looked closely at those papers, huh," he said quietly.

She swallowed. "Yeah."

"You've put a lot of thought into this, Theodora." He almost sounded impressed. "You know, I respect that. And I respect the extracurricular work you've been putting in, too."

"...What do you mean?"

Now Armstrong leaned a little closer. His smile was flat, plastic.

"I'm sorry to tell you, Theodora, but I'm afraid your...personal relationships are a matter of gossip in this sort of environment. And when a donor is in town, offering to sponsor research, word gets around. Isn't that why you and Mr. Adler were at the Geltner House?"

"I wasn't on the clock," Theo said automatically. Dr. Armstrong's expression turned to a purse-lipped parody of sympathy.

"Of course not. I believe in your professional integrity. But unfortunately, people are going to draw certain conclusions. To have one of our visiting artists influencing her, well, significant other into taking his patronage to a different museum—it looks like she's trying to get involved in how we run our institution. It looks like unprofessional interference."

The bland, colorless phrase made Theo's gut lurch. *Unprofessional interference* was one level above *fireable offense.*

"I'm concerned," Armstrong continued, still dripping with faux sympathy, "that I may need to find another artist for this project. I'm afraid I'm not satisfied that you really understand what's important here."

Theo's mouth was dry. "What *is* important here?" she managed to say.

"Discretion." The word came out sharp. Toothed.

Armstrong took a step toward her, his hands coming to rest on the Minister's case, and the phantoms howled in her ears.

"Tell me," he said softly. "Why were you really at Geltner House, Theodora? What were you looking at?"

"I..." She couldn't think straight. Misty hands still pawed at her back. Voices whimpered and wailed in her ears. And standing over her was Al Armstrong, whose expression said he knew exactly what she'd looked for that day.

Princess Penedjmet, half-formed under her wig and jewelry. The Minister, broken and misshapen. Body parts mixed with papier-mâché, fillings gouged out of teeth. And the Brother Priest. Jay. His cracked vertebrae a silent witness to murder, even while his shattered soul raged in agony against the maker who'd torn him apart.

She remembered choking to death. A voice in her ear, apologizing calmly as Jay died.

"Well?" Armstrong prodded.

"It was a hunch!" she blurted out. "I tried to get my boyfriend to sponsor a different project so I could do the art on it. I thought maybe I could do like you were saying I could here—concept art, illustrations." She swallowed. "But, but—I didn't mean to be indiscreet. I swear."

The cold look faded. An expression of almost fatherly concern replaced it. Theo felt sick.

"I understand," Armstrong said. He clapped her on the shoulder. "You're in a tough spot, aren't you? It's so hard to be a woman in a male-dominated field. I applaud your go-getter instincts—I really do! But, well, it just doesn't look professional. I really hope you'll reconsider what you've been doing."

Theo swallowed. "I will," she promised. Bruises were rising on her back where the ghosts clutched at her. One of the voices was nothing but a wail of pain. "I really, really will."

The doctor bent and wiped a smear of dust off the Other Woman's case. For a moment, his scalp was visible between his thinning hair: a balding patch on the crown, like a monk being tonsured in installments. He looked up, and new lines marked his eyes and mouth with tension. His hand was pressed flat against the glass, bloodless in its pressure.

He doesn't believe me.

"I guess I don't know as much as I thought I did," Theo tried. "Will you still let me work on this exhibit?"

The doctor shook his head. He sounded kind and understanding, and Theo didn't believe it for a minute. "I don't think that would be for the best," he said. "But I'm sure we can find some other special projects for you. After all, it's important to support our artists and craftsmen. You might pay off a mortgage soon."

Yeah. Sure. Theo made a show of glancing back and forth between Armstrong and the door. If he was going to stop her leaving, now would be the time.

"Now, why don't you get some rest?" Armstrong added. "You're under a lot of stress. Don't bother racing in early tomorrow. And don't worry, no one needs to know about this. It was a misunderstanding."

She could've collapsed in relief. Instead, she just picked up her bag and retreated. Behind her, Armstrong patted the case of heads like a man petting a favorite dog.

Theo made it to the door and opened it, but didn't step outside. She let the door close as if behind her, and then slipped into the electrical closet, breathing shallowly. She waited there until another set of foot-steps passed by and the door opened and closed again.

Theo waited, heart in her mouth. Five minutes passed. Ten.

Finally, she stepped out of her hiding place again. Dr. Al Armstrong was gone. She hurried back toward the main hall, pulling out her phone.

"He did it," she whispered. The weeping of the dead followed her.

CHAPTER 20

I will not see a good woman suffer.

—*Excerpt from the so-called Petrichor Codex,*
Castille, 1715

Seth's hotel overlooked a plaza and a small patch of parkland, with the shape of museum buildings just visible through a thicket of trees. The temperature outside edged into the nineties, but inside there was air conditioning and ice.

He concentrated on the scene, fixing it in his mind. He was here and now: in America of the twenty-first century. A world that was far different from the one his heart and clay knew.

But the past intruded on the present. Faced with the forces that he had been taught to fear from the cradle, he couldn't control his instincts. The blood froze at the thought of those spirits, voiceless and shattered— clawing at the physical world in their desperate need to feed and find their names. To blot out a man's name was to sentence him to a half-existence of insanity.

While a living man, Anhurmose of Waset swore that such a fate was worse than death. Better to die than to linger in a warped, evil form.

Seth Adler knew that Anhurmose was a liar. When it was he who was looking at death, Anhurmose decided to linger.

The thought of the nameless dead gripped him. The nameless were broken things, half-made and half-mad, lacking pieces of their souls. Men feared to go among the oldest tombs. Striking a name from a monument condemned that ghost to never reach the realm of the gods.

He, too, was a half-made thing. But he retained his mind, his sanity. His own heart in his chest. If he had gone mad, it was so quietly that he hadn't realized it.

...And yet here he sat, waiting to go among ghosts.

His phone rang. Theo's picture.

"Djed? What news?"

"I'm in Building H." She kept her voice low, but he heard an echo from tile or concrete. "Dr. Armstrong thinks I've left. I'm in the upstairs bathroom now—east side."

She was hiding from the curator. Which meant—

"It's him?"

"Jay and Al. Alan Armstrong. He seemed to know a hell of a lot about that archive fire that conveniently messed up all the records." Her tone turned bitter. "And he knows we've been looking at Geltner and the provenance. Said I should stop asking questions or else."

Kill him. No. Get everything I can on Armstrong. Find pressure points for his employees. Do I have any trusts or standing donations to the Heritage Museum? Cut off his support.

"Are you in danger?"

"I don't think so," she said. "He's left for the day. But he took me off the project—I don't think we'll be able to get back in here anytime soon."

Seth stared out at the city. "What about the fakes?"

"Real," Theo said softly.

That was it, then. Even if the six pseudo-mummies in the museum had been made of a single body, it meant at least two victims. Two desperate, damaged spirits, grasping for Theo in their need for help. They were beyond dangerous—chaotic beings of pure pain—and they had already proven it at Geltner House.

Choking to death.

"Do you want to help them?" Seth said.

"Yes." Theo's answer was immediate, breathless. "God, Seth, they're hurting so much. They didn't ask to be like this."

"Even after...?" The Brother Priest.

"You saved me. I'm still alive. They don't even have that." Her voice shook. "They've been like this for years now. Just begging for anyone to help them. We *can't* leave them like that!"

He breathed deeply, composing a prayer in his mind. His instinct still screamed at him to run. The spirits touched the world around them and polluted it. Innocent people were in their path.

But they were suffering. And in their suffering, they harmed others. If they could be quieted, lives might be saved.

That was what he told himself, anyway.

"We won't leave them," Seth promised. "Listen, djed. Are you safe for the moment?"

"Yeah. Mostly. I'm hiding in the women's room on the second floor."

"Stay quiet and keep your head down. I'll be there as soon as it gets dark." Rising, he paced, thinking hard. "Nighttime is the time of the dead. If we give food to them and speak the calming spells, we may be able to get some answers out of them. I'll bring offerings and talismans to protect us both, and we'll quiet them as much as we can. That will reduce the damage they cause for the moment. Then, in the morning, we find a way to move against Armstrong."

Another donation, probably. Curators were not as exalted as their professional credentials suggested. A substantial check to the right people could get Armstrong removed from his position, leaving Seth and Theo free to get to the fakes again. Remove them from the building—burn or bury them to dispel the spirits.

But if they were going to calm the restless spirits long enough to get rid of Armstrong, they would have to move tonight. Armstrong knew enough to remove Theo from the project. He'd doubtless revoke her access first thing tomorrow. Perhaps increase security, too.

Act quickly, before the enemy has a chance to gather their forces.

"I'll be ready," Theo promised. Her voice was tight: he recognized the sound of someone working through pain. "See you soon."

"Be safe, djed," he murmured. *"Ankh wedja seneb."*

Theo breathed out. *"Ankh wedja seneb,* Anhurmose. *Meri tje."*

Building H was partially visible from his window. Part of it was obscured by the bulk of the university annex, but he could see the shapes of the façade easily enough. His one good eye spotted cornices and decorative ledges.

"I'll come in through the third floor," he said. "Southeast corner. Two hours."

"Be careful."

She rang off. He set the phone down and went to gather food and drink for the dead.

* * *

The southeast corner of Building H was relatively hidden from passersby. Here, a clump of elderly maples shadowed the craggy edifice of the building. Across the street, a pharmacy's security cameras were angled just far enough to catch part of the maples, but the other side remained out of sight.

Seth had scaled this building a few days ago, but then, he'd gone up the west side: with its fire escape, it was barely a challenge. Now, with heavier traffic on the street facing the west side, he'd switched to the southeast corner.

He crossed the street from the alley just after sunset. Even the most dedicated museum employees were beginning to trickle out. A few Hondas and Chevys lingered in the staff parking lot.

He slipped into the shadows and looked up at the building. Despite everything, a smile curled the corner of his mouth as he saw the gargoyle squatting on the cornice above. The heavy granite blocks fit together cleanly. Pillars and pilasters decorated the corners.

Climbing buildings had become much less fun in the twentieth century. Steel and glass and flat façades, like a world made of mirrors. If he had to break into places to get his tomb artifacts back, he could at least have an easy way up.

A quick standing leap got him high enough to grab the second-floor cornice. As a pair of security guards rounded the corner below, he crouched beside the gargoyle, imitating its pose. They didn't even look up.

He scaled a Grecian column, gripping the deep indentations. The concrete was streaked with moss and dirt. He'd be leaving marks, if anyone tried looking.

Below, the security guards continued on their way.

No alarms on most of the windows. Careless. Bracing himself against a false portico, Seth pressed his gloved fingers to the glass. Friction pads caught, and steady pressure forced it upward. The elderly window latch gave way. He slipped through the gap and perched on the sill, considering his next move.

This room had been used for cutting audio- and videotape a decade ago; now a reel-to-reel sat under a dirty sheet and a rogue's gallery of old electronics littered the steel shelves. Dust covered everything and would make his footprints clear the moment he put his feet on the ground.

Simple enough to confuse an investigator. Seth twisted and put his back to the door, closing the window and walking backward. A whiff of déjà vu accompanied the movement—a vague memory of rock underfoot, kepi-wearing soldiers under a Rajput sun.

He could hear someone breathing now. Familiar.

Through the door. He found himself in a long gallery above the cavern of the storage area. Narrow walkways bordered with metal rail-ings, and below, the shrouded shapes of crates. Passing along the walk-way, he followed the sound of the familiar breath and heartbeat.

Theo sat on the tile floor of the bathroom, her chin resting on her knees. Her pupils were huge, blown wide with nerves and the darkness.

She let out a breath and rose, her legs wobbling. He gathered her into his arms and pressed a kiss to her hair. She was shaking.

"Djed," he murmured. "Can you hear me?"

She blinked, coming awake. "'m fine," she said at last. "They're—they're awake. All the time now."

"Theo."

She kissed him. "I'm fine," she repeated. In the dimness, there was only the thinnest ring of malachite green around the dark pools of her pupils. Shadows deepened the hollows in her thin face. "They're hurting, and I can't help them."

"Yes, you can." He shifted, tugging on the strap of his satchel. "Let's go."

CHAPTER 21

No plan of operations reaches with any certainty beyond
the first encounter with the enemy's main force.

—Helmuth von Moltke

The touches were constant now, and the whispers were growing. Like
being in the room with a hidden clock, constantly ticking and driving
you crazy. There were few words, just sighs and murmurs—sensations
rather than real voices.

They were afraid. Their fear hung in the air, thick and smothering
like summer heat.

When Seth had arrived, the voices went quiet. Maybe he'd frightened them. As he wrapped his arm around her waist and helped her out
of her hiding place, the rush of sensation receded, leaving Theo tired but
clear-headed.

"Where are they?" he said.

"First floor. Down there, with the crates." Theo pointed. "Three
mummies, one torso with a partial mummy case, and two...two heads."

"Are they speaking to you now?" he said gently.

"Muttering and crying. Can you hear them yet?"

"I hear nothing. But you're the priest here."

They descended the steps. Theo pointed out the few cameras and
their blind spots. One section at the bottom of the stairs was awkward:
the only way to avoid being seen was to use a rickety shelving unit as a
ladder. Seth lowered her down, and then simply jumped—dexterous and
quick, like a cat leaping off a perch.

I do good work, Theo thought, admiring the movement.

Though it wasn't all her. The body was like new clothes to him: just
a shell around the real person. She'd given him the tools, but it was his

169

will and experience that made them do things—good or bad.

She wondered if he saw it that way. His recent surge of memories frightened her: made her not afraid of him, as she had once been, but afraid for him. She couldn't fix pain.

Maybe that was why the ghosts called to her so strongly.

Only the emergency lights were on now. The room glowed a faint blue from strips of cool LEDs. It gave an eerie luminescence to Seth's right eye, and the scars on Theo's hands stood out, waxy white.

Seth took a pouch from the satchel, tucking it into a zippered pocket, and handed the satchel to Theo. "Wait here," he said, low-voiced. "I'll fix the cameras."

He tugged on his gloves, grabbed one of the support beams, and simply climbed it. Nonchalant as if he were walking down the street. Two of the cameras hung from the third-story walkway, and he went hand-over-hand down the underside of the walkway, holding on to the metal braces that supported it.

Despite the weakness in his right side, he moved easily, almost lightly for such a tall man. In moments, he'd reached the first camera. He wedged himself between two struts, looped an arm around another one, and pried open the camera's case.

It took him less than a minute to deal with the first camera. The second followed quickly. He dropped twelve feet down to the floor and rose to his feet, peeling his gloves off.

Theo grinned at him. "Y'know, most guys just try to impress the girls with fancy cars."

"Hard to get a car through a top-floor window," Seth replied. "Unless you're a very careless driver. We have about forty minutes."

Theo nodded and opened the satchel.

Seth had packed flatbread and a thick, home-brewed beer that smelled like sourdough. Theo unwrapped a pair of clay offering vessels already painted with prayers, and a small pot of real kohl. Hastily scribbled hieroglyphs and English translations covered a small sheaf of notebook paper.

As she ran her fingers over the paper, something brushed her scalp. A hand, a small hand: five points of pressure. It tentatively touched her hair and carded through the loose strands. Theo's breath caught.

"Hello," she said.

Another hand touched her cheek, lightly. Theo closed her eyes and listened.

This wasn't like the attack at Geltner House. That one had been too powerful, too agonized, to be reached. These touches lightly stroked across her cheeks and hair, and voices hissed behind her: *Sorry, sorry, sorry.*

"It's OK," she told them. "We're going to help you."

Seth was cocking his head, listening to something in the distance. Now he turned. "Theo?"

"They're here, Seth." Theo held up a hand, cupping the air. Fingertips brushed over it. For a moment, red mist streamed through them. Her heart jumped. "Look! Look! They're here!"

"Well," he said. "Serapis be praised."

She knew him too well to take that at face value. Serapis had been a Greek invention, a combined god created during Alexander the Great's time. Seth loathed the invented deity and refused to sacrifice to it.

A sudden memory flashed across her mind: a high school boyfriend, sitting petrified in his chair as Mom and Dad interrogated him. (They had a good-cop-bad-cop routine TV couldn't beat, only it was more like Money Cop, Country Club Cop.) Seeing him shrivel under the cool, polite questioning, slowly picked to pieces, and later hearing him say his goodbyes with a stiff "It's been really interesting to meet you." That had been the end of that boyfriend.

Parents, ghosts. Every relationship had its problems.

Seth had turned away and was listening again, seemingly on guard. Theo kissed her palm and held it out, wordlessly sending the gesture toward his back. Maybe the ghosts would carry it.

Maybe she was just being a flaky artist again. But she'd fix this, too— somehow—once they had the fakes taken care of.

Seth stirred, but it wasn't the kiss. His expression sharpened as his gaze raked the walkway. He'd heard something.

"Better get started," he said. "I'm going to check the perimeter. We've been interrupted by enough security guards in the past, I think."

Theo nodded. Seth vanished into the shadows.

The ghosts swept around her, some stroking, some tugging. At least three: a light touch, a harder touch, and one that tapped and fluttered rather than poked.

Theo knelt beside Princess Penedjmet's case. She spread out the offerings and went to work with the kohl. Seth's hastily written instructions included vital symbols for the priest to wear, and she painted them onto her hands and face. Then she sketched more symbols on the floor with a stick of chalk. The eyes of the ka to look out upon the world, the heart scarab for memory and self, and the crooked scepter to open the mouths of the dead. More complete, more appropriate for the purpose, than her hasty attempts with the lip balm.

"Brothers and sisters, awaken," she whispered. The words rippled through the room.

She poured beer into the cup and laid one piece of flatbread in the clay dish. The voices rose and echoed in her ears. More words, now: *fear* and *help* and *afraid* and *sorry, sorry, sorry, please.*

The first prayer was the simplest, a three-sentence invocation. She recited it six times, each time placing one more slice of bread in the dish and adding more beer to the cup. The touches and taps died away, and the voices hushed. A wisp of smoke curled from the center of the plate.

Slowly, she fed them. Small pieces, building them up, reciting the words that the ancients had spoken. Preparatory and welcoming phrases, calling on the spirits to be welcome, to be at peace, to be known and recognized by the gods.

"It's one of those days, huh?"

Theo almost dropped the beer bottle.

"Aki?" she said. "What are you doing here?"

"Imhotep texted me," Aki said. He wore his "meeting with the higher-ups" clothes—a blazer and khakis. After the meetings, he must have gone right back to work without changing. "He said shit's about to go down."

"I told him to stay away," Seth said from his place by the door. "He didn't listen. And they haven't replaced the window I broke, so he climbed up."

"You're gonna get yourself killed," Theo told Aki.

"Yeah, well, I'm still half hungover from the other night. Death doesn't feel so bad right now. You figured something out?"

"I'll keep him out of trouble," Theo said to Seth. "You should probably go back to watching the door. If anyone finds us, we're gonna need more pull than I've got to get out of this."

Seth nodded and disappeared into the corridor. When he was gone, Aki knelt down next to Theo. His expression turned worried. "You OK? Are you possessed or something?"

"Nope."

"Ghost shit?"

"Yep."

"Tell me in ten words or less."

"'Mummies are real. One murdered. Could be Dr. Armstrong.'" She counted the words in her head. "'Seriously.'"

"...All right. Anything I can do?"

"Just hang tight for a sec. I've got to do these offerings and get them calmed down so we can ask them some more questions. Remember, I'm sort of a priestess now."

Aki's eye twitched, but he stepped back. Theo finished her prayer, gathered up dishes, and walked to the south wall. The bread smoldered on the plate, and she trailed smoke behind her like a censer.

Another invisible hand gripped the back of her shirt. Theo flinched but kept a straight face as the ghosts pawed at her again.

As Aki watched warily, Theo dropped to her knees again and added another slice of bread to the plate. Bow and chant: a prayer to the dead things that haunted this place. The tyet on her chest throbbed, sparks of pain flickering across the skin.

Please, let this work. Please, let us be able to help them.

She made her circuit of the room as Aki watched. The beer and bread were offered; the dishes marked; the sacred markings drawn. The rising tide in the back of her mind lapped at the edges, waiting—but not yet cresting. She sank down on her knees, laid her hands on her thighs with palms up, and began to intone the next prayer.

It was another new one—one Seth had brought, along with the vessels and the food.

In the name of Isis and Osiris, in the name of Amon, in the name of Anubis who shall bring these vessels before you, and in the name of she who shall not be fed by your hearts, I offer to you. Behold, your name is known to the gods and is not forgotten. Behold, you are given food and drink. Behold, you are remembered. Behold, you are sacrificed unto. Behold, you are worthy.

So says Theodora, daughter of Amy and Phillip, who offers to you.

She poured the beer and filled the plate one more time.

"Theeee-ohh."

The word sighed through the room. The back of her neck prickled. Hairs rose on her arms as the voices washed over her, carried on a breeze that smelled like must and old age.

"Aki?" Theo said. "Aki, did you say that?"

"What?" Aki looked over at her. He was standing near the door, shoulders hunched, hands shoved in his pockets, but watching for anyone who might see them. "I didn't say anything."

"Thee-oh. Theeo. Theo."

"One second." Theo turned back to the dishes. The touches of the ghosts were growing stronger, more desperate.

"Theo. Theo. Theo. He bleeds."

Theo stiffened. "What?"

"Bleeds. Falls. The maker comes."

The voices rose into a howl. Theo reeled. Aki yelped as she convulsed, dropping the offering vessels.

"He comes! He comes! The maker's fire comes upon us!"

CHAPTER 22

Your servant humbly informs you that this device is beyond his understanding... Though he accounts himself learned in the arts and practices of war, he cannot imagine the wicked ingenuity of that which he sees before him.

—Words of an anonymous Persian oarmaster,
ca. 680 ACE, upon encountering Greek fire
for the first time (Lampos Manuscript)

The night was full of movement. He couldn't hear it as Theo did, but he sensed it: invisible and silent, a cobweb wavering and thrumming in the air. His skin prickled.

He hadn't really understood the task at hand until he came here and felt them all around. They jarred his senses. Scraped his bones. Broken minds haunted this place, and his every instinct screamed at him to grab Theo and *run*.

The phony Unknown Master, this pair of thieves and murderers, had chosen a scorpion as their maker's mark. It couldn't be a coincidence. The gods spoke this way, if they spoke at all: with omen and sign. A curse mark to warn of splintered souls.

Seth stepped out into the night and flattened his back against the outer wall of the building, turning statue-still and listening. By now, the sky was almost fully dark. The city's ambient light blotted out the few stars that were trying to peek through.

Keeping to the shadows, he walked the perimeter of the building. A few security guards a block away did the same. To his shabti eyes, they were patches of life in the shadows. No sudden movements or alarm from them. He stayed out of sight and stepped back into Building H.

The air felt different. It jangled like a sistrum in an unskilled hand.

He circled the ground floor and climbed up onto the catwalks. Theo and Aki were talking. His ears could catch their words, but he deliberately tuned them out. That was not his business.

The upper floors were clear. He walked only in the tracks others had left in the dust and kept his gloves on. Most of the locks were old and could be sprung with pressure in the right place, but aside from marking entrances and exits, he had little to do in those rooms.

For a moment, he leaned on the catwalk railing and looked down at the ground floor. Theo's chalk hieroglyphs were a spark of the familiar in the strange scene. She was kneeling again, praying over the offering dishes.

His eye lingered on the body of the woman swathed in gold. A false princess. He wondered who she had been in life.

Whether she'd died choking, as he had.

He walked the perimeter on the ground floor once more, keeping an eye out for cameras, watching the shadows shift and the distant figures of patrolling guards.

A click. A door. The front door, by the empty guard station.

Footsteps.

Seth listened. Male, by the size and weight of his steps. No one he'd met before. Strong heartbeat—healthy, middle-aged. Leather-soled shoes.

"Hello?" A man's voice, definitely. "Who's there?"

Seth waited.

The man came into view. Thinning dark hair, broad frame, solid build, wearing a suit with a violently fuchsia shirt underneath it. He carried a canvas bag slung over one shoulder and had one hand tucked in his pocket. There was a bulge there—the right size for a small gun.

Seth recognized him. They'd never met, but the man's picture was on the museum site.

Armstrong.

Seth stepped out in front of him. "You can't go in there," he said. "There's work being done."

The doctor's eyes widened at the sight of him. Seth could hear his pulse jump.

"Mr. Adler," Armstrong said. "What are you doing here?"

So Armstrong had done his research too. The curator's voice was level, but his heart was still racing. Seth shifted his stance, moving slightly forward onto the balls of his feet.

"Dr. Armstrong." He nodded to the other man. "I apologize, but some of my experts are currently on-site. The board of directors has asked that nobody else enter while the specimens are being examined."

"Examined?" Armstrong's voice sharpened. "I didn't hear anything about this."

"Hm, really? I suppose you didn't get the meeting invitation."

The story wasn't going to cut it. Armstrong pushed forward, trying to shove past Seth, but Seth shifted to block him.

"Let me in!" Armstrong hissed. Seth could smell him now. A reek of alcohol on his breath, and oil and metal in his pockets.

"Go home," Seth said. The doctor pushed again, but his strength was purely mortal. Seth was immovable.

Frustrated, Armstrong fell back a step. "You can't keep me out of my own building," he said breathlessly. "It doesn't matter what your girl-friend told you. This is *my* museum. *My* exhibit. And this is *not cleared with the board.*"

"Things change," Seth said flatly.

The two men watched each other. Sizing each other up.

Then Armstrong moved. His right hand whipped out of his pocket. A gun? Seth twisted, already knowing the shot would go wide—narrow line of fire—ready to break the man's arm—

It wasn't a gun. Something, small and weak, struck him in the chest. *Pain.*

Sudden and complete. His body burned. Muscles stiffened and con-vulsed, heart racing out of control. He couldn't even stagger: he was paralyzed, locked in its grip.

As suddenly as the strange force overwhelmed him, it abated. Seth fell.

He landed on his right side. His breath was locked in his throat. Armstrong stepped over him, reeling in some strands of wire that had shot from the strange weapon.

With a heavy kick, Armstrong rolled Seth over onto his front. His limbs weren't obeying him. He could only lie there, twitching in the aftershocks, as the man knelt over him. One knee pressed into the small of his back.

A streak of black. A cord, around his neck.

He reached for breath that wasn't there. Relentless pressure on his back and in his neck, choking the life out of him. He fought to get a hand underneath him, to rise and fight back—throw the man off, break every bone in his gods-cursed body—

His hands scrabbled at the concrete. Still his body refused to obey. And the relentless pressure choked him.

"I'm really sorry about this," said Armstrong's voice behind him. Seth clawed at the wire as his vision darkened. "At least the cleanup is going to be easy."

CHAPTER 23

HISTORY, n. An account mostly false, of events mostly unimportant, which are brought about by rulers mostly knaves, and soldiers mostly fools.

—*Ambrose Bierce,* The Devil's Dictionary

The voices pressed against her ears: wailing, shrieking, begging. She felt Aki bracing her, keeping her from falling, but for a moment she lost everything but the ghosts.

Theo raised her head, taking deep breaths, and forced her eyelids open. It was agonizing, but—

But she'd felt this before. Ghosts in the graveyard with Meren, ghosts in the museum. "Aki, you have to hide!"

"Why?" Aki was holding Theo steady, but there was a crazed look on his face.

"No time." Theo pulled herself away from Aki and braced herself against the nearest case. "Find a corner. Hide. Someone's coming!"

A heartbeat's hesitation. But Aki nodded and sprinted for the dark overhang of the catwalk. Theo saw a flash of movement as he crawled between two crates, vanishing into a gap.

Just in time. Footsteps clicked on the concrete of the entryway. Theo flattened her hands against the case and swallowed hard, trying to stifle the nausea.

Dr. Armstrong appeared in the entrance. His tie was askew and sweat dampened his bright Hawaiian shirt and suit jacket. He carried a canvas tote bag slung over one shoulder. It sagged with the weight of something heavy.

"Theodora," he said. "I should have guessed you'd be here. Are you OK?"

"I wanted to take one more look." No kidding. "I was inspired. Um, why are you here?"

"Well, you know how it goes in this business," Dr. Armstrong said. "Sometimes a project just blows up in your face."

"Is that, uh...has that been a problem lately?"

"That's life." Dr. Armstrong's smile was wide, his eyes glassy. "It's hard to find people who are willing to really put in the work."

He pulled a gun from his jacket. It looked like a Glock. Police-issue. Theo took a step back, pressing against the glass case.

"Um, Doctor?" She tried a shaky laugh. "I don't think that's, uh, that's how you make people put in the work."

"You'd think so," the doctor said. If he fired, he'd put a hole in Theo's chest. His aim was steady. "But standards have been falling everywhere lately. No one cares about quality anymore."

Where are you, Seth? "Is that what this is about? Quality?"

"Among other things. Put your hands up, please, Theodora. And back away from the case, slowly."

Theo did as ordered. A chilly wind rippled through the room, but Theo heard only muted whimpering from the ghosts. Her throat prickled, remembering the strangling ache.

"Thank you. Turn around, please, and put your hands behind you."

Panic spiked. "No!"

"Theodora." Dr. Armstrong raised the gun. His smile was still locked in place. "Please, I don't enjoy this any more than you do. This would've gone much better if you weren't here. Put your hands behind your back now."

No chance. If he got her tied up, she was dead meat. She needed a distraction, fast.

Seth, come on, come on, please...

Something moved in the shadows, but it wasn't Seth. Aki crept between two crates, moving slowly and silently. He'd found a crescent wrench somewhere.

Dammit, Aki! You're mortal!

"You're the Unknown Master!" she said. Armstrong's mouth tightened. "Or one of them. It was a partner gig, right? You do the paperwork and the research, and some other underpaid slob has to do all the heavy lifting."

"So you really did figure it out," he said quietly.

"I had to. Nothing was adding up." *Eyes on me, you son of a bitch. Eyes on me. Don't look behind you.* "So I started digging. It got harder when the Egyptians cracked down, didn't it? But you still could've sold to the private collector market if your partner hadn't lost his nerve."

Dr. Armstrong's lips were taut and white. "That's enough!"

Eyes on me. "You love these things," she said quickly.

The gun wavered a fraction of an inch.

"Don't you?" she continued. "You added a maker's mark and every-thing. Even if they weren't making you any money, you wanted every-one to see 'em. So you messed up the archives with a quick fire and sneaked some fake provenance into the back catalog. Stuff gets lost all the time in places like this, doesn't it?"

"Theodora. Stop talking. You don't understand this kind of art."

"Oh, trust me, I do," she said fervently. "You start a project for a paycheck. But you put your time into it—blood, sweat, tears. And you fall in love with it a little."

That shot landed. The gun wavered again, a little more. Armstrong's eyes flicked to Princess Penedjmet for a fraction of a second.

"Tell me something," she said. "Why real bodies?"

"Why not?" Armstrong said quietly. "Good work needs good mate-rials."

More movement in the shadows. Aki crept closer. A few more steps...

"Like Jay?" Theo said.

The doctor's eyes widened, and the muzzle of the gun rose. "How did you—?"

Aki swung. The crescent wrench struck a glancing blow and split open the doctor's scalp. Blood colored his graying hair. His fingers clenched around the trigger guard.

As he stumbled, Theo pounced. She jammed her knee into his leg and sank her nails into his hands, trying to pry the gun loose. Aki fumbled with the wrench.

Armstrong whipped his head back, slamming the back of his skull into Aki's face. Aki yelped and clutched at his nose. The blood-slicked wrench almost slipped from his fingers.

Still grappling, Theo tried to knee Armstrong in the groin. Both of her hands were occupied with his right, but his left was free, and he struck a glancing blow at her face. Theo's head snapped back, ears ring-ing. She lost her grip on his gun hand.

Armstrong jammed the gun into Theo's stomach. She froze, pressed up against the Other Woman's case.

"That's enough!" Armstrong snarled.

Aki still clutched the wrench, his other hand pressed to his face, blood seeping through his fingers. His nose was broken.

"Back off!" the curator bellowed. "Both of you! Back the *fuck* off!"

He grabbed Aki's arm and shoved him toward Theo. Aki swung wildly, but he overcorrected and smashed into the nearest glass case. Armstrong jumped back from the spray of shards but kept the gun on them. Theo caught the stumbling Aki. He mumbled thanks, but his eyes were fixed on Armstrong.

The doctor unslung his tote bag and dropped his jacket. Without the camouflaging suit coat, Theo saw heavy muscle lining his arms and shoulders. A former football player with a lot of gas left in the tank.

"It's a shame," he said tersely. His mouth worked like he was chewing on something. "You're right, Theodora. I do love them. But you had to involve your goddamn sugar daddy, didn't you? Get him asking questions, waving money around. I know when my job's in trouble." Teeth flashed as he grimaced. "I don't love them enough to leave evidence behind."

He pulled a gallon can out of the bag. Its lid was stained yellow, and Theo caught a whiff of something sweet and nutty.

Linseed oil. Useful for painting and refinishing. Museums bought it by the gallon. One of the most volatile substances Theo had ever worked with. Linseed-soaked rags ignited when they dried.

2006. Someone spilled some linseed oil.

Armstrong began pouring a line of oil from the center of the room toward the electrical closet under the catwalk. A great place for a fire to start. Theo remembered the building records she'd pawed through: outdated wiring, flammable insulation.

"Oh, Jesus," Theo whispered. Aki surged forward, but Theo clutched his arm hard, holding him back. If their clothes got soaked, one little spark would mean the end.

Armstrong dumped the last of the linseed oil and dropped the canvas bag into it. One very big rag to soak it up. He turned and gestured with the gun.

"I'm not happy about this," he said to them. "We could've had a great exhibit. Good money, good publicity. This kind of stuff makes careers! But all you cared about was your fucking *research*."

"Dr. Armstrong, please," Theo pleaded. "There's more going on here than you realize. Nobody is gonna lose their jobs. I just wanted to help the mummies!"

He shook his head. "Too late."

"Dr. Armstrong!"

"Too late," he repeated. "You got a donor involved. I know when I'm beat. Now I have to make sure these fakes don't get any more attention."

Seth should be back by now. Armstrong must have done something to him. The doctor spoke ancient Egyptian well enough to sight-read it: did he have any of the old prayers memorized? Could he speak the spells that affected the shabti body? Or was it a shot to the heart that anchored that shabti form? Losing his real heart might kill him as easily as it killed a normal man.

Beside her, Aki was tense as a wire. The ghosts wailed in her ears.

Armstrong knew the old language. But Seth knew the old prayers, and she held the old magic. Once before, she had called on a disembodied ghost to obey her, and sent it into an old body.

She raised her eyes to Dr. Armstrong. "Behold," she said.

Armstrong's brow wrinkled. "Behold what?" he said curiously.

"Behold. Behold, I bring an offering before you. An offering which the King gives unto the Osiris-spirit."

A strange expression of fascination spread across Armstrong's face. He recognized an offering formula. The woman he was about to shoot was reciting ancient funerary texts.

"To the Osiris-spirit is given bread, beer, and oil. To the Osiris-spirit is given a temple of learning and a place of writing. To the Osiris-spirit is given flame. Let the Osiris-spirit take upon itself that which it is given, and be satisfied. Blessed and holy is the Osiris-spirit, who goes before the dawn upon golden wings, and let him come unto me and rise once more to full health."

Theo recited the whole prayer without a hitch or a stammer. Her gaze held Armstrong's. If looks could kill, he'd be history. But he only listened, curiosity in his pallid face, and let her finish.

"That's a strange formula," he said. "Were you doing some home study, Theodora?"

"I've learned a lot, I promise. I can hear them now."

"Excuse me?"

"I can hear the ghosts. Of your *art*. They've been guiding me all this time." Theo smiled at him. "And you poured oil…an offering which their maker gives. It's theirs now. And I think they'll take it."

A scrape. A crack. A creak.

And Princess Penedjmet sat up.

Armstrong's finger tightened on the trigger. The shot echoed brutally loudly off the concrete walls, making the metal catwalks ring. It drowned out the tinkling of glass as the case broke.

The princess half-rolled, half-fell out of the case. Breaking free like a cicada from its shell, brown and withered.

Beside her, Aki flinched violently. He whispered under his breath: *"Holy shit, Grandpa, you were right."*

The princess tottered toward them. The bandages hung loose around her thighs, revealing clean white fibers under the artificial aging. The golden plate was too heavy for her. Clumsy brown fingers worked at the braided rope, struggling to unpick the knot. Her mouth gaped soundlessly, withered lips folding around tea-colored teeth as the papier-mâché struggled to flex.

Another creak. A crackle of old leather. Bandages tore. The Minister sat up.

Armstrong gaped as he watched them rise. The spreading pool of linseed oil lapped at the edges of the cases, but his attention was fixed on the mummies.

Penedjmet staggered to a stop. Both arms dropped, but one still swung back and forth with the force of her motion. White lines showed clearly through the broken glaze and patina now. One of her elbows, the one made of monkey bones, bent the wrong way.

The Minister struggled to rise, but his lack of feet slowed him down. The old wooden struts replacing his lower legs snapped. He flopped awkwardly over the side of the coffin. Dust rose as he clawed at himself, fingers snapping, bandages tearing. One wooden leg was left behind in the coffin. He got his hands on the floor and began to crawl toward Theo and Aki, slipping on the oil.

"I miss art school," Aki mumbled.

"Don't move!" Armstrong shouted. But he couldn't tear his eyes away from the crawling figure.

Theo was between Aki and Armstrong now. "Go," she breathed. "Go, go, go!"

Aki knew it wasn't the time to argue. He darted for the door. Theo leaped forward, toward the Minister and Armstrong. Armstrong fired, but his concentration had been shattered: a white-hot line slashed across Theo's arm, and the bullet cracked into concrete. Aki was already down the hall.

He'd find Seth. Or call the police. The situation was now officially beyond *lose our jobs* and well into *lose our lives,* and Aki knew it.

On the other side of the room, the Other Woman threw her lid off. The severed heads of Tilamentu and Khnumwaset vibrated soundlessly in their box, jaws yattering.

Glass shattered as Hai-Ti sat up. That one was weak. With trembling bandaged paws, it could only swipe at its face, brushing away scraps of gauze.

Armstrong's focus darted from one to another. They moved like puppets, struggling to move their limbs. Cartonnage and papier-mâché cracked as the spirits pushed the bodies beyond their limits.

Dr. Armstrong fired again. The bullet tore through Hai-Ti. The fake flopped backward on its broken spine and nearly fell out of the case. It groped at the ground, upside-down like a child falling out of bed.

"What did you do?" Armstrong roared. *"What did you do to my mummies?"*

"I told you." An awful calm rested on Theo. "I did my research."

Armstrong gaped. For a moment, the gun hung loose in his hand.

"This isn't appropriate behavior, Theodora," he said dazedly. "I thought you'd be more sensible. The benefits of working on this project..."

She stared at him, cold-eyed. "Thank you for your time and consideration, Dr. Armstrong. But I've decided to take my career in a different direction."

The boilerplate words jolted him back to himself. He raised the gun.

"Then I regretfully consider our agreement terminated," he said.

CHAPTER 24

Thine enemy the Serpent hath been given over to the fire.

—*The Papyrus of Ani,*
trans. E.A. Wallis Budge

The door held. The hinges didn't. They broke, and the door slewed to one side and crashed to the floor.

Armstrong wheeled, the gun moving to cover what must be a squad of policemen. Theo dove to the ground and scrambled behind the nearest case.

It wasn't the police. A single figure stalked over the fallen door, face a mask of fury.

He looked like hell. His trousers were torn at the ankles and knees, gloves gone. A livid red line stood out around his neck.

Armstrong fired twice. Seth lurched with the impact. Theo screamed, but Seth didn't fall. He shook his head like a dog trying to clear its ears and broke into a run.

Armstrong fired again. Fresh red stained Seth's chest.

In one dive, Seth tackled Armstrong to the floor. The gun flew out of the curator's hands and skittered across the concrete, right past Theo. She didn't dare touch it.

Seth crouched over the struggling curator, one hand braced on the floor, the other around Armstrong's neck. He said nothing as he dug his thumb into the hollow of the man's throat and choked the life out of him.

"Seth!"

Theo's scream broke the spell. His lips shaped her name. Armstrong strained weakly against him.

"Seth, don't!" she cried. "Don't kill him!"

Seth didn't let go. Just held his grip, inhuman strength crushing the curator's windpipe. Armstrong's eyes rolled up as his face turned maroon.

Theo dropped to one knee, grabbed his arm with both hands, and began to pry at the fingers that felt like steel bands. "Seth. Don't kill him!"

Her touch, or his name, seemed to finally pierce the fog. His fingers loosened a bare inch, and Armstrong gasped for air.

Seth's voice was low. "He was going to kill you."

"We can't do anything to him, Seth."

"The spirits. You know what he did to them. What he was going to do to you—" The fear flashed in his eyes. "Theo, you don't—you shouldn't see this. Go."

"No." She slid her fingers under Seth's, loosening his hold. Heavy bruises were already rising on the curator's throat. "Seth. Listen to me. The authorities don't know he hurt the spirits and they don't know about the bodies yet. But if you kill him, they'll find DNA or fingerprints—Seth, you're *bleeding.*"

She wrapped her arms around his shoulders, kneeling next to him. *"Anhurmose."* A shudder ran through him. "Don't do it."

He released the man. Armstrong slumped to the floor, barely breathing. Seth looked down at him with unbridled hatred in his face—but Theo pressed her face into his shoulder, and the tension seemed to leave Seth in one long wave.

"He should be dead," Seth told her. Armstrong wheezed for breath.

Seth rooted through the curator's pockets, taking spare clips and removing the ammunition from his gun. He found a small black box—a Taser—and crushed it in one hand.

"And they say that war never changes," he muttered and threw the remains of the Taser away.

Theo stood, and he rose stiffly and put his arm around her again. She leaned into him again, willing them both to be calm.

"We're going to regret this," Seth told her. "He can accuse us of anything he likes."

"He can try. Don't you get it? There's no evidence for *any of us.*" She pointed to the tottering Penedjmet.

She could feel the shivering in Seth as Penedjmet staggered closer. But she knew he understood what she was saying. Any physical evidence of Theo and even Seth could be explained away by Theo's visits to the building—but in turn, they had almost nothing solid to use against Armstrong. The remains he'd mutilated were in such ruinous condition, acid-stripped and covered in powerful paints and solvents, that the likelihood of matching him to their deaths was next to zero. And testimony from still-incoherent ghosts meant nothing to the law.

"I want him dead," Seth told her, low-voiced.

"Me too." Theo's voice was muffled by the fabric of Seth's shirt. He gently touched her face, his hand shaking. "But he made ghosts, and they hate him, Seth. And they've just eaten the biggest offering they ever had. They won't leave him alone now."

"I pray you're right, Theo—ah! Damn!"

Theo's shoulder had bumped his chest, and Seth hissed in pain. His shirt was still wet with blood.

"I overdid it," he said ruefully. Theo pressed a hand to his chest, trying to stem the fresh flow. "This new body is wonderful, but—but the clay would at least heal faster—!"

Theo pressed the heel of her hand to the heaviest bleeding. "Oh, God, not again. We need to get you to the hospital!"

"No." Seth flinched, but he stayed upright. The fury that had driven him was draining away. "No hospital. Almost no hiding it last time."

"Back to the motel. Aki got clear—we'll call him for pickup."

"I know. Saw him running." A hitch in his breath. "Dammit, it feels like 1918 all over again."

"Don't turn your back on me!"

Armstrong was on his feet, barely. He slumped over the remains of Princess Penedjmet's case, hands resting on the wood framework. His fleshy face was bright red, and his voice was a strangled rasp. On the floor, his wavering duplicate glowed in the viscous surface of the spreading linseed oil.

"Don't," he repeated. "You can't leave. You can't!"

"Be silent," Seth said tightly. "This farce is over."

Armstrong inched toward them, clawing sideways along the case. "You can't do this," he said. "I'll tell everyone. You're finished!"

Theo ignored him. She didn't have any more patience for him.

"You *cunt!*" the old man bellowed. "Doesn't matter if you fuck the whole board of trustees! You're done!"

Theo could feel Seth's muscles tensing under her hands. "Seth, *don't*," she begged. Then she shot a narrowed glare at Armstrong. "It's *all* done," she said. "The cameras are out. No one can prove we were here.

The ghosts get to decide what happens next...and if I were you, I'd start praying."

She turned to the swaying puppet-corpses. "When you're done," she said quietly, "we'll come back for you. We'll feed you again. Maybe we can find your real names."

Jaws gaped. Papier-mâché tore, enamel cracked like beetle shells. A breath of exhalation rose, ruffling the back of Armstrong's hair.

And they began to move again. The Other Woman came first, crawling, dragging her legless trunk. One arm propelled herself forward, her body flopping like a fish, leaving a slug trail through the spreading yellow oil. Her other arm cradled two chattering lipless heads: Khnumwaset and Tilamentu.

Behind her came the bent shape of Hai-Ti, twisted to one side, one arm dangling from a single strand of old rope. The Minister was beginning to get free of his case at last. Penedjmet struggled to drop the heavy golden plate that dragged her down.

"No," Armstrong whispered. "No! Stop it!"

The dead did not stop.

"Stop it!" Armstrong shouted. "These items are the property of the Heritage Museum of History! I did not authorize this!"

Theo laughed. "Dr. Armstrong, you can't own people. We had a war about it and everything."

The creatures moved closer. She could feel Seth's heart racing, but he held steady, jaw set. Behind them rolled a wall of red mist, streaming like smoke and swirling around their misshapen bodies.

Armstrong's expression flashed raw panic. He grabbed at Penedjmet, his fingers crushing the brittle bandages. Penedjmet thrashed, her pendant limbs swinging wildly, and Armstrong lost his grip. He staggered back with his face twisted in disgust. He kicked at the pool of linseed oil, splashing it across Penedjmet, and staggered back with his lighter clutched in his hand.

The corpses halted. Armstrong raised the lighter, baring his teeth in a snarl.

"Back off!" he bellowed. The tiny flame danced between his fingers. "You're all covered in oil. One more twitch, and I'll light you up!"

The mummies shivered as one. Their jaws gaped. They breathed out, and the red mist rolled over Armstrong. It tightened in a coil, crawling up his arms, plucking at his fingers.

The dancing flame sputtered and shot up. Sparks pattered down on

Armstrong's shoulders and chest. And a few stray drops of oil spray kindled in his clothes.

Horror slashed across his face. Too late.

The flames leaped up, deep saffron orange. They crawled up his body with shocking speed, flicking out long agile limbs and hooking their claws into him as they climbed. A scream tore from him, choking and crazed, as he fell back and clutched at his face. An eruption of black smoke swallowed him up.

CHAPTER 25

I say, O Osiris in truth, that I am the spirit-body of the god,
and I beseech thee not to let me be driven away, nor to be
cast upon the wall of blazing fire.

> —*The Papyrus of Ani,*
> *trans. E.A. Wallis Budge*

Flame leaped from man to floor. From floor to wall. It crawled with an
unholy speed, seeking out particles of oil on the walls and in the air.

Heat washed over them. Seth stiffened. A smell—the reek of burning
cloth and oil and man—

Theo cried out. She called his name, telling him he was hurting her.
How was that possible? She was—no, she was in his arms. Concrete
under his feet. He ran, heedless of the pain in his chest and side. Hurtling
down the hall, chased by the heat of the growing fire.

It would eat everything. Paper, wood, oil, dried flesh: it was a full
meal for any blaze. If any of the nameless things still existed in its upper
floors, hidden behind closed doors and buried in crates, they would be
gone within the hour.

Not for nothing do we burn offerings for the gods.

He smashed the door open and barreled out into the warm summer
night. With the heat behind him, the night air chilled the sweat already
risen on his skin. He pelted across the lawn, clutching Theo to his chest,
and didn't stop until he reached the copse of trees on the north side of
the street.

"Put me down!" Theo was shouting. Crying. "Put me down, put me
down, put me down!" She seemed locked in some kind of trance.

"Djed. Shh." He set her down gently, still holding her close. "Shh.
You're safe."

She struggled, trying to twist away from him. Her eyes were huge, pupils blown wide in terror.

No. Not terror. She pulled herself loose and lurched forward, landing hard on all fours. Even as he reached for her, she started back toward the building. Fire glowed at the windows.

"Go back!" she was saying. "Go back, go back, now! We have to save them!"

Her words broke through his numbed stupor.

"They're dead!" Seth shouted. He grabbed her arms even as she strained away from him, toward the building.

"But they're awake, Seth!"

"They're dead, Theo! They should be gone."

Tears streaked her face. "But if their bodies burn—that's it! There won't be anything left to help them!"

The house of death and dead things. Half-formed souls, monsters' monsters. Things that should have lain quiet in museum cases or never been made at all.

I bet you're going to look great in the exhibit. Right, guys?

A face and a voice, smeary through the glass. Viewed from a dozen angles at once. A dozen pairs of eyes on the shelf, roused from sleep by an artist's magic.

Unquiet, half-formed spirits, clinging to their half-formed shabtis.

His heart thundered in his chest. It was his own heart: *ib*, the core of the soul. His original corpse was locked up safely in Chicago: *khet*, the physical body. Personality and vital essence: *ba* and *ka*, still present. His shadow and his name were his. He was dead, but every part of his soul was his, and he was whole.

He looked up at the purple sky and the distant wink of pale stars.

The dead shouldn't fear dying. But he was dead, and he still remembered the agony of burning alive in that forest more than a hundred years ago. He remembered Maximilian, starving to death in the traces of Crusade. He remembered choking on his own breath, dying of a disease that the people of his time hadn't begun to understand.

Death wasn't the end of suffering. How long had those crazed spirits cried for help?

The fire was already glowing in the windows of the old building. The alarms would be sounding any minute. Dry bone burned quickly and cracked in the heat: in minutes, they'd be shards. The last pieces of their bodies destroyed, and more of their souls ripped away.

The memory of the fire in the forest sent cold sweat springing to his skin. But long before that, in a kingdom now long gone, he'd clutched his brother's hand and wept as he begged for *someone* to help him.

"Theo," he said. His throat tightened against the reek of smoke. "Theo. Pray for me."

"W-what?"

"Pray for protection. Say a spell over me."

She licked her lips. They were cracking, with a line of pale pink flesh split to show a thread of red.

"Repeat after me. I know the words, but I'm not a priest. Say them, Theo. Now!"

She threw her arms around him and clung tightly. His heart thundered against her chest, finding a rhythm that reflected his fear and hers. His lips pressed against her hair as he bowed his head over her, his hands pressed against her back.

Suddenly, absurdly, he became aware of her scent. She smelled like sweat and soft fabric and lilac shampoo. Her favorite, always. Familiar.

He said the words, and she repeated them back, barely understanding the language but speaking with a terror and an awe that filled them with power. The murmured prayers rolled over them both. Invocation after invocation, plea after plea in a dead language.

Then he turned and ran toward the fire.

* * *

The security guard was gone. Fled already, or perhaps Armstrong had dismissed him when he came in. That was fine by Seth: one less witness.

He slammed his palms into the frame of the glassed-in security door. Three rapid blows bent it out of place, and the glass cracked. He ripped the door out of its place—there went the silent alarm, no doubt—and dropped it to the ground.

Smoke was already thick in the corridor, tinting everything blue-gray. Seth stifled a cough.

There: the deserted guard station. Someone had left a half-empty bottle of water on the desk. He tore part of his sleeve off, soaked it in water, and wrapped the cloth over his nose and mouth. Then he sprinted down the corridor.

The vast storage hall was an inferno. Flames crawled up the huge stacks of crates, crawling like Theo's scorpions. The fire flared blue-green as it ate up the paint and chemicals soaked into the wooden crates. Plastic containers were beginning to melt, their sides sagging and dripping down the piles.

The remaining panes of glass in the display cases were already cracking in the heat. The ancient, dry wooden supports burned like torches, soaked as they were with hundred-year-old lacquer. All around the cases, fire licked across the concrete floor in intricate loops, following the original trail of linseed oil.

One of the nearest crate stacks was already beginning to collapse. Molten plastic slag slithered to the ground, almost obscuring the first pile of bones.

Gods. It was the thing Theo called Hai-Ti. Its head was wrenched and turned backward. The sternum and ribs stood out in his vision, clear in their reality against the parody of flesh and form.

Paper and cloth tore as Seth ripped the bones free of their fake corpse. He shoved them under one arm, kicked the pieces of the thing that had been called Hai-Ti aside, and wiped his stinging eyes.

He found the Minister next. On legs that were poorly constructed, with only a few ribs and a scrap of skull to power him, the creature had failed to escape his case. Seth smashed the glass with a chair and ripped the bones free, leaving behind the lie.

The bones wept.

Heat washed over him, baking him dry. The fire rampaged through the hall. A few desultory sprinkles of water dampened the ash, but the old suppression systems couldn't do much to stop the oil-fed fire from eating up paper and paint. He leaped over another fallen crate and landed hard, rolling on the hot concrete, barely avoiding another pool of burning oil.

Princess Penedjmet lay behind one of the cases, weighed down by the golden plate. She gave up the bones of her skull with barely a sigh.

The thing labeled Other Woman slumped against a wall, twitching feebly. It raised a hand to him, and the bones of its fingers and forearm stood out in his vision—human. It cradled two faux heads in its lap. He tore off the arm and took the jaws and teeth of the fallen heads.

Life left them with their bones. He kicked away the remnants as he had before. Sparks settled in the husk.

The smoke was too thick now. He couldn't see. Couldn't breathe.

Did he have a choice?

Yes. And he'd chosen.

Idiot.

The men in the forest would be laughing at him now. Napolitano and Liebermann, always arguing. Schwartz and Red Schwartz—card games and laughter until the forest silenced them all. Sgt. Dorff, rolling his Bull Durham in newspaper, grimacing as the smell of oily smoke wafted up the slope toward their camp—

The Germans were advancing. Scorpions poured from the sergeant's mouth.

His lungs burned. The pain of breathing was almost worse than the pain of suffocating. Fire eating everything up—crisping cloth and cooking flesh, unable to escape—

Tonight, for the second time in four thousand years, he'd been strangled. Now, for the second time in a hundred years, he burned.

His scream caught in his throat. The bones in his arms blackened, their lacquer falling away in flakes of ash. A streak of epoxy lit up, a streak of red that burrowed into the bone and cracked it open.

Seth yanked off his shirt and covered the bones with it. Clutched the bundle to his chest, bent his head over it. The heat crisped his hair.

The burning oil had spread, and the door was blocked by a sheet of flame. The crawling fire reached the topmost layers of crates and made the leap to the rafters, swarming up toward the third floor and the wires. Sparks showered down. Plastic and foam insulation melted, spreading shining pools of lava-hot liquid across the floor.

He squeezed his eyes shut against the glow and the heat. Boiled in his skull, like bones floating in the pot. Burning, as his brother had burned under the sacred signs. As Adder had burned.

Where was the sergeant?

Which way?

Sparks landed in the cloth bundle. He stifled them with his hands, each one a pop of pain against the skin of his palm, and hugged the bundle closer to him. The bones clacked and scraped as he moved. Dry as dust, dry as firewood.

Huns! Huns in the treeline!

Benutze den Flammenwerfer!

The smoke smelled of gasoline. Petrol. Wet leaves and mud underfoot, slipping. What was—?

Way out. Where was the way out? His mouth tasted only ash. Bones, cooked to cinders. The pools of liquid plastic were closer now, leaving scorch marks on the cracking concrete. A cloth draping into a long shining streak of blue dropped sparks, and the shining, bubbling surface caught fire.

Another case shattered. The shards sprayed across the floor. They fell into the liquid plastic and skidded, sending molten-hot droplets flying.

The drops struck. Seth recoiled. Searing liquid plastic burned through the legs of his trousers and burrowed into his skin. No blood rose: veins and arteries seared closed before it could reach the surface.

Hunched over the bundle of bones. They would burn, just like him. He fell to one knee and bent his head. Couldn't fall to the floor, couldn't roll—he'd only burn faster.

Adder had died this way. *Benutze den Flammenwerfer.* The word didn't mean anything to Adder. Only a few half-remembered syllables from the times when he once spoke German, lifetimes before. Bring the—fire? *Flamethrower.*

His hands were burned red. Second verging on third degree, now. The skin swelled. Cracked.

Red lines appeared between the broken pieces of flesh.

Fire.

Anhurmose screamed. Adder and Seth screamed.

The clay roared.

The veneer of humanity sloughed away, but the creature could not die. The beating heart was reunited with its own soul, bound to live by the magic that connected them. The husk of clay spoke to the magic it had been imbued with. Its orders said it would live.

The golem staggered forward. Into the sheet of flame. Its surface cracked and split. A core of lava roiled underneath, humanity nothing but a broken shell. Like continents on the shifting mantle of the planet.

The fragile bundle in its arms began to catch flame. The fire crawled through the linen threads, scorching them, tracing woven patterns onto the bones inside.

No.

I promised her.

The golem took another step. Then another. A falling drop cloth sent a billow of flame gusting over him, but he hunched closer over his bundle. Blood boiled away.

Death fell over him like a shadow. The lava began to crack and seize.

I promised her.

The voices of the ghosts followed in his wake. Hands laid upon him from beyond the grave, words in his ears.

Who am I?

Help me!

A little farther! Five more steps!

His good eye was sealed shut by fire and molten clay. The blind one gaped open still, seeing only flickers of movement in the darkness. But the strongest voice, a woman's voice, whispered in his mind.

Five more steps! Yes! Turn left, turn left!

Blind and deaf, the golem clung to its bundle and the only thing it had left. Five more steps. Turn left.

Another flicker of light in his dead eye. A woman's shape.

That's it! Keep going! Watch out, there's a beam—

The golem stumbled and fell. The bones in its arms cracked. Voices wailed as their remains suffered. The golem hunched over them, struggling to climb to its feet, cracking and crumbling. Baked dry.

The heart wasn't enough. The magic wasn't enough. The golem burned alive. With it burned Seth Adler, and Faruq and Rachid and Adder, and Maximilian D'Anjou and Hermes Aegyptos and Aelfred the Black and the barbarian Eats Cold Meat and the *don de herdade* Vicente Jose Maria Vasquez de Gregorio. A hundred more voices joined in its mind, overwhelmed above all by the scream of Anhurmose of Waset. Burned alive, together with half a dozen unknown souls.

"Seth!"

The scream ripped through the soul of the dying golem. A woman, not the murmurings of the strongest ghost. A living woman.

"Seth! Seth, I'm coming in! Where are you?"

No. *No.* The golem lurched to its feet. Fire blazed now in the remains of its skin, but its clay knew that voice as deeply as it knew its own heart. The voice of its maker, who'd once intoned the sacred words.

The golem lived because she willed it. The soul and mind were the man's, and his alone. The heart was his, but it belonged to her.

Anhurmose walked. Still clutching the bundle of bones. He clambered over the fallen beams, his clay rising again, molten and living under the licking flames. Adder had died to fire, but Anhurmose feared curses more than fire. He pressed through.

And then—relief.

The warm air of a summer night felt like a bath of ice water. He staggered a few paces more and fell to one knee, still cradling his burden. Cracks spread across his skin as the fresh air struck his super-heated clay.

"Seth!" The voice called to him in a way that nothing else ever had. Anhurmose bowed his blind head and raised his hands, palms flat, holding up the offering he'd brought to lay at the feet of the goddess.

"Oh, no," the goddess moaned. "Seth! *Anhurmose.* What are you now?"

Hands flung fabric over his head and shoulders. His clay burned too hot: the fabric burst into flames, eaten up in seconds. Black ashes fell away.

"Oh, no..." A hitch in the goddess's voice. Footsteps: she was retreating from him. "I can't even touch you. Isis, Osiris, you *better* be listening right now!"

Cloth rustled as she dropped to her knees and raised her hands to the night sky. And she began to speak the holy words.

Health. Life. Strength. She stumbled over the words, her language as broken and misshapen as his body. Addressing both him and the gods with the fluency of a frightened child. *Be calm, be healed, be quenched.*

Wrong words for a wrong thing. Perhaps that was why it worked.

The flames died as clay began to soften into flesh. Scorched and seared veins opened, blood flowing. A thin whine came from his throat as new nerves branched through the skin.

The charred bundle fell from his hands. Bones bounced across the cold asphalt. She did not accept the offering.

"Oh my God," she was saying. "Seth, talk to me. Please!"

She commanded. He opened his mouth.

"Netjeret."

She gingerly reached out a hand. He was still burning hot to the touch, and she flinched as her fingers brushed his skin.

"Goddess? What? Seth, we're getting you out of here! You can't die!"

No. No, he wouldn't.

The voices of the dead retreated. Flesh flowered from within, obedient to the magic's command. He raised his head and opened his eyes.

A figure swam into view. A woman. Pale as a painted figure, the shining knot of Isis resting on her breast. Golden-maned, green-eyed, parted pink lips, glowing with the life that called to him as she spoke.

"Hear me," she breathed. "Hear me, Ra. *The cavern is opened for him, and the eyes are opened for him. Sunlight falls upon him within the darkness. Conceal him within the Imperishable Stars. His name is Anhurmose, and he is Ra, who himself protects himself. He will not die again."*

Life kindled within him. The heart and soul rose in response, united with the clay that already loved her as creator and loved her now as the woman. Not a goddess. A living woman. *Theo.* Reciting the same prayer he had whispered for her before he ran into the fire.

Seared skin crackled and fell away in flakes. Flesh, clean and new, replaced it. Theo's breath came fast as she traced sacred sigils in the air, repeating her ungrammatical prayers.

He fell to the concrete and bowed his head again, willing the agony to end. He held on to Anhurmose while the woman kneeling beside him worked the magic of an artist and a priest and dragged him back from the brink of annihilation.

* * *

Cold. Colder than ever before. He lay on stone, slumped in a trough of icy water. A chill washed over his aching body, soothing the burns, but his mouth was dry as the desert. He called for drink, and the movement sent a wave of pain through him.

"Did he just say 'moo'?" a man's voice said.

"Water. Water." He was pleading now.

"He's asking for water," a woman called out. Hurried footsteps, harsh and loud on hard floors. Indoors, someplace with tiled floors that echoed. A fine house. His house?

"He moos for water?"

"It's the Egyptian word." Footsteps drew closer now. The woman's voice, colored with worry and fear. "He must be really out of it."

A hand slid down to his back, gentling him to raise his head as she set a cup to his lips. His eyes were still closed, unwilling to risk the light, but he let her raise his head so that he could drink.

The water tasted strange. Metallic. They were putting the medicines in his drink. He obediently swallowed the water and lay back down in the water, the mere movement exhausting him.

How long had he been sick? Was he wounded?

A fall, he remembered. A fall from a platform, in the village where the rebels were. But he was...burning?

"Seth," the woman said. She was at his side, stroking his hair, the other hand still cool against his skin. "Seth, can you hear me? Do you understand me?"

The words made no sense. Curious babble, as if someone were hissing and slurring on the tip of their tongue rather than speaking true words. But something in the string of noise was comforting, and he relaxed into the woman's touch.

A foreigner, then? Nofret had wanted a servant to assist with the weaving. But the hands that stroked his aching head were too soft to be the hands of a weaver. Had she acquired a chamber slave or a maid-of-all-work?

"I don't think he can hear you," the man's voice said. Was that Bet, his scribe? No. Bet spoke no other language than their own. "Look at the weird flexing in his face. His eyeballs are going crazy. He's having bad dreams or something. What's that called?"

"I think," said the woman, "it's called having bad dreams."

"Oh. Yeah."

"Whatever he's thinking, having us talking in here isn't going to help." The woman stood. His cheek and scalp tingled, missing her soothing touch. "Thanks for watching him while I was out, Aki. I can take over now."

"No worries," the man said. "I got some drawing done while I was watching the Human Torch here. You're into some weird shit, Theo."

Theo.

Something clicked in his mind. Words. Syllables and sounds. Slotting into place, meanings assigning themselves to formerly incoherent masses of noise.

The man was *Aki.* Akeela Lee. Lunatic but loyal, prone to poor decisions under the influence of tequila. Closest friend of the woman, *Theo,* who breathed life into clay.

His cracked lips parted. "Theo."

"Seth!" Theo said. She almost knocked over a chair in her hurry to reach him. "Seth? Can you hear me?"

"Theo." He swallowed. "How long?"

"About ten hours," she said. "You've been in pretty bad shape, Seth. We've got you in the bathtub in my motel room. For the burns. You're healing fine—just relax, OK?"

He couldn't remember anything. "What happened?"

"You saved some people." Her hand returned to his cheek, and he turned his head, leaning into her touch. "They're already dead, but you saved what's left of them. They're not going to hurt anyone, I promise."

Ghosts? He remembered, vaguely, but the fear seemed so far away now.

"You're not allowed to die anymore," she told him fiercely. There was a sob in her voice. "Never. Again. You're going to live forever, and you're one of the only people I know who *can* do that, so it's a done deal and you can't ever go back on it. Live. Forever."

CHAPTER 26

Friends help you move. Real friends help you move bodies.

—Anonymous

Aki had found them in the deserted plaza near Building H. He'd yelped when he saw the burned Seth but claimed he couldn't leave "my dumbass bro" to suffer alone, and Theo wasn't sure which of them he meant. He'd helped her pour bags of party ice onto Seth's body in the motel bathtub and chatted like they were talking shit in the bar after work.

He couldn't look directly at Seth, though. The sight of charred skin made him turn green. He later claimed that looking was against the bro code.

Both of them had to go back to work in the morning. It would be too strange if they were missing after...something...happened. Whatever the story ended up being. Aki rigged up a webcam that Theo could check on her phone, and they moved Seth into Theo's bed.

So Aki and Theo went to the museum in the morning, and were of course surprised to learn that Building H had caught fire during the night. Dr. Armstrong was missing, and everyone knew Dr. Armstrong was obsessed with the Building H collection. The museum directors said nothing, but everyone had theories—ranging from Dr. Armstrong being arrested for cocaine possession to him running off to Thailand.

The cops interviewed Theo. The log showed her entering Building H that afternoon, shortly before Armstrong did. Yes, and she'd exited a few minutes after that. Where'd she gone? Back to the motel. Aki could confirm that they'd been together all evening.

She was under suspicion. A mysterious fire in a graveyard, a mysterious fire in a museum annex...but Dr. Ferrara of the Geltner House Museum volunteered that Theo had no reason to set the fire. In fact, she had been investigating the mummies' provenance and seemed to be interested in them.

"I told Dr. Armstrong that I thought they were fakes," Theo told the police detective. "He started acting condescending and told me I was wrong. Then he threw me out. I don't know what happened next."

By mid-afternoon, fire investigators sifting through the wreckage found a can of linseed oil, along with the remnants of fibers. Some of the glass cases had been smashed before the fire broke out.

Nobody was doing much work. Theo, perched on a sawhorse in the exhibit hall with her tablet, lived last year's chaos over again as she watched the Heritage people. They clustered together, talking in low voices, going quiet when a security guard or an executive walked by; furtively checking updates on concealed phones and shooting endless messages to each other. All wondering what was happening and what their future was going to be. If someone in their department was an arsonist.

Around four o'clock, it happened. Word spread through the department like a ripple in a pond. *They found a body.*

A single body, probably a man's. The remains of a lighter in one hand. Theo quietly put down her tablet, went to the bathroom, and hid for a while.

Should she pray? She didn't know. Some part of her hoped his spirit wandered for a long, long time.

For the rest of the day, she kept her head down and focused on her work. It was a relief to go back to the hotel.

After twenty-four hours, Seth had mostly healed. Dark gnarled lines remained where pieces of new flesh joined together, but some of them were beginning to fade. Fine black stubble covered his scalp.

Aside from those first words begging for water, he'd said nothing. Not eaten, not drunk, barely breathed. But he was healing.

Aki got over some of his squeamishness once most of the charring was gone. He made a store run for fresh bandages and Neosporin.

Theo opened a bottle of beer. Instead of bread, she poured honey into a bowl. Remembering what Herodotus had written about "offering incense of all kinds" to the gods, she lit a scented candle. It smelled like pumpkin spice.

Aki watched silently as Theo recited the few healing prayers she knew. Generic appeals to the gods, barely a step up from the rote invocations of *ankh wedja seneb* that filled the pharaonic writings. (The ancient Egyptian "have a nice day.") But Seth operated on different rules. They couldn't take him to a hospital.

She looked at him afterward. His color seemed better. She touched his cheek, and he turned his head, leaning into her touch.

* * *

Two days after the fire, LeDieu found her in the exhibit hall. Theo was covered in sweat and sawdust: surprise, surprise, one of the frames was being a problem child. She stood up and found the archivist watching her steadily over the pile of frame pieces.

"You called him condescending," LeDieu said abruptly. "Did you mean it?"

Theo nodded and mopped her face with a stained rag. "Armstrong? Yeah. He got angry that I was researching the fakes instead of listening to him."

LeDieu was silent for a moment. Thinking. Theo waited, wiping her hands on the rag.

"When I was your age, I had an affair with a classics professor." The other woman shrugged one shoulder. "Older man. Married. I didn't care, but Alan Armstrong found out."

"And he understood," Theo said quietly.

"He said he understood," LeDieu repeated. "He told me I was the victim of a predator. I wasn't...but Alan and I were competing for the same position. I couldn't afford to look guilty. So I said yes, the man lied to me, I didn't know about his wife."

Theo said nothing. Just waited, the rag now motionless in her hands.

"Alan understood me to my face. And he understood me to everyone else. Including the selection committee." LeDieu's mouth twisted. "He told that story over and over again for months. People started wondering how stupid I was, that I didn't know my boyfriend was married. It's one thing to be ruthless in this business, but stupid? Alan got the promotion. I got the archives."

"I know," Theo said. "I told him something wasn't right with the fakes. The provenance. But he didn't want me asking questions."

"You didn't stop looking."

"No."

"But you wanted to," LeDieu said.

"Yes."

LeDieu's eyes were sharp. "You remind me a lot of myself at that age, Speer. Ambitious enough to grab an older man. Hungry enough to want every opportunity. Dumb enough to trust Alan Armstrong."

Theo met her iron-hard stare. "One difference," she said. "You went with the lie."

That was what it came down to. Theo and LeDieu regarded each other, sizing up like a couple of boxers. Then LeDieu nodded and left.

Maybe Theo had passed some kind of hazing ritual. Or maybe LeDieu recognized the truth in her story. Either way, the tide of the rumors started flowing in a different direction. Nobody said it to her face, of course, but the ones who thought she was Armstrong's butt-kisser seemed to get the memo that they'd been wrong. Theo breathed easier.

When she came back to the hotel that night, the dead man was awake.

* * *

The hotel room still smelled like smoke. The curtains were shut tight: couldn't have any passersby looking in and seeing anything strange. The webcam still sat on top of the bureau, pointed at the bed, but Seth was awake.

He looked...alive. His skin was still reddened, his eyes bloodshot, but when Theo came barreling into the hotel room he was sitting up in bed.

Theo stifled a sob as she scrambled onto the bed. He reached out for her; she felt his shoulders shake with suppressed laughter as she pressed her face against his chest. Tears dampened his skin. He ran his fingers through her hair, murmuring in Kemetic, and kissed her neck.

He smelled like a fire in a paint factory, with charred meat on top of it. The hotel would probably have to throw out these bedsheets.

But he was *alive*. He was alive, and Theo would happily give his gods ten million cans of beer if this wasn't some kind of wonderful dream.

"I can't believe it," she breathed. "I can't believe it."

"Believe it," said Aki from behind her. "I told you to dump him, but nobody ever listens to me."

Seth raised his head. "You."

"Yeah?"

"Get out."

Muttering something about needing better one-liners, Aki got out. Seth tightened his arms around Theo and pulled her onto the ash-strewn sheets.

She couldn't believe what she saw. The cracked and burned skin had grown back, new and clean. Fingers that had charred into stumps were now long and square-nailed. So thoroughly healed that even calluses and scars were gone.

No. Not completely healed. She ran her hands over his body, feeling the sleek skin over muscle, and her fingers detected something her eyes couldn't.

Gingerly, she traced the shapes. Loose and fluid lines of scar, barely perceptible in the texture of the flesh. On his chest, the heart-scarab and the ankh. On his back, where lava had burst through the charred skin: the djed pillar, for strength.

Theo remembered drawing those shapes. No paint or ink, just tracing in the air and praying it would stick to the blazing being too hot to touch. The only thing she could think of when he was dying.

"How...? How is this possible?"

He shook his head. "I don't remember much. Just fire and pain, and a voice, guiding me out. The ghosts, I think."

"You *heard* them?"

"Who else could it be?" Seth touched his chest, wincing as he moved, and felt the outline of the ankh and the scarab. "I had an offering to make to—someone. I don't remember. Everything burned, I was burning up...but I lived this time."

"Oh my God," Theo whispered. There didn't seem to be anything else she could say.

"I should have died. I'd burned before, in the forest. But you made this body, with my own heart in it." Seth looked down at his hands. A strange look crossed his face. "I'll have to get my archery calluses back."

The look on his face—annoyed, baffled—thinking about the hard work he'd now have to do, *dammit, this is going to cut into my schedule*—pushed Theo over the edge. She stifled a sob (she was happy. Why was she crying?) and covered her face.

"I'm sorry," she said through her tears. "I'm sorry, I'm sorry, I'm sorry. I shouldn't have—you shouldn't have—they were already dead—"

His hands covered hers. Gently, so gently, he pulled her hands away from her face. "Look at me," he murmured. "Look at me, Theo."

She looked. He was clear-eyed. Even the spiderweb marks remaining from his resurrection in the graveyard looked paler. Renewed, like the rest of him.

"I made a choice," he said. "A stupid choice, but I made it."

That wasn't very reassuring, and Theo's face showed it. Seth fumbled for the right words.

"I didn't—damnation." He chuckled as he rested his forehead against hers. "Theo, you didn't force me to risk my life. You and I, we know there is life after death...but they died the way I did, the first time, and they couldn't forget it."

Theo swallowed another sob. She kissed him, quick and clumsy, and he caught her chin and kissed her back, harder.

"They will," she said. "They're broken, but they're still here. I don't know if he killed them all, but they were so afraid of him. *You saved them.* Thank you, Seth. Thank you. Thank you, thank you, thank you—"

He kissed her again. Theo touched his neck and jaw, skating lightly over the new scars, tracing the blessings she had etched into the substance of his very form. *Live.*

"I love you." She kissed the corner of his mouth. "Thought I'd lost you. I felt sick. Please don't die again, Seth."

He cradled her to him. "Meri tje, Theo."

They stayed there, holding each other. Theo rested her head against his chest, and he stroked her hair, murmuring in a language she didn't recognize—not English or Egyptian. For a few moments, everything was peaceful.

Then Aki came back in, carrying a bulging Burger King bag.

"All good?" he said. "Done being dramatic? Cool. Theo, I got you double fries so you don't steal mine again."

Theo closed her eyes, relaxing against Seth. "Aki," she said, "how the hell are you still so normal? After all this?"

"There's a living dead guy in the room, and I'm a hetero dude with a female best friend. Normal is overrated."

EPILOGUE

While we can never know what occupied the ancient
mind, our shared humanity suggests that the thoughts of
the average Egyptian peasant in the fields and the average
office worker on the subway might not be as different as
one might suspect. Both would ask themselves: am I doing
this right? Is this going to take all day? What is my wife
going to think?

—*Excerpt from "Kemetic-American:*
A Speculative Examination of the Ancient Egyptian Mind
Within the Modern Framework," by Dr. Wayne Van Allen

Chicago, one month later...

The loft was ugly. Not as bad as it might have been, but it was still
one big room with caked-on paint in bile yellow, warped brown linole-
um, and a persistent cat smell. There was no cat.

Theo's new lease listed so many no-nos that she'd probably lost her
security deposit by moving in. But it was close to the train, had a skylight, and it wasn't being paid for by anyone but Theo. She could live
with that.

Half a dozen friends from the Columbian had helped her move. In
accordance with the ancient rituals of moving, Theo paid them in pizza.
The pizza was from Lou Malnati's, so she got top-notch help from
them—except for Dave, who was from Boston and thought that pizza
wasn't pizza unless it had been ironed flat.

Fortunately, she also paid them in beer. That solved everyone's
problems.

The sun was setting when the guys left. Only Aki stayed, exercising
his Best Friend Privileges to hang out and fill up on leftover pizza. Most
of the furniture was roughly where it should be, but piles of books,

movies, art supplies, clothes, and five canvases on stretchers turned the main area into a serious tripping hazard.

Aki flopped onto the couch and groaned. "I think my arms are broken. So much for my art career. Oh, God, the darkness is coming...I can see a light...Mother...arrrrrghhhh..."

He gave a rather impressive death rattle and collapsed sideways onto the couch. Then: "Ow."

"Did you fall on my keys?" Theo said.

Aki's voice was slightly muffled by the cushions. "I fell on your keys."

"Well, don't break them. The landlord charges for a new set." Theo dodged as Aki tossed the keys at her. "Watch it! I almost dropped my beer!"

"Your beer sucks!"

"He's right, you know."

Theo jumped. Seth stood in the doorway, a wrapped bundle propped on his shoulder. He wore jeans and a long-sleeved shirt, and his hair was tousled by the brisk summer breeze outside. He smiled at Theo's wide-eyed look.

"Stop sneaking up on me!" she told him. His smile widened.

"No."

"Jerk." Theo put down her beer bottle and hurried over to kiss him. He cradled the bundle against his side and slid his free hand into her hair, drawing her up to him.

"I'm glad you could make it," Theo murmured.

"Mmm. My pleasure. No more than ten hours at the office every day from now on, I promise."

"You're the best."

"I thought I was a jerk."

"You can be both at the same time. It's like flavors—they go together." She gave him another quick peck. "You can be a sweet and spicy jerk."

Behind them, Aki made a disgruntled noise. He was still flopped over the couch, and his eyes were closed. "You two give me diabetes."

Seth frowned. "I thought you were going to get rid of him."

"He helped me move your body. He's got a lot of cred built up."

"Damn right!" Aki yelled from his prone position.

"Hm. I'd hoped to do this in private. But, ah, I brought you a housewarming gift." Seth held out the wrapped object. It was about eighteen inches tall but heavy, almost as heavy as metal. He'd carefully wrapped it in a length of white linen.

"You didn't have to—"

"I wanted to. There are some things every home should have. And since you already have a village idiot..."

"Yeah, whenever you look in the mirror!" Aki added. Theo threw a cushion at him. It flopped onto his stomach, and he looked up at her with a deadpan expression. "Nice shot, Tiger."

"Sue me. I'm still new at violence. Seth, please, put that down and come in. There's still some pizza left. I think."

"I thought I smelled Lou Malnati's."

Theo grinned. "So that's why you came!"

"Guilty as charged. I've gone native."

Theo led the way to the kitchen, which was about ten steps. The loft had a skylight, but not much else.

"It's small," Seth said. "Is there enough room here?"

"Probably not," Theo admitted. "But it's cheap. That's apartment life, right?"

Aki poked his head up over the back of the couch. "Apartment life that your parents don't pay for," he said.

"Yeah. Still getting used to things, I guess. I was living in a bubble—I get it. But..." Her mouth twisted. "Someone help me out here."

"Shit sucks?" Aki suggested.

"To carry oneself is to bear a heavy burden."

"Did you just call her fat?"

Theo rolled her eyes. "Yes, thank you, all of that, except the last thing. But I'm on my own now—figuratively speaking—and there's a lot to adjust to. I'm gonna have to repaint all of my walls, for a start."

"No kidding. This place looks like it was built out of cold polenta." Aki, still sprawled on the couch, stretched out as far as he could and grabbed a beer with the tips of his fingers. "You'd better repaint ASAP. I'm thinking something classic, like Pantone 1505."

Theo giggled. Seth, who didn't understand color chart jokes, shrugged and ate some pizza while waiting for the mortals to start making sense again.

Theo made some room on the couch by picking up Aki's legs and moving them until the rest of him followed suit. Seth sat down, and Theo perched on the armrest, leaning against him. He put an arm around her again and drew her closer. She relaxed against his shoulder and let out a contented sigh.

"This is heaven," she said. "Let's just stay like this forever."

He laughed. "When you find the right spell, let me know."

"Oh, no. I'm not messing around with"—Theo wriggled her fingers in the air—"that stuff. Booga booga boo."

At the word "boo," Aki suddenly broke out in an unconvincing fit of coughing. Theo frowned at him. "Are you OK?"

"Fine," Aki wheezed. "Fine. Fine. Totally. Just—pizza. Stuck in my throat."

"Careful," Seth said. "If you die, we'll have to drag your body back down four flights."

"Yeah, not all of us can be self-cleaning corpses like you."

"Efficiency, Aki. I know you're not familiar with it."

"Super-efficient. Pioneering flameless cremation. RIP, Seth Adler, finding eternal rest in a vacuum cleaner bag."

"And yet here I am, alive," Seth said lazily. "With Theo. And there you are...not even someone's *bu*."

Aki reddened. "Hey! Hey! Private information! I told you that under duress!"

"Tequila is not duress."

"Wait, what?" Theo said. Aki was glaring at Seth now. Was this a guy thing?

At that moment, Theo's phone rang. She squirmed, working to fish it out of the pocket of her jeans. One word flashed up on the screen: *Mom.*

"Oh," she said. "Guys, I should take this."

"What is it?" Aki said. Wordlessly, Theo leaned over and showed him. "Oh, *shit.* I'm out!"

"Probably a good idea." Theo gave him a quick hug. "Thanks for everything, Aki. See you on Monday. And if you don't start talking to Sandy—"

"I'm out I'm out I'm out!" But Aki eyed Theo's phone. It was still ringing. "Are you sure you're gonna be OK?"

Seth laid a hand on Theo's arm. She squeezed his fingers, and looked up at her best friend. "I'll be fine," she said. "Really."

Aki nodded and pushed out of the apartment, carrying one of the half-finished pizzas. Theo felt a rush of gratitude as the door closed behind her friend. Even if he was a pizza thief, he was more like her brother than her actual blood relations were.

Seth pressed a kiss to Theo's shoulder. "Answer it," he said. "If you're sure."

Theo nodded and answered the call.

"Dora?" Her mother's voice was shrill. "What's going on? What are you doing?"

"Mom—"

"The landlord called and said you broke the lease! What were you thinking?"

Theo took a deep breath. "Mom!"

"Don't take that tone with m—"

"Mom." Theo gripped the phone. "I'm going to hang up now."

That got through, finally. Amy Rose Clarendon Speer did not get hung up on: the thought seemed to short-circuit her brain. There was a short gasp, and then blessed silence.

"Mom," Theo said. "Listen to me. OK?"

"Dora—"

"I paid off the lease. I've got a new place now. I love you, and I'm grateful that you still want to provide for me, but I have to take care of myself."

"Where are you living now?" Amy Rose demanded. "Is it with that man? You moved into a love nest instead of telling your mo—"

"It's not a love nest. If it was, it wouldn't smell this bad. And I didn't tell you because I knew you'd scream at me and call me ungrateful again."

"I don't scream at you," Amy Rose retorted. "How can you do this to us? Where did you get the money, anyway? From that man? You're just living off him!"

"It's none of your damn business where I got the money," Theo said flatly. Seth *had* loaned her some of it—and they'd drawn up a repayment plan together, fair and square. He'd wanted to make it a gift but had bowed to her pride.

There was still a gap between them. There always would be, in some ways: power, experience, and money were all on his side. But maybe Theo could learn to live with that and quiet some of the doubts in the back of her head.

After all, they both knew that there was more to life than the ordinary things. In the world of the extraordinary, an artist-priestess was a fair match for a living mummy. And she would never use her prayers and visions against him, just as he would never use his worldly power against her.

That'd be hard to explain to her mother, though.

"You *did* get it from him!" Amy Rose shouted. "How could you do this to me? To us? You're ruining your life, Dora!"

"Goodbye, Mom."

Theo hung up. She dropped the phone on the couch and leaned back, taking a deep, deep breath.

The phone rang again. Theo looked at it. Then she kicked it off the couch. It landed on the rug, face down, its ringing muffled.

"That felt good," she murmured.

"She really hates me, doesn't she?"

Theo looked over at Seth. "How much of that did you hear?"

"All of it," he said. Damn magical senses. "So I'm 'that man' now. Seems I'm debauching a matron's respectable daughter."

"If it helps, the Heritage people thought I was vamping you. Kinda evens out."

Seth laughed. "We can take turns corrupting each other."

"Yeah." Theo took a deep breath and stretched, resettling her shoulders. The phone was still ringing, but it was almost inaudible, still muffled by the rug. The cheap-ass rug she'd chosen and bought, herself, with her friends helping her carry it up the stairs. "New place, new start. All me, all mine."

At that, a strangely hesitant look flickered over Seth's face. "Perhaps..." He frowned, trying to find the words. "There is that additional...thing that I would suggest adding."

He picked up the object he'd brought and carried it over to her. Despite its weight, he handled it carefully, like it was fragile.

She unwrapped it and found herself looking at the face of a god. A handmade clay statuette, no more than eighteen inches tall. The god wore a simple shendyt kilt and stood in the stiff, one-foot-forward pose the Egyptians had liked so much, but it was clearly a modern piece. His head was a ram's.

"I've seen him before," she said softly. "Who is it?"

"It's Khnum. He made the first of us out of clay. Or so the story goes, anyway."

Theo gently traced the statuette's face. The ram's face was solemn and dignified, with a tuft of beard on its chin and gently curved horns that swept back from its forehead. A few fingerprints dotted the clay. Newly made: not to fake an antique, but simply because it was wanted.

"Did you make this?" she asked.

"No. Ah, I commissioned it. Does that matter?"

"Of course not. But it's just right—it looks like something you might have wanted to make." She turned the statuette over, examining it. The details were fluid, halfway between Western realism and Egyptian stylization. "It's *beautiful*, Seth."

"It is. I mean, I'm glad you think so." He reddened. "I wanted you to have it and think it was beautiful. I don't look at art the way you do, but I thought it would make you think it was—that it was, not that I made—I'm not explaining this well."

She hugged him with one arm, careful to cradle the statuette in the other. She could feel his pulse racing under her cheek.

"It *is* beautiful," she murmured. "Like your shabtis." She felt, rather than heard, the tiny hitch in his breath. "I do remember talking to them, you know? I used to look at them and think *someone made you to be loved.*"

"I remember too," he said, and tightened his hold on her.

They lingered there for a long moment, arms around each other. Safe.

But the statuette was still in Theo's arms, and she was afraid she'd drop it. "Let me go," she said, wriggling. "I know where I need to put Khnum."

Reluctantly, Seth let her go. Taking the statuette in both hands, Theo crossed the tiny apartment. Tucked next to the bed was a tall cabinet she'd set up herself while the guys were bringing in the heavier furniture. It was just cheap particleboard, but it hid a secret.

The main shelf was divided into two halves, front and back. The backing of the cabinet slid to reveal the hidden half.

In the little space stood an open can of beer and a plate of Melba toast. Two gift-shop *ka* statuettes knelt on either side, saucers balanced on their sculpted wings. The saucers held tiny toys in the shape of food: hamburgers, a thumbnail-sized plate of cookies, bread, salad, and even a jar of jam. (Twenty dollars on eBay could buy you a lot of dollhouse food.) Just for the hell of it, she'd added a real box of orange Jell-O. Incantations and prayers lined the cabinet, calling on forgotten ghosts to eat, drink, and be welcome and content.

Below, on the bottom shelf, sat a small wooden trunk. It held six linen-wrapped bundles, each with a name carefully inked in hieroglyphs. The bundles were tied with ribbon and sealed with wax, and more prayers covered the inside of the trunk.

Penedjmet. The Minister. Hai-Ti. The Other Woman. Tilamentu. Khnumwaset. These were all that was left of them, labeled with the only names they had for now.

Seth was working to get the Brother Priest from Geltner. He, at least, might have a name: Jay, or perhaps Jason Wolff. If they had both his name and his body, they could lay him to rest properly and stop his crazed ghost from wandering. Theo was already studying the ceremonies for the dead. But here, these others could be safe and hidden while the living searched for their names.

She carefully placed Khnum between the offering plates on the upper shelf. The ram-headed god beamed benevolently down at the ersatz feast.

"What do you think?" she said to Seth. "He should probably go where he'll do the most good, right? And I think the ghosts will need him more than I do right this second."

Seth looked over the unorthodox shrine. "Djed," he said, "I don't think these ghosts could need anything more. Gods help any man who breaks in."

Theo laughed. "The landlord probably won't be happy either. Though there's nothing in the lease that says I can't have ghosts. Just pets. And they're definitely not cats or dogs, right?"

"To hell with the lease. But there *will* be ghosts in your home. Most people would not be comfortable with this."

"It's definitely weird," she said. "I'm flaky, not stupid. But—" She glanced at the shrine again, then held up her hands. "I've made weird things. Not just your new body—those shabtis, the ones I made to find you last year. That's not a bad thing, but I was still playing with stuff I don't understand. It's not the ghosts' fault that a greedy psycho was doing the same thing."

Seth looked down at her.

"You've adopted them," he said quietly.

Theo blushed. "We all need our hobbies, right? What's wrong with that?"

"Nothing. You know I respect your *hobbies*." He ran a hand through her hair, tracing the curve of her ear with the pad of his thumb. "I just prefer it with you and me. Alone."

He kissed her again, and she relaxed into his arms. One of her feet rose to caress his calf.

"You don't seem that bothered," Theo said. "I thought having them around would, uh, discourage you?"

"I'll get used to them." His hand slid down her hip. "Of all people, I should know that there's hope after death."

Theo thought about that for a moment. Then she looked at the ceiling.

"OK, you guys," she said, "take a walk around the block. An hour at least."

They were still weak from their battle. They had no words. But the air moved, and the dead laughed as they streamed out.

AFTERWORD

The Forger of Faces was inspired by several real events in the history of Egyptology and art. Medieval Europeans used Egyptian mummies as apothecary stock. The English word *mummy* comes from the Arabic *mumiya,* which refers to a type of bitumen (asphalt). The dried, blackened mummies looked like they contained bitumen, and their remains ended up in everything from medicine to oil paint! To this day, artists can still buy paint labeled Mummy Brown—now fortunately human-free.

Napoleon's 1798 expedition into Egypt was lavishly documented by French scholars brought along specially for that purpose, and their publications launched a new craze for all things *Égyptien.* Now there was a different kind of demand for mummies. Foreign travelers would purchase mummies and bring them home to display or unwrap with friends.

With all this interest, forgeries were rampant. The early history of mummy forgery isn't well documented, but we do know that at least two individuals in the United States were creating faux mummies by the early twentieth century. As a result, several American universities and government buildings acquired fabulous mummies (always a princess or a priest, naturally) that later turned out to be fakes.

I'm happy to report that these days, when the fakes are detected, people often embrace them. As Dr. Armstrong points out, a modern fake is a scam, but an old fake is often seen as a curiosity or a prank from the past. People consider them interesting works in their own right.

One well-known example is the Mississippi Capitol Mummy. This supposed princess, on display for decades, was finally X-rayed in 1969. "She" turned out to mostly contain newspaper and animal bones over a wooden frame. Judging by the choice of newspaper, she was probably created in Milwaukee around 1898, perhaps by a German-speaking immigrant.

Despite being a fake, the Mississippi Capitol Mummy is still regularly displayed today. She's a novelty and a bit of Americana. In a way, she's a window into our own past, showcasing the work of some anonymous nineteenth-century forger who fooled the public for decades.

Today, mummy forgery is a fairly small segment of the Egyptian forged antiquities market. It's high-risk, low-reward: modern tech makes the fakes easier to spot, and people are much less blasé about trading human body parts. But the phony mummies haven't vanished completely. Some are still being made.

One, in particular, inspired *The Forger of Faces.*

In the year 2000, authorities in Balochistan recovered what appeared to be a 2,400-year-old female mummy. She wore a gold crown, and her burial goods mingled Persian and Egyptian iconography. Experts speculated that she was the daughter of a Persian king who married an Egyptian and died in her new land.

But the gold-draped Persian princess was all too modern. The young woman under the bandages had died in the mid-1990s. The circumstances of her death remain unknown, and she has never been identified.

So much for the bodies of the story. What about the spirits?

The Forger of Faces features multiple cases of splintered souls or incomplete ghosts. Seth gives Theo prayers to help feed and soothe the dead, and points out when the wrong prayers would enrage them. While not fully accurate, this approach does have some parallels in history.

The long history of ancient Egypt means that we can't really say "this is what they believed." Beliefs evolved and built on each other over centuries. The writings we collectively refer to as the Book of the Dead are actually dozens of different texts written thousands of years apart, springing from very different stages in the Kemetic religion. I've tried to ground Seth in the religion as he knew it in the early Middle Kingdom, circa 2000 BCE.

We do know that the ancient Egyptians believed the soul was made up of different parts. The number of parts depends on the era and the text you consult, but a man's soul traditionally included his heart *(ib)*, vitality *(ka)*, personality *(ba)*, and name *(ren)*.

The complex Egyptian funerary rituals evolved over the centuries as a way of empowering and sustaining these different parts of the soul, enabling them to be united as a final perfect otherworldly form *(akh)*. Mummifying the physical body allowed the *ba*-spirit to reunite with it at night, when the sun was in the underworld, and rise from it each day. The heart would also be carefully preserved, as the heart was the center of wisdom and memory. Offerings would be made in tombs to feed the dead. Chanting their names would strengthen and honor them. When the *ba* rejoined the body at night, it would presumably take strength from the offerings it had received.

But what happens if one of those parts is lost?

I don't know of any authentic Egyptian literature that depicts a truly splintered soul, but the notion of attacking or damaging someone after death was very much in the air. Discredited kings, such as the "heretic pharaoh" Akhenaten, would be destroyed postmortem by having their names erased from their sculptures and coffins. Offerings were stopped and mummies were destroyed. If anything was left, it would be a soul without a name, body, or heart to anchor it.

And we do know that, in the ancient Egyptian mind, it was possible for a ghost to affect the living. A 20th-dynasty ghost story (one of the few extant) depicts a ghost whose tomb has collapsed and whose offerings have stopped, leaving him desperate. He is able to reach out to the living and beg for help.

It was also believed that neglected ghosts could turn dangerous and even demonic. One text features a husband pleading with the soul of his deceased wife, asking why she's cursed him with misfortune when he's been honoring her tomb. In this case, the husband isn't at fault, but his reaction tells us that it would be expected for a truly neglected ghost to act the way his wife seems to be. If he really had forgotten her, it would make sense to him that she'd lash out.

There were also powerful spirits that had never been human. Scholars often refer to these creatures as demons, but they appear as both helpful and harmful. Some guard the deceased while others torment and attack the unworthy. Medical texts list spells for driving away the demons believed to cause certain ailments.

In the Book of the Dead, some demons would be named as part of ritual formulas. Speaking the demon's name would give the dead man power over them—perhaps one of the earliest examples of the "true name" clause in world mythology. The creature and its realm would be described and named, and the dead would state definitively that it has no power over them. As it was written, so would it be.

Take this example from the Papyrus of Sobekmose: "O you cavern, secluded from the gods, hidden from the akhs, dangerous for the gods. The god who is in it—the One Who Makes the Buri-Fish Fall is his name...the One Who Makes the Buri-Fish Fall does not have power over me. The kharu-demon shall not come after men. The male adversary shall not come after me. I live on the offerings that are within you" (Paul F. O'Rourke, 2016).

I've been privileged to meet some of these demons face-to-face. During a trip to the mortuary temple of Seti I in February 2022, we were escorted down the dark tunnel of the Osireion—the temple complex commemorating the death of Osiris himself. In that tunnel, I first encountered the painted figures known as the Inert Ones. They were depicted as tormented shadows, upside down. Was this to rob them of their powers? Or did they exist in a nightmare world where everything was backward, the way shadows appear upside down and trailing behind you? Are they what the gods themselves become in the darkness of the night?

There's a lot more work to be done in this area. And I'm a writer, not an Egyptologist. But if you strip a ghost of its name and parts of itself, force it into a new form, and surround it with other screaming ghosts— well, that sounds close to a demon to me.

Seth also refers to another concept from ancient Egyptian culture: *ukhedu* or *wekhedu*. Like many concepts from distant times, we don't completely understand the idea of what *ukhedu* was or what it meant to the ancients. However, we do know that *ukhedu* was associated with poison and disease.

Scholars say it probably derives from the verb *ukhed* or *wekhed,* meaning "to suffer." Readings of the medical Ebers Papyrus suggest that *ukhedu* meant "abscess," "inflammation," "decay," or simply "pain." *Ukhedu* was said to travel through the body and affect every part. The more *ukhedu,* the worse the patient, until death resulted.

The medical concept of *ukhedu* thus bears a striking similarity to the religious concept of *isfet,* or chaos. The conflict of order versus chaos was a cornerstone of ancient Egyptian thought, and the red desert was held to be the seat of chaos. Hungry ghosts were inherently chaotic, and the bad luck and disruption they brought evokes the creeping sickness of *ukhedu.* It seemed appropriate for Seth, a man who died of a wasting disease at a time when such diseases weren't well understood, to link *ukhedu* and *isfet.*

In closing, I'd like to recommend some fascinating books about archives and art forgery. These books were a great help while writing *The Forger of Faces,* and I recommend them as entertaining and informative reads in their own right.

Egyptian Fakes by J.J. Fiechter

A cool and academic look at the history of ancient Egyptian art forgeries from the 1800s to the present. The book has particular interest in the career of a man named Oxan Aslanian, who produced some remarkably successful Amarna-era forgeries, among many others. He may have also worked with Nazis. Eek.

Provenance by Laney Salisbury and Aly Sujo

For me, *Provenance* falls into the category of "too crazy to be fake." It's the true story of con man John Drewe and reluctant forger John Myatt, two men who scammed the art world by not just forging pieces but doctoring the records to insert their fakes into art history. An interesting look at not only the forged paintings, but the work that goes into determining authenticity.

Veritas by Ariel Sabar

A tale of scholarship, obsession, cuckoldry, and Coptic grammar. A divinity professor gets hold of a Coptic gospel hinting that Jesus was married—and it just so happens to match all her personal theories and beliefs. Then it turns out to be a forgery by a disgruntled ex–East German scholar who runs a porn website on the side. This was one gift horse with some majorly bad teeth.

In Vino Duplicitas by Peter Hellman

People really forge wine? Apparently so. The weird true story of Rudy Kurniawan, a super-taster with a shadowy past, a love of fine wine, and spending habits so heavy that he turned to duplicating legendary vintages for cash. Also a good example of how the little details can ruin a major scam.

Thanks for reading!

ABOUT THE AUTHOR

Catherine Butzen was born and raised in Chicago, Illinois. Surrounded by world-class museums and with a family library overflowing with everything from computer manuals to Norse myths, Catherine developed an enduring love for history and writing. Her first book, the horror adventure *Thief of Midnight,* was published in 2010.

Today she lives and works in Madison, Wisconsin. Her interests include sewing, archery, languages, cybersecurity, and being a font of strange but occasionally useful trivia.

You can find her at catherinebutzen.wordpress.com, or on X @cjbutzen.

Thinklings
TIMELESS BOOKS • QUALITY AUTHORS

www.ThinklingsBooks.com
Facebook.com/ThinklingsBooks
@ThinklingsBooks

Thinklings Books started out when three speculative-fiction-loving editors—Deborah Natelson, Sarah Awa, and Jeannie Ingraham—got together and formed a writing group. We called ourselves the Thinklings, in honor of C.S. Lewis and J.R.R. Tolkien's group, the Inklings.

Over time, we found ourselves agonizing more and more about how messed-up the publishing industry had become. Why couldn't good books get published? Why were so many bad books published just because their authors had big Twitter followings? We wished there were something we could do about the problem . . . and then we realized there was.

As a developmental editor, a substantive/line editor, and a proof-reader, the three of us knew good writing when we saw it—and we knew how to make it even better. We had a lot of experience walking our clients through the publishing process—both traditional and self-publish—and we had contacts with marketing and design experts. We had some amazing unpublished books lined up and ready for production. We had, in fact, everything we needed to make a great publishing company. All that was left was to actually do it.

So we're doing it.

Spectacular Reads. Every Time.

IT'S TIME TO TAKE OVER

Fodder of Humble Village is a soldier for the plot of each new story, and, frankly, he's really sick and tired of getting speared, disembowelled, and decapitated so the good guys can look glorious. In fact, he's not going to take it anymore.

The Plot Bandits
the complete four-book . . . uh, trilogy . . .
by Katherine Vick

TRAPPED BY CRIME.
FREED BY MAGIC.

When Skate tries to burgle a shut-in's home, she gets caught by the owner—a powerful undead wizard. He makes a deal with her. Now, she'd better find out exactly where her loyalties lie.

Skate the Thief

&

Skate the Seeker

by Jeff Ayers

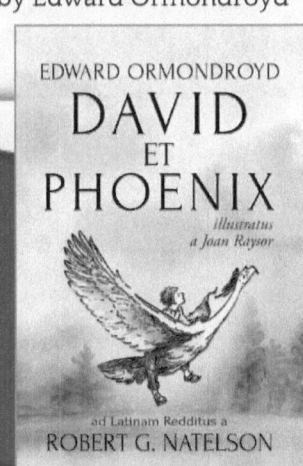

A BOY. A MYTHICAL BIRD.
A WORLD FULL OF MAGIC.

David and the Phoenix
by Edward Ormondroyd

THE ENGLISH ORIGINAL.

THE AUTHORIZED LATIN TRANSLATION.

AND YOU THOUGHT COLLEGE WAS TOUGH BEFORE

Try getting bitten by a werewolf. And being hunted by madmen. And being stalked by a very suspicious secret organization.

Hunter's Moon
by Sarah M. Awa

RIDICULOUSLY MAGICAL. MAGICALLY RIDICULOUS.

Crafted as a slave to serve Time, the clockwork man escapes to seek out his imagination, his purpose, and his name.

The Land of the Purple Ring
by Deborah J. Natelson

THE CLOCK IS TICKING

Plans seldom survive contact with the enemy, a truth thrown at Mercedes when an ordinary trip turns into a battle for survival.

Bargaining Power by Deborah J. Natelson